PRAISE FOR

The **Patron Saint** *of* **Butterflies**

A Book Sense Pick
A NAIBA Book of the Year
An ABC New Voices Pick
An Oprah's Book Club Teen Reading List Selection
A Cosmo Girl Book Club Best Beach Read

"An exceptional and powerful story. . . . This grim tale
of realistic fiction will have teens enthralled, unable
to put this book down until the final page." —*VOYA*

"Readers will be amazed by Agnes and Honey's strength to
enter a brave new world of Big Macs and automatic doors—and
independence and unconditional love." —*Kirkus Reviews*

"Readers will be fascinated by a glimpse into a lifestyle
not often seen." —*Booklist*

"[A] stunningly original debut novel. . . . The author offers . . .
memorable characters and a fascinating exploration of
family, faith and love." —*The Buffalo News*

"*The Patron Saint of Butterflies* is a truly amazing book. . . .
The writing has a wonderful style and quality, shifting
between two teenage best friends." —Flamingnet.com

"This is a stunning, incredible, and heartfelt novel."
—TeensReadToo.com

"*The Patron Saint of Butterflies* . . . pulls readers through the pages
with a persistent urgency to discover what happens to the two
main characters. . . . Galante is a very talented writer, and fans
will eagerly look forward to her next book." —Teenreads.com

The
Patron Saint *of*
Butterflies

CECILIA GALANTE

BLOOMSBURY

NEW YORK BERLIN LONDON

Published by Bloomsbury U.S.A. Children's Books
175 Fifth Avenue, New York, New York 10010

The Library of Congress has cataloged the hardcover edition as follows:
Galante, Cecilia.
The patron saint of butterflies / by Cecilia Galante. — 1st U.S. ed.
p.   cm.
Summary: When her grandmother takes fourteen-year-old Agnes, her
younger brother, and best friend Honey and escapes Mount Blessing, a
Connecticut religious commune, Agnes clings to the faith she loves while Honey
looks toward a future free of control, cruelty, and preferential treatment.
ISBN-13: 978-1-59990-249-4 • ISBN-10: 1-59990-249-4 (hardcover)
[1. Cults—Fiction. 2. Communal living—Fiction. 3. Christian life—Fiction.
4. Saints—Fiction. 5. Butterflies—Fiction. 6. Identity—Fiction.
7. Connecticut—Fiction.] I. Title.
PZ7.G12965Pat2008   [Fic]—dc22   2007051368

ISBN-13: 978-1-59990-377-4 • ISBN-10: 1-59990-377-6 (paperback)

Typeset by Westchester Book Composition
Printed in the U.S.A. by Quebecor World Fairfield
1 3 5 7 9 10 8 6 4 2

All papers used by Bloomsbury U.S.A. are natural, recyclable products
made from wood grown in well-managed forests. The manufacturing processes
conform to the environmental regulations of the country of origin.

This book is dedicated to Ruth VanLokeren
and to Fannye Jo Plummer.

In a room where people unanimously maintain a conspiracy of silence, one word of truth sounds like a pistol shot.

—Czeslaw Milosz

¹saint: \'sant, *before a name* (͵)sānt *or* sənt\

noun

1: one officially recognized especially through canonization as preeminent for holiness

2a: one of the spirits of the departed in heaven . . .

3a: one of God's chosen and usually Christian people
b *capitalized*: a member of any of various Christian bodies;
specifically: LATTER-DAY SAINT

4: one eminent for piety or virtue . . .

Zebra Longwing:

The Zebra Longwing is one of the most beautiful butterflies in North America. Usually black in color, its long, slender wings are highlighted with vivid yellow stripes. Small white spots freckle the edges like a dusting of snow. Although these butterflies roost in colonies at night, they disperse at first light to look for food. Zebra Longwings thrive naturally in the southern part of the United States, as well as most of tropical America.

PART I

AGNES

"Please tell me what to do," I whisper, staring at the crucifix on the wall. "Is there any other way to get out of here right now without telling a lie? Could you just give me a sign to let me know? Maybe blink your eyes or nod your head or something?" Clasping my hands under my chin, I bow my head, close my eyes, and wait. Around me, the other twenty-seven kids in the room continue chanting the afternoon prayers, their lips moving methodically over the Latin words. The air in the room is warm and stale. My knees are grinding into the thin carpet and I can detect the faint smell of sweat under my blue robe. Some days, afternoon prayers can feel like they go on forever. I count to ten and raise my head again. The Christ figure on the cross remains frozen in his agonizing position: hands and feet nailed to the wood, ribs exposed, eyes raised heavenward. My shoulders sag. No sign this time.

Well, that's it, then. There's simply no other way. It's just that the thought of having to tell a lie makes me mad. Furious, even. I've done so well this whole week, and now I'm going to blow it because of Honey. This is *her* fault. If she hadn't taken off after Emmanuel called us into the Regulation Room this morning, I wouldn't even be in this situation. Why does she have to go and do things like that? It's not like it was the end of the world or anything. Peter and I had been called in there with her, and then Emmanuel told the two of us to go back down to the East House. Honey had been ordered to stay behind for some reason, but I'm sure it wasn't a big deal. At least, I don't think it was. I just can't get rid of the feeling that something might not be right this time. Four hours have passed and there's been no sign of her. She's run off before after Regulation Room visits, but never for more than an hour. Lie or no lie, I've got to find her.

Behind me, a throat clears. I turn my head slightly and lock eyes with Peter. He has pushed his light brown hair, which usually hangs in his eyes, off his face. He's part of the reason we got into trouble this morning, and I know he feels guilty for Honey's prolonged absence. "Are you going to go find her?" he whispers. His teeth, large and crooked, look too big for his small mouth. What Honey sees in him is beyond me. Peter knows as well as I do that if anyone finds Honey outside today, she'll get in even bigger trouble than she did this morning. It is Ascension Week here at Mount Blessing, and no one is allowed outside except to walk to and from the Great House for meals.

Mount Blessing is the religious commune just outside of Fairfield, Connecticut, where I was born. I live here with my parents and my little brother, Benny, along with about two hundred and sixty other people, including Honey. Mount Blessing was founded by our leader, Emmanuel, who wanted to create a community of holy people, separate and apart from the sinfulness of the rest of the world. There is no one in the world quite like Emmanuel. My dad told me once that the reason so many people keep coming to live here is because Emmanuel can make broken people whole again. And it's true. There have been people who have come here messed up on drugs, feeling lost or even suicidal. After spending a week or so with Emmanuel, they become completely new people, striving to live good, religious lives. He heals them from the inside out. And sometimes from the outside in. After Emmanuel laid his hands on little Frankie Peters, who has been stuttering since first grade, he began to talk just as well as the rest of us. And just last year, Grace Willoby's facial tics vanished completely after Emmanuel prayed over her. Dad tells us all the time how lucky we are to be living with such a saintly man, and I know he's right.

Now I glance at the clock on the wall. One thirty. Taking a deep breath, I look back at Peter and nod my head. His whole face relaxes as he closes his eyes and resumes chanting. But I cannot even look at the crucifix when I turn back around. Bowing my head, I make the sign of the cross over my chest and try to control the quavering in my whispered voice.

"I know telling a lie is a sin, but I have to go find Honey and I just can't think of any other way to get out of here right now. I will make it up to you with an extra penance tonight. I promise. Please forgive me." I squeeze my hands so tight that my knuckles turn white. "Please." Reaching under my robe, I pull out *The Saints' Way* from inside the waistband of my jeans. *The Saints' Way* is a book about how to live our lives, using the life stories of saints as examples. All the adults at Mount Blessing have the book, but Emmanuel gives each child a personal copy on his or her twelfth birthday. I got mine two years ago, and I'll never forget it.

I was both nervous and excited that morning: excited to be turning twelve and nervous about going in to see Emmanuel, who would present me with the book. It is always a huge honor to have a private meeting with Emmanuel, but it also made me a little shaky. Standing in front of him is an intimidating experience, what I imagine looking directly at God would feel like. Anyway, Mom ironed my best dress and helped me pin my hair up into a neat bun, and Dad was waiting for me on the front porch when I came out. The sun had just risen and the air was still cold and purple.

"You ready?" Dad said, inserting his hands into the sleeves of his big blue robe. Everyone at Mount Blessing wears blue robes—all the time.

I nodded and straightened out the folds in my own robe. "I think so."

"You look nice," Dad said, holding out his hand. "Especially your hair." I wanted to tell him that being twelve meant that he didn't have to hold my hand as we walked toward the Great House, but I didn't. It's not every day that Dad compliments me, and I didn't want to ruin the moment. We stood outside Emmanuel's room and Dad rang the buzzer that would let him know we were there. In a few seconds, the red light above the door began to blink. My mouth was as dry as sand as we walked inside.

Emmanuel's room is enormous, even bigger than the whole first floor of the house I live in with Mom and Dad and Benny. At any given time, there are usually between ten and twenty people in there, but this morning it was empty—except for him. He was sitting in his huge chair, a beautiful, hand-carved piece of furniture that had been made especially for him, eating grapefruit sections out of a glass cup. He didn't have his blue robe on for some reason, and without it, he looked different, almost human. Dad and I fell to our knees, bowed our heads, and waited.

Emmanuel cleared his throat. "Come in," he said.

Dad and I stood back up and tiptoed over the plush white carpeting, past the baby grand piano and the wall of wooden wine racks, which held numerous slender bottles of wine. Next to the wine racks was an oil painting portrait of the Blessed Virgin, which Emmanuel had painted himself. Her face was a cloudy gray color and her eyes, which were wide and black, stared back at me as I made my way across the room.

"I hear it is someone's birthday," Emmanuel said, placing his empty glass on a table next to his chair. It made a light clinking sound against the wood.

I nodded mutely and stared at his pressed white shirt and casual gray slacks. I still couldn't get over how different he looked without that robe on. He even had *slippers* on! Dad nudged me with his elbow and I gulped.

"Yes, Emmanuel," I said quickly. "Thank you."

Emmanuel wiped his gray beard with a cloth napkin and then raised his eyebrows. "You know what happens on your twelfth birthday, don't you, Agnes?"

I nodded again, swallowing hard over a lump in my throat. I couldn't believe the moment was actually here, that it was finally happening. When Mom and Dad had been presented with their books, it had been such an exciting day for them. They told me how they had spent hours that evening leafing slowly through the pages and then sliding the slender volumes onto their new home on the bookshelf. Each night they would pull their books back out and read another page.

I watched as Emmanuel leaned over and took a small book

off the little table. A gold ring on his finger glinted under the light. "Come here," he said to me. I stepped forward on shaky legs and stared at the book in his hands. "You are an adult now," Emmanuel said. There was a pause, and I realized he was waiting for me to make eye contact with him. I raised my head and studied the sharp planes of his narrow face, his bushy eyebrows, and his watery gray eyes. Even his beard, which rested—neatly trimmed—against the top of his collarbone, looked virtuous. He smiled at me. "You are an adult now," he said again. "Capable of leading the life of a saint." He held out the book. I took it from him with trembling hands. It was heavier than it looked, with a black cover and the title, *The Saints' Way*, inscribed in gold lettering. "Study this book," Emmanuel continued. "Learn all you can from the greatest living examples ever to walk the earth." I nodded, pressing the book against my chest. "And then live your life accordingly, as a saint would."

"I will," I whispered.

Emmanuel nodded and smiled again at me. "I have great faith in you, Agnes. Your name means *lamb*, which symbolizes purity and innocence. You are capable of doing remarkable things. Do not ever forget that."

My eyes filled with tears; it was such an emotional thing to hear Emmanuel say he had faith in me, that I could do something remarkable. Imagine! *Me!* "I won't forget," I said, feeling my voice get stronger. "I promise."

Next to me, Dad beamed.

In the last two years I've read *The Saints' Way* at least six or seven times all the way through, earmarking the stories I like best. Now I turn to Saint Rose of Lima, who has become one of my favorites. Born in South America, she spent her entire life trying to make up for the sins she committed. Her tolerance for pain and suffering was nothing short of spectacular. Skimming the list of her favorite penances, I try to determine which one I will do tonight:

- *Tie a length of rope around the waist until it is tightly uncomfortable.* Check.
- *Fast for three days. (Only water and the occasional citron seed.)* Check.
- *Sleep on a bed of broken glass, rocks, or other sharp objects.*

Placing the book back inside the front of my pants, I retie the itchy string around my waist, tightening it until it cuts into the soft flesh. I started wearing the waist string three months ago, after I got mad at Benny and yelled at him. Now, every time I feel it chafe against my skin, I offer up the pain for any failings I have committed that day. I also fast pretty regularly—skipping breakfast and dinner at least three days a week. Fasting is a big thing with saints in general. Saint Francis of Assisi and Saint Catherine of Siena used to go weeks without any solid food. My personal record is four days, but then I fainted in the pool and almost drowned, so I had to start eating again. But I have never slept on a bed of broken glass or rocks. I'm sure it will hurt, but like the others, it will be a great test of my will.

Smoothing my robe back into place, I stand up slowly, taking care not to distract anyone, and walk toward Christine in the back of the room. Christine Miller, an older woman in her late fifties, is in charge of all the kids at Mount Blessing. She has three or four young women who help her—especially with the little kids—but she's the one who calls the shots when it comes to us coming and going. She watches me wind my way through the room, narrowing her eyebrows a little. Her long black braid hangs over one shoulder and little wisps of loose hair curl around the sides of her face. I stop in front of her, hesitating as her lips pause midchant.

"I have to go lie down upstairs," I whisper, rushing over the words. "My stomach is killing me."

Christine studies me for a moment. I am counting on her knowledge of what went on this morning, hoping it will persuade her to let me leave. She and I will never talk about what went on inside the Regulation Room—or that the reason the three of us were summoned there at all was because she went and told Emmanuel that we were misbehaving—but I know she feels bad about it. She always feels guilty when one of the kids has to go to the Regulation Room. She's been in charge of all of us for fifteen years now, but she's still pretty much a softie.

"Go ahead," she whispers, reaching out and straightening the belt cord around my robe. "I'll come up later to check on you."

Afternoon prayers won't end until 2:45, which means I have a little over an hour to find Honey, assess the situation, and get the two of us back before Christine realizes I've left the building. I sneak out the back door, fastening my hair into a bun at the nape of my neck, and head toward the barn, which is where Honey escaped to the last time. The barn is all the way on the other side of the grounds, only a ten- or fifteen-minute trek if I use the main path. But since it is Ascension Week, I walk along the back road, staying low to the ground to avoid being seen.

The sky is a brilliant bowl of blue. I hate that. On days like this, when everything hurts the way it does, I wish the sky would turn black and that it would rain and rain until I felt better again. I move as quickly as possible, bent over at the waist, clutching the hem of my robe in one hand, pausing briefly to stuff my pockets full of small stones. The welts on my rear end and the backs of my legs make the awkward movements painful. I grit my teeth and offer up the pain for the lie I have just told.

The smell of green is everywhere. The five or six apple trees that line the path are just starting to blossom; from a distance, they look like enormous pink cotton balls. Bright gold petals dot the field like splayed fingers, and every few moments the lonely *caw* of a crow splits the silence. Up ahead is the schoolhouse, a large brown building shaped like an A-frame, where all the children at Mount Blessing attend school. Honey, Peter, and I are in ninth grade this year. There are only two other kids in our class: Amanda Woodward, who is incredibly smart, and James Terwilliger, who can swim three lengths of the pool underwater. I like that we have a small class. Benny's first-grade class has seventeen kids in it, and Honey told me once that public schools can have as many as thirty kids in one room. That would drive me crazy. I don't know how I would think!

Honey complains about it all the time, but I love living here at Mount Blessing. I can't imagine living anywhere else or being anything but a Believer. That's what we're known as, the Believers, because that's what we do. We believe. Specifically, we believe in two things: Christianity and Emmanuel, which, when you think about it, is everything we could possibly need or want. I've never left the grounds of Mount Blessing, but I wouldn't want to. I actually get hives when I think about it. It's so huge and dangerous out there, and so full of sin. How could anyone possibly be a saint with all those temptations surrounding them? I feel sorry for the men at Mount Blessing who have to go into the outside world to work so they can help pay the bills. My father, for example, works at a mattress company in Fairfield. I asked him once what it was like having to leave every morning and sell mattresses, and he touched my cheek with his finger. "There's no place in the world I'd rather be than right here," he said. "But if Emmanuel wants me to work, then that's what I'll do."

There are rules here that we all have to follow, like wearing the blue robes, going to three daily prayer services, not eating red or orange food (which is symbolic of the devil), and things like that, but they're not a big deal. When you think about it, if a place with two hundred and sixty people living in it didn't have rules, it would be chaos! The really important rules—ones we abide by to live as holy a life as possible—are the ones that really count, anyway. These are known as the Big Four, and they were probably the first things we learned when we started to talk. The Big Four is what being a Believer is all about:

I. *In all things, strive for perfection.*
II. *Clothe the body, adorn the soul.* (This is the reason for our robes. We need to spend our time worrying about perfecting our souls, not our wardrobes.)
III. *Waste nothing.*
IV. *Tempt not, lest you be tempted.* (Temptations include things like television, magazines, radios, or anything at all that has to do with bringing the outside world into our community.)

Emmanuel created these rules, and there is nothing more important to a Believer than following them. It's not always easy, especially the striving for perfection one (as you can see), but like Emmanuel says: The only thing worse than not being perfect is not trying to be perfect. So I keep trying.

It really bugs me that Honey doesn't. Try, I mean. And not only does she not try, but in the past year or so it feels like she has just turned her back completely on everything having to do with Mount Blessing. Honey's always been kind of a rebel—once, when we were about six years old and Emmanuel invited all the kids into his room to listen to him play the piano, she stood up in the middle of a very slow, beautiful piece, and said, "I'm bored!" Can you imagine? Just to be invited into Emmanuel's room is in itself a huge deal. But being in there *and* getting to listen to him play the piano is doubly special—like getting to celebrate your birthday twice. Dad says that listening to Emmanuel play is like hearing the voice of God whisper in your ear, and I couldn't agree more. Lately, though, Honey's contemptuousness toward Emmanuel has been getting worse and worse. I don't know what started it or if it's going to end, but I get horribly upset whenever I think about it.

She also does nothing to hide her scorn for what she calls my "saint-wannabe" campaign. She thinks that trying to become a saint is a first-class joke or something. "Human beings aren't supposed to be perfect," she says whenever I remind her of the first of the Big Four rules. "You're just beating your head against a wall, Agnes. The whole point of being human is to make mistakes. That's just the way it is." But that's *not* just the way it is. Emmanuel says that most of us are using only an eighth of our capacity as human beings, and that if we really tried, we could do so much more—even attain perfection. Honey guffaws whenever I try to argue about it with her, and she usually ends up storming off. It's maddening; it really is.

But my resentment vanishes now as I spot her in the tall grass. She is lying on her side, facing away from me, behind the red barn. Her blue robe is a few feet away, flung in a heap beside a cluster of dandelions. The back of her white T-shirt is streaked with grass stains, and her jeans are smudged with mud. For some reason she is missing her shoes. I look around, but they are nowhere to be found. Her breathing is slow and steady and when she inhales, a small whistling sound comes out of her nose. I lie down silently in the space behind her, being careful not to touch anything. I am not sure where it hurts the most. It amazes me that even after all these years my body still fits along the curve of her back. The front of my knees still align perfectly with the backs of hers and there, right along the slope of her neck, is the little freckle I used to stare at just before I drifted off to sleep next to her in the nursery every night. I lean in a little closer until the tip of my nose touches one of her long red braids. Her hair smells like wet grass. Around us, the air pulses with the steady thrum of singing crickets and the sun, warm as bath water, caresses our skin.

"Did Christine send you out looking for me?" Honey's voice, drifting out from beneath her arm, is clotted with sleepy tears.

"No." I pause. "She didn't say anything. I think she

knows you needed some extra time today." This is most likely true. It is no secret that as Mount Blessing's only orphan, Honey is Christine's favorite. After Honey's mother ran away one night—leaving three-week-old Honey behind in the nursery—it was Christine who took care of her. Even when Honey got too old to stay in the nursery and was sent to live in the Milk House with Winky Martin, Christine came down every night to tuck her into bed. And while it's been years since Christine has gone down to check on her, it is obvious that she still holds a special place inside for Honey.

Now Honey snorts. "How big of her."

I stay quiet. It *was* Honey who had gotten us in trouble this morning, Honey who was caught kissing—with her *tongue!*—Peter behind the pool. She made me stand watch, but then Amanda Woodward—who is always sticking her nose into everyone else's business—had popped out of nowhere and started yelling about how she was going to tell on us and so we all paid the price. But it was Honey who had gotten the worst of it.

"Well, if Christine didn't send you, how'd you get out of afternoon prayers?" Honey asks, finally removing her arm and turning over to face me. Her forehead is dirty, her cheeks streaked with dried, salty tear tracks. The white, crescent-shaped scar above her lip is the only unsoiled spot on her face.

"I said I had a stomachache. Christine told me to go lie down. She thinks I'm upstairs in the East House."

Honey's eyes narrow. "*You* lied?"

I sigh heavily. The waist string is cutting so tightly into

my skin that the area around it feels numb, and my pockets, bulging with stones, are pulled tight against my thighs. "Don't remind me, okay? I was worried. You'd been gone for so long. I didn't know what happened."

"Wow," Honey says. "Didn't you almost tell a lie last week when Christine asked you where your consecration beads were?"

I nod, automatically moving my hand to the wooden beads around my neck. "But I didn't."

"Still. An *almost* lie last week. And now a real, full-blown one. What's happening to you, Agnes? You're never going to end up in *The Saints' Way* if you keep going like this."

For a moment I am genuinely stung. After everything I have just gone through for her, she is still not going to give me a break. *Still.* I open my mouth, ready to tell her off, when she turns her head. A blue bruise has blossomed on her cheek, wide and dark as a plum.

"Oh, Honey." I reach out to touch it with my fingertips and then, thinking better of it, withdraw my hand. "Does it hurt?"

Honey pokes at the mottled skin roughly and then winces. "Sore." There is a pause. "But not half as sore as my ass."

I bite my lip. Given the situation, now is not the time to start reminding her of the sinfulness of curse words. "He was hard on you," I say quietly. "After Peter and I left, I mean."

Honey gives me one of her *Sometimes I can't believe we're even friends, you're so stupid* looks. "Um, *yeah.*" She takes a deep breath and then shakes her head.

"Do you . . . want . . . to talk about it?" I ask gently.

"Well, you know, the man's a perfectionist," Honey says. "Gotta get it just right every time. The bastard." I gulp hard. It makes me nervous when she speaks ill of Emmanuel—even if he did just punish her. Emmanuel never punishes us unless we really deserve it. Honey may not think so, but kissing a boy—with your *tongue* no less—is definitely a sin. A carnal one, too, if you want to get really technical about it, which is one of the worst kinds.

"But I screamed my head off," she continues. "Made a whole big scene, just like I always do. Pissed him off royally."

I stare at the sky. Emmanuel has a no-crying rule in the Regulation Room. No matter how bad it gets, if you cry out, it will only get worse. I've learned to hold my breath, taking tiny gulps here and there so that nothing but air emerges from my mouth, but Honey always carries on like she's being tortured or something, just to make him mad.

"'Course, I paid extra for that," she says bitterly.

"What do you mean?"

She rolls back over so she is lying on her stomach. "Lift my shirt up."

"What?"

"Lift my shirt up. Take a look at my back."

I sit up on my knees, tucking my robe beneath my legs. Honey's never asked me to do anything like this before. Sticking out my arm, I let my fingers hover tentatively at the edge of her shirt before dropping them again. "I don't want to."

"Oh, just *do* it." Honey sighs, letting her forehead drop against the ground. *"God."*

I lift her shirt gingerly, as if it might hurt, and hold my breath. Nothing prepares me for what I stare down at. Underneath the slashes of violet belt stripes there are letters scrawled in red marker, large and sloppy, across the tender skin:

H-A-R-L-O-T

My nose starts to wiggle, a habit of mine that started when I was three years old. *Wiggle, wiggle, wiggle.* Somehow it prevents the tears from coming.

"Nice, right?" Honey asks, craning her neck to see over her shoulder. "That was Veronica's idea."

"Veronica?" I repeat, letting go of her shirt.

Honey nods. "Yup, Veronica. Sweet, pure, chaste Veronica who can do no wrong."

I stare disbelievingly at a blade of grass, feeling the blood pound behind my eyes. If Emmanuel is Mount Blessing's spiritual father, Veronica is our spiritual mother. She's second in command here, just one rung below Emmanuel, and is just as holy and virtuous as Emmanuel himself. The story of Emmanuel finding her twenty years ago while teaching one of his advanced divinity classes at a college in Iowa is legendary at Mount Blessing. Dad has told it to Benny and me numerous times over the years. My favorite part is when Emmanuel finally approached Veronica, who, as a college sophomore, had answered yet another one of his theological questions with a wisdom well beyond her years.

"You have an almost otherworldly knowledge of divinity," he had said to her. "Have you ever studied it before?"

Veronica was really shy back then, so shy that she could not even look Emmanuel in the eyes as he addressed her. She was also very self-conscious of a skin rash that covered her arms and hands. It was so severe that it made her skin bleed, forcing her to keep her hands hidden inside her shirtsleeves at all times. "No," she answered. "Never."

"Then how do you know so much?" Emmanuel pressed.

According to the story, Veronica ducked under his steady gaze. "It's not really me," she answered. "It's something bigger, something inside of me that knows. I can't explain it."

But it was explanation enough for Emmanuel. Back then, Mount Blessing was just starting to form, with nine Believers—all of whom had left their homes and come to live with Emmanuel in his little house next to the college. Soon after her conversation with Emmanuel, Veronica became the tenth Believer. Two weeks later, after leaving Iowa and moving to Connecticut where he would begin Mount Blessing, Emmanuel introduced Veronica in a formal ceremony to the other members. She was dressed in the very first blue Believer robe, and her hair, which smelled of lemons and rosewater, shone in the light. The red rash on her hands was completely gone. "Look carefully," Emmanuel said to the tiny congregation. "She is the closest any of you will ever come to being in the presence of the Blessed Virgin."

Every female at Mount Blessing—except Honey—strives to be like Veronica, beginning with how she wears her hair, swept off her face and knotted at the nape of her neck, to the way she holds her arms out straight during an entire prayer service, just like Jesus on the cross. I've spent prayer services—two, three hours at a time—just watching the way she moves her lips or the fervent way she closes her eyes when she utters certain phrases. She is the epitome of perfection, the example of what we are all striving to become. And she is brilliant. Sometimes even Emmanuel will defer to her while he is preaching and let her explain things in her own words. That is why I don't want to hear Honey's reason—if there is one—about Veronica's participation in this. It just wouldn't make any sense.

"What's a harlot?" I find myself whispering instead.

"It's a whore," Honey says. Her voice is matter-of-fact, but when she starts talking again, it trembles around the edges. "Veronica said that's what I am, running around trying to kiss boys like I do. Like I make a habit of it or something. It was one time, for God's sake. *Once!*" The silence between us is deafening, interrupted only by a soft *neigh* from one of the horses in the barn. I take her hand in mine and stroke it tenderly, my fingertips caressing the rough patches along her knuckles.

"You're not a harlot, Honey."

"Yeah," she says, pushing her hair off her face. "I know." Her gaze is fixed on something I can't see in the blue canopy above us. She points with her index finger. "Hey, look! It's a Spangled Fritillary!"

I squint at a small orange butterfly swooping down toward some Queen Anne's Lace. Only a butterfly could distract Honey from the conversation at hand.

She stands up slowly, watching as the small insect floats from one flower to the next. "Look how gorgeous. And so many markings on the wings." She turns to look at me. "Did I tell you Winky and I started aerating the garden this morning?" I nod. "Winky found some wild fennel and turtlehead in the field, too. We're going to transplant them tonight after dinner. The garden's going to be so beautiful this year. I bet we'll have over a thousand butterflies." The butterfly soars past us suddenly and, after grazing the tip of more Queen Anne's Lace, disappears from sight. Honey watches, shading her eyes with her hand.

A small, sudden shout interrupts the moment. "Agnes! Are you up here?"

Instinctively, Honey drops back down in the grass. "Who's that?"

The voice floats over us, louder this time. "Honey! Agnes! Where are you?"

"That sounds like Benny," I say, peering in the direction of the voice. Standing up straight, I wave my arm through the air. "Benny! Over here! We're over here!"

"How'd *he* know where to find us?" Honey asks.

I lean up on my tiptoes. "Probably from when he followed us the last time. Remember?" My little brother is so small that I can see only the top of his white-blond hair as he turns and then swerves through the tall grass like a marshmallow on a stick. He's a nervous little kid to begin with, but he gets even more nervous when he doesn't know where I am. At all times. I love him to pieces, but sometimes it feels like he is suffocating me.

"Nana Pete's here!" Benny says, bursting out all at once from inside the field. His blue robe flaps around him like a tent and his enormous black glasses slide down the bridge of his nose. A constellation of freckles stand out like tiny ants across his face.

"Nana *Pete*?" I say. "What are you talking about? Are you sure?"

Benny is holding his knees with his hands, breathing hard. He lifts his head at my barrage of questions. "I'm telling you, she's here! Mom just came down and got me out of prayers so I could go get you! She's waiting for us in the Great House!"

Honey looks at me accusingly. "You didn't tell me Nana Pete was coming."

I stare wide-eyed at her. "She wasn't. At least, she's not supposed to be. Dad said she wasn't coming until August, just like always."

Nana Pete is Dad's mother. Despite living all the way down in Texas, she comes up to visit us at Mount Blessing every summer without fail. Sometimes she takes a plane, but more often than not, she drives her big green Cadillac, which she calls the Queen Mary. There's nothing she likes more, she always says, than a "good ol' road trip." And while she is Benny's and my paternal grandmother, she has made a point to include Honey in every single thing we've ever done with her, starting when we were just little kids living in the nursery. In fact, I can't ever remember a single time with Nana Pete that didn't include Honey.

Benny slaps his knees. "Can we go? Please?"

Honey laughs out loud and tosses her robe carelessly over one shoulder. "See you guys later."

"Oh, come with us," I say. "You know she'll ask for you as soon as she sees us."

"No more Great House for me today," Honey says, walking on ahead. She looks over her shoulder. "But tell her I'll see her later. Maybe after dinner."

"Where are you going?" I ask uncertainly.

Honey spits out a blade of grass and wipes her mouth with the back of her hand. "Back to the East House, I guess.

Christine probably thinks I've committed suicide by now or something."

I cringe at her offhand comment. Suicide is a mortal sin. "Okay," I call after her. "I'll see you later, then."

Honey lifts her arm in response but doesn't turn around. Benny tugs at my arm, leading me in the opposite direction, but I find it hard to take my eyes off Honey as she moves farther away from us. Her head is held high, her back straight and proud.

It's so strange. Every once in a while, even though I know it's wrong, I find myself wishing that I could be more like her.

HONEY

It's the middle of May, which means that the field behind the horse barn is full of new butterflies. On any other day, I'd be running around like a nut, numbering the different species, examining their wing patterns, and writing everything down in the little notebook Winky gave me. Not today, though. Today those tiny buggers could have wings of pure gold and I wouldn't give them a second glance. After tearing off that damn blue robe, I lie down in the grass instead, turning on my side when it hurts too much, and stare at the sky for a while. I'm supposed to be down in the East House with Agnes and all the rest of the kids, saying afternoon prayers, but that's just not gonna happen. If I was in that room right now, I would probably punch someone. And if Christine wants to give me a hard time about it later (which she won't), she can go jump off a cliff.

When the noise in my head gets too loud, I pull the tiny ceramic cat out of my front pocket and hold him up over my face, directly in line with the sun. George is a Siamese, about the size of a large pecan, and so small that most days I forget he's even there. He's the only thing I have left of my mother, Naomi, who left him behind just before she took off. Sometimes I wonder just how demented she really was, thinking that a four-inch ceramic cat could actually take her place. I don't know whether to cry or laugh when I think about it.

"Hey, Georgie," I say, studying the soft brown markings

along his nose and ears. "How are you? You get squished at all from everything that went on in there?" His blue almond-shaped eyes stare back at me. I turn him around, checking every angle. The tiny chip in his tail is still there, but everything else looks intact. "You're a tough cat, you know that?" I lower my arm so that I can see him up close. He is trembling.

"Hey," I whisper. "Why're you still shaking? It's okay. We're out of there now. Those psychos are history. They're not thinking about us at all anymore." I wrap my cold fingers around the figurine and bring him down against my chest. My heart feels like a tiny, untethered ball knocking around under my rib cage. "It's okay, little guy. It's okay. Deep breaths, remember? In and out. In and out." The sun, a bright lemon disk, warms the cold skin on my face and legs. "In and out, George. That's it. In. And. Out." My arm, heavy as a log suddenly, sinks down across my eyes.

I try not to think about it, but the whole Regulation Room scene unreels itself like a movie in my head. Emmanuel's thin lips loom in front of me, followed by Veronica's ice-blue eyes. I can't stand Emmanuel, but I hate Veronica with an intensity that frightens even me. I hate that she is beautiful, not because I'm jealous, but because her beauty has been wasted. No one as mean as Veronica deserves to carry around a face like that. She has milky white skin, a high forehead, and large, perfectly round blue eyes. Agnes says they are the color of sapphires. I think they are the color of death. I also hate that she is the only person in this place—aside from Emmanuel—who doesn't have to play by the rules. As the queen of Mount Blessing, she calls her own shots—no questions asked. She doesn't want to wear her robe one day? Fine. She wants to buy a television for

Emmanuel's room, even though all electronics are forbidden at Mount Blessing? No problem! In fact, why not buy a gigantic color television that will hang on the wall of Emmanuel's room like a fish tank?

I hate that she is cruel. Not cruel like Emmanuel. Emmanuel's cruelty is freakish, something almost inhuman. Part of me wonders if he was just born that way, that maybe he doesn't even have a choice. Veronica, on the other hand, is a whole other deal. She's *learned* how to be cruel over the years, and the more powerful she's become, the meaner she's gotten. She used to leave Emmanuel's room whenever one of us kids was brought in to be interrogated. Eventually she got to the point where she could stay, but with her eyes riveted on the floor and her fists clenched in her lap. Pretty soon, though, she was participating in the question-and-answer drills, even interrupting Emmanuel at times to ask us to "clarify" something further. Now she even takes over occasionally in the Regulation Room, the way she did this morning. Despite all this, everyone still considers her to be on the same level with the Blessed Virgin Mary. It makes me want to puke when I think about it.

But most of all, I hate that the Believers here refer to her as the mother of this place. As far as I'm concerned, the words "Veronica" and "mother" should never be in the same sentence. Yeah, I know my own mother ran off and left me, so what do I know about mothers, right? I guess I should be grateful that I have some kind of pseudomother stand-in at all. Well, I'm not. I might not know anything about what having a mother feels like, but I'll tell you what: I do know what having a *bad* mother feels like. And I'd bet my life that having a bad mother is worse than not having any mother at all.

I don't remember falling asleep, but the next thing I know, Agnes is snuggling in next to me, exactly the way we used to when we were kids sharing the same crib in the nursery. Her breath is soft as a rose petal against the back of my neck. Something inside my chest swells as our breathing aligns itself. For a moment it feels as though the old Agnes, the one I've known since we were born, is back. The new Agnes, who seems to have sprung whole and fully formed from inside the bowels of Emmanuel's room after he presented her with that freaky *The Saints' Way* book on her birthday, just doesn't do things like that anymore. (I didn't get the book on my birthday, which is two weeks after Agnes's. Agnes was all upset for me, but I told her to relax. Emmanuel probably thinks it would be wasted on me and for once he'd be absolutely right. I'd probably burn the damn thing if I got it.) I hardly recognize Agnes anymore. Now, as if the rules we have to follow here aren't enough, she has become completely obsessed with becoming an actual saint. She walks around with this glazed expression on her face, mumbling prayers under her breath, trying to be perfect. Half the time she doesn't even eat.

It's been a long year, watching and listening to my best friend turn into a robot-girl. I miss her. I miss the light and easy way things used to be with us, the way she used to be able to make me laugh so hard I practically peed in my pants. I can't even remember the last time she was funny—about anything. I miss sitting in the old apple trees on the path to the barn and talking for hours, about any and everything. When we got hungry, we would just reach up and pluck an apple, warm and sweet from the sun, from one of the branches and eat it. I miss the way we used to steal extra snacks from the snack tray after dinner—usually plastic bags filled with dried cereal—and run down to the frog pond so we could eat it without being seen. If Agnes stole anything now, she'd probably have a heart attack. I miss the dumb jokes she used to tell me and the way her eyes would fill up with tears when she watched the sun go down at night.

Most of all, though, I miss running with her in the rain. Agnes is small, so you wouldn't know it by looking at her, but she can run. *Fast.* When she takes off, it's like a set of wings sprout from the back of her shoes. No one—not even any of the boys—has ever beaten her. Not once. It's like trying to keep up with a cheetah. We used to spend the majority of our free time, especially in the summer, racing against each other. I liked running in the heat, but Agnes would literally drag me down the hill to the bicycle ring whenever the skies threatened rain. Her eyes would gleam with excitement as the wind whipped up the dust around us and the air began to fill with the strange metallic scent of the coming storm. We flew across the ring over and over again as the drops fell, going faster and faster as the rain picked up speed.

It's been over a year since we ran together. Whenever I suggest a race, Agnes just shakes her head. It's just as well I guess, since she can barely even muster the energy to walk the quarter mile to school every morning, let alone run a race, thanks to all that ridiculous fasting. The whole thing pisses me off. It really does. Agnes said once that running against the rain made her try harder, that it forced her to reach down inside herself to a place she usually didn't go. If you ask me, that place was the only thing that kept her normal.

Now I don't know what's in there.

After Agnes and Benny leave to go find Nana Pete, I get up slowly and head back down to the East House. I'm dying to go down to the butterfly garden and see how things are going with Winky, but I don't dare. I've already been missing for four hours. After the last Regulation Room visit I was gone for one hour, and the time before that, almost forty-five minutes. I don't know how much longer Christine will let me get away with doing this kind of thing, but I don't want to find out.

Except for the occasional whistling of a bird, the grounds are eerily quiet. Even the wind is still, as if it too understands this week's rule of silence. Ascension Week is one of the holiest times of the year, when the Believers celebrate Jesus Christ's ascent into heaven. For the next seven days, talking is allowed only at the barest minimum, and then in the lowest tone possible. Any activity that takes place outside is strictly prohibited. Even school is canceled for the week. Everyone is inside somewhere, either praying or participating in "Ascension activities," which will culminate at the end of the week with the Ascension March.

So when I hear a strange noise suddenly, like the crunching of gravel, I freeze in my tracks. A strange car emerges from around the bend in the dirt path, moving slowly up the hill. Darting behind a lilac bush, I peer out through the leaves. Sleek and compact as a bullet, the car is the color of gunmetal. Its glossy exterior is spotless, and the tiny silver hood ornament catches the sun in a flash of light. The little hairs on my arm stand up as I catch a glimpse of Veronica sitting behind the wheel. She is not wearing her robe. No surprise there. Gold bracelets encircle her thin wrists and a blue scarf, knotted at the throat, covers her blond hair. I hold my breath as the car passes in front of me. There's no telling what will happen if Veronica catches sight of me now, especially after all the trouble I got into this morning. I hunch down farther against the bush, but the car rolls on past and continues without pause up the remainder of the hill.

Spooked, I run the rest of the way down to the East House without stopping and poke my head in cautiously. The prayer service has obviously ended, as a bunch of the older kids are crowded around the window in the front of the room.

"Did you see it?" I hear Peter ask. "I think it's called a Mercedes. My dad told me Emmanuel was ordering it from somewhere in Long Island."

I roll my eyes. Out of all the boys in my group, Peter is definitely the most gullible, which is why I dared him to stick his tongue in my mouth this morning. Thinking about it now, the way he nearly lunged at me with his mouth wide open, I feel sick to my stomach. I should have picked someone with a little more backbone, someone who at least would have made going into the Regulation Room afterward worth it. Peter was too easy. Plus, he gave me up in a heartbeat when Emmanuel demanded an explanation, pointing at me from across the room with a trembling finger. "It was Honey's idea," he whispered. "I didn't even want to." What a jerk. His little ears, which turn pink when he gets embarrassed and had appealed to me earlier, now just looked stupid. To tell you the truth, though, I wasn't really surprised. Peter is a carbon copy of his parents, especially his mother. Mrs. Winters practically kisses the ground Emmanuel walks on. She's been telling that poor kid what a godlike person Emmanuel is since he was old enough to talk.

You know, some days I think I am going to lose it when I think about the fact that I don't have the faintest idea who my mother (or father) are, but other times I seriously believe that their absence has given me an advantage over the rest of the kids here. Think about it: I am the only kid in this place who doesn't have a second set of authority figures yammering in my ear day in and day out about how *divine* Emmanuel is. And while everyone around me seems to think that my parentless "situation" is pitiful, I think it has actually provided me with room to think for myself. Poor Agnes and Benny and Peter and all the rest of the kids don't have any room left in their heads to have an original thought. Not only are their brains crammed with all of Emmanuel's and Veronica's crap, but they have their parents' crap on top of it. They can't win.

Now I look at my group, which is made up of the twelve- to fifteen-year-olds, over in the corner, rubbing their knees and stretching. The littlest kids are wandering around the room in a kind of daze, their eyes rheumy from staring at the cross on the wall for so long. Six-year-old Iris Murphy, who is always making a fuss about something, is crying about the shooting pains in her legs. Christine rubs her back, trying to console her.

Ducking into the bathroom across the hall, I splash cold water on my face and then look at myself in the mirror. Horrible. Swollen, puffy eyes, splotchy skin, three bright red pimples on my chin. I squeeze one of them until it bleeds and decide against squeezing the rest. Pulling the rubber bands off the bottom of my braids, I shake my hair loose, snatching out pieces of grass. Christine told me once that when I was born, my mother laughed and laughed to see her hair on me. Saffron red, with the same tiny curls just around the ears. Of course at Mount Blessing, red hair, like everything else red, represents Satan and hell and all that good stuff. So while my mother may have thought my hair was cute, my flame-colored tresses have only added to my already damaged reputation here. I guess I can't win either.

I've had exactly one conversation about my mother with Christine, who told me that aside from the red hair, Naomi was just eighteen years old when she arrived, and that she played the violin. Really well. In fact, she was so good that Emmanuel himself took notice and invited her on more than one occasion into his room to play for him. Which is no little thing. Emmanuel used to be a classical pianist, and while I'd personally rather stick needles under my fingernails than have to sit in his room listening to him play, I have to admit, the guy knows his stuff. For real. I mean, he doesn't even have to look down at his fingers or anything when he plays. So Naomi must have impressed him quite a bit with her own musical abilities.

"Actually, she was taken into his spiritual inner circle almost immediately," Christine had said, getting a faraway look in her eyes as she remembered. (Even after twenty-five years, Christine has never been made a part of Emmanuel's inner circle. I don't know why she hasn't, but sometimes I wonder if that made her jealous of my mother.) "Like a month after she got here, which is practically unheard of. But

Emmanuel was so taken with the way she played the violin that no one was really surprised when it happened."

"But *then* what?" I asked. "What happened that made her run away, especially if Emmanuel was so amazed with her?" I paused and bit my lip. "Was it me?"

"Honestly, Honey," Christine said. "I just don't know. One day she was here, visiting you in the nursery, and the next morning she was gone. No one ever saw her again."

I didn't press things after that. For one reason, I believed Christine, who, when I really thought about it, didn't have any reason not to tell me the truth. But there was another smaller part of me that didn't really want to know. What reason could ever be good enough for abandoning your own child?

Now, braiding my hair again quickly, I blow my nose, run my tongue over my lips, and slide my arms back inside my robe. Fastening the silk cord loosely around my waist, I glance down. Where the heck are my *shoes*? When did they come off and how did I forget to put them back on? Well, I'll have to look for them later. Thank God my robe just barely covers my feet. I stroll nonchalantly back into the room, taking small steps so my feet don't stick out, and look around. Peter spots me instantly and breaks away from the little group at the window.

"Hey," he says, trying to act all casual. "Where have you been?"

I shrug and bend my knees so the robe covers my feet again. "Around."

"Yeah," Peter says slowly. "Well." He clears his throat. "You know . . . I just wanted to tell you that I'm sorry that I—"

"I'm *sick* of prayers!" Iris shouts suddenly, interrupting Peter midsentence. She is wriggling away from Christine. "I want to go back to school!" The room erupts with laughter as Iris bursts into tears. She has wild, curly blond hair and a stubby nose. "And no one's listening to me! My legs hurt! They've been hurting all day!" Poor Iris. She says whatever's on her mind, no matter what the consequence. It won't get her into too much trouble here with Christine, but she's always getting it from her parents, who, after Peter's parents, are two of the most devoted Believers at Mount Blessing. They have no qualms about telling Emmanuel every single thing she does wrong. Like me, Iris is no stranger to the Regulation Room.

"Go upstairs and lie down, Iris," Christine says. Her voice sounds tired. "I'll be up in a minute to rub your legs." I turn back to Peter and chuck him softly under the chin with my fist.

"Yeah, I know," I say. "But thanks for saying it." Peter's face changes from one of relief to one of alarm as Christine walks up to the two of us.

"Honey," she says, her dark eyebrows knitting themselves into a line above her blue eyes. "I was just going to have someone go look for you." She touches my arm as Peter drifts back over to the window. "Are you all right?"

I nod and stare down at the floor. Christine moves her hand up to my shoulder. When I look up, her eyes are rimmed with tears. "You're sure you're okay?" she whispers.

I shove my hands into my pockets and shrug. "Yeah, of course. I'm fine."

I guess Christine has been the closest thing to a mother I've ever known. Once, when I had the chicken pox, she stayed up with me for two days straight, taping a pair of mittens around my wrists so I wouldn't scratch myself. Another time, when my fear of the dark started to get really bad, she brought a tiny yellow night-light in the shape of a heart and plugged it into the wall next to my crib. It was no larger than a belt buckle, and to this day I don't know how or where she got it, but I still have it. When I was younger, I guess, the fact that she was nice to me sort of canceled out the fact that she also ratted me out to Emmanuel every now and then. But I'm older now. And I know better.

Christine is a huge Emmanuel fan. *Huge.* Her devotion to him stems back twenty years, when he healed her of some weird compulsive disorder and then convinced her that she couldn't live without him. I've heard her story about joining Mount Blessing at least a thousand times. She used to tell it to all of us when we lived in the nursery, sort of a last-resort bedtime ritual that she would launch into whenever she got bored or sentimental.

Christine was more or less an old maid before Emmanuel came along. At least that's how she tells it. At the age of thirty-six, she still lived with her mother in a little town in Iowa, worked at the local library, and had never been out on a date. As if that wasn't bad enough, she also had some kind of ailment that made her face and body do all sorts of weird things. Her mouth would squish itself up into horrible grimaces, or she would start to make clicking noises with her tongue. Other times, she would yank at her hair or stamp her feet. She had no control over these things; she said it was as if her body and her brain lived on two separate planes and operated independently of each other. There was no known cure for the disorder, and her life ahead looked bleak and hopeless. Until Emmanuel and his first followers moved into the house next door. Christine had heard little things about him from the women she worked with at the library; apparently he was already making a name for himself at the college, where he taught divinity classes, inviting students of his to "healing services" he held at the house. And after a few neighborly nods and a wave here and there from the front porch, Emmanuel invited Christine to come to one of the services, too.

"There was so much love in that room," Christine always said, closing her eyes during this part of the story. "All just radiating from Emmanuel. There were seven or eight other people in there, seated in a semicircle at his feet, but I hardly even noticed them. I couldn't take my eyes off Emmanuel. The light from the lamp next to him made his skin look as if it was glowing. He held out both of his hands as I came into the room and gave me the most beautiful smile. I started to get nervous. 'Come closer,' he said gently. I took a few steps, and as I got close enough Emmanuel reached out, put his hands on my head, and started to pray in Latin. As he prayed, his hands began to tighten, until the pressure on my skull was so intense I thought he might push me through the floor. There was no pain, but I remember the heat from his hands, how it traveled all the way down my body. Then suddenly he tilted my head back so I was looking directly into his eyes. They were the strangest color I had ever seen—a sort of milky gray with little specks of gold and green. 'Be still,' he said, gazing at me with those eyes. 'Be still.'"

I don't know if I believe anymore that Emmanuel has magical healing powers the way I used to think he did when I heard this part of the story. But after that night—and to this day—Christine got her body back again. The foot stamping, the clicking noises, the hair pulling, all of it, just disappeared after Emmanuel prayed over her that night. Lately I've been thinking that maybe she wanted so badly to be healed that her body did it for her. Or maybe her belief in Emmanuel was stronger than the wacky way her brain was wired, and once she had something to replace that part of it, it withered and died. I don't know. It's hard to say. Whatever the case, it was enough for Christine to pack her bags when Emmanuel moved East, kiss her mother good-bye, and follow him. Twenty-five years later, she has never looked back.

Now, back at the East House, Christine clears her throat and adjusts the rope of braid along her shoulder, all business again. "Well, then you're just in time. We're about to start making the banners for the Ascension March."

I bite my lip, stifling a scream. There's no way I can sit around now and start making *banners*. My head is pounding and it feels as if it has been stuffed with cotton. I've got to get down to the butterfly garden or I'm going to freak out. "Did you know Nana Pete's here?" I ask, thinking quickly.

Christine blinks. "Yes, I know. Agnes's mother came down a little while ago and told me."

I look up with my best pleading stare. There is no need to explain to Christine the special relationship I have with Nana Pete—it was Christine who let me tag along whenever Nana Pete took Agnes out of the nursery for a visit. But she winces now, as if reading my mind.

"And . . . you want me to let you go visit with her?" she asks. "*Now?*"

I nod my head vigorously.

Christine puts a hand on her hip. "Honey, you just missed the whole afternoon prayer service. During Ascension Week!" She lowers her voice. "I can't keep giving you special treatment all the time. Emmanuel is going to find out about it."

"Just this once," I beg. "Please, Christine. It's a surprise visit, which means she's probably not even going to be staying very long. I just want to go down and see what the story is. Please let me go." Unlike Agnes, I'll lie until I'm blue in the face if I have to. Anything to get out of here. Christine takes a deep breath and looks uneasily around the room. Peter and the boys are in deep conversation again about the new Mercedes. Amanda Woodward is sitting in the opposite corner of the room, reading a book.

"All right," she whispers finally. "I guess it is sort of a special circumstance." I quell the urge to jump up and down. Christine grimaces and lowers her voice. "And find your shoes before dinner, got it?"

I nod. "Got it."

Cresting atop the wide hill behind the back door, I glimpse the slanted roof of the Milk House, where I have lived with Winky Martin for the past seven years. Unlike the other houses on the compound, which are set in a kind of semicircle around the Great House, the Milk House sits alone in an opposite field, an island adrift in a grassy sea. Its name originated years earlier, when Emmanuel founded Mount Blessing with his first ten followers, and they used the house for storing milk from the community's three cows. As the community grew, the cows were sold off and the house was left empty. The Milk House itself is tiny, with just a first floor and side steps leading up to an open loft. The original shelves used to store the milk bottles still run the length of each downstairs wall, and wide wooden beams meet in a *V* across the ceiling. When it rains, a smell like damp hay and violets fills the rooms.

When I was first sent to live in the loft here at the age of seven, which is the cutoff age for the nursery, I cried for a week. It was the first time since I had been born that I was going to be separated from Agnes, who was going back to live with her parents. (Another Mount Blessing rule dictates that all children be separated from their natural parents at six months of age and raised in the nursery until the age of seven. This is supposed to ensure that Emmanuel remains the primary parental figure.) I would still spend the majority of my days in school, and Christine was instructed to come down every night to make sure that I was in bed, but without Agnes next to me in the little cot we shared for so long, I literally thought I was going to disappear. Even worse than that, now I was going to have to share space with Winky Martin.

I saw Winky just about every day as he pushed a mop around the floors of the Great House, but I, like the rest of the kids, had always kept my distance. I wasn't really sure what it was, but there was definitely something wrong with Winky. In the head, I mean. Some people even said he was retarded, but I just found him frightening. He grunted and wheezed, his meaty face shining with perspiration as he moved his mop back and forth across the floor. Even under his blue robe, his heavy, awkward shape was apparent, and when he walked, he led with his head, swaying it back and forth like a giant agitated bear. Agnes clutched me when we heard the news, her blue eyes big and round. "It'll be okay," she whispered. "Don't worry. Just hide under the covers whenever he comes in."

I did just that for the first week, listening to his muffled grunts from under my blankets, squeezing my eyes shut and clutching George so hard my palms got sweaty. I stared at my little yellow night-light and waited for Winky to climb the steps up to my room and do something horrible to me. But the dreaded footsteps never came. In fact, it seemed as if Winky didn't even realize—or much care—that I was there in the first place. And then one night, after I climbed into bed, I noticed a strange book under my pillow. It was large and heavy, like a dictionary, with an enormous orange and black butterfly on the front cover. Over the picture, in an arc, was the title *The Encyclopedia of Butterflies*. The inside was jammed with information about every butterfly known to man. It was the most beautiful book I had ever seen. I pored over it, savoring every drawing and photograph, memorizing whole passages about the flight patterns and mating habits of the tiny insects. There were butterflies with fantastic names, words I had never even heard before: whirlabouts, skippers, emperors, sulphurs, and monarchs. It took me two weeks to read the book from cover to cover, still under my blankets, with George perched on the mattress next to me.

After that I began to poke around downstairs. There wasn't much to look at, since Winky's entire room consisted of a dresser with four drawers, a single bed (unmade and wrinkled), and a chair covered with a green corduroy material. The items on top of his dresser consisted only of a blue hairbrush (minus half its bristles), a clock, and three other books about butterflies. But his bed was messy. I liked that. My bedspread upstairs, stretched taut the way Christine had taught me, was just another reminder of the "strive for perfection" rule we had to follow, which, in my book anyway, is complete crap. Who in their right mind seriously thinks that a human being can go through life without making a mistake? It's impossible! I'm constantly trying to get this through Agnes's head, but she just won't listen. She doesn't listen when I point out some of the other inconsistencies of the Big Four either, especially the one about tempting not lest you be tempted, which is supposed to explain why there are no TVs or magazines or radios anywhere on the grounds. But why is it, I've asked her, that Emmanuel himself—and now Veronica—is exempt from this rule? Why is Emmanuel's room full of material things like stereo equipment, a baby grand piano, expensive wines, and that enormous color television? Agnes says that Emmanuel is entitled to these things, since he has achieved a "plateau higher than temptation." Like she even knows whatever the hell *that* means.

Anyway, for this reason alone, Winky's unmade bed made me happy. It was the first time I had ever come across anyone who dared dismiss Emmanuel's rules, however trivial. I sat down on the edge of his soft mattress and swung my legs and wondered what other rules he broke.

It wasn't long before I found out. One night, after hearing strange noises coming from downstairs, I crept to the top of my stairs and peeked over the railing. I could hardly believe my eyes when I saw Winky sitting in his green chair staring at a tiny black-and-white TV. The screen was no larger than a piece of loose-leaf paper and the picture, which at times skittered up and down, was fuzzy at best. Guys in rimmed hats and black-and-white-striped uniforms stood around a gigantic baseball field, and a crowd roared every time one of them hit the ball. When someone got up to bat, Winky shifted restlessly in his seat and grunted. I sat still as snow and watched the rest of the game from the stairs. When it ended, Winky stood up, burped, unplugged the television, and pushed it back under his bed. I crept back to my own bed, listening to my heart pound in the dark as Winky's snores filled the house. Segregated or not, the Milk House was starting to feel like home.

Now I tiptoe around to the back of the house. Winky is on his knees in the middle of the garden, tamping down soft dirt around the pepper bushes in the back row. Perfect. I back up slowly and sneak into the house. Moving as quietly as possible, I angle the tiny TV out from under Winky's bed, set it on the orange milk crate next to his slippers, and plug it in. *Days of Our Lives* is nearly over, but I watch the last ten minutes of it breathlessly, trying to figure out what I missed. I think someone may be plotting to kill Hope, but I'm not sure. It's just a hunch. I keep an eye on Winky, peeking out the window every few minutes. He once caught me watching this show and flipped his lid. He doesn't care if I watch baseball with him, but he thinks everything else is trash and he doesn't want to be responsible for me watching it. My mouth waters as a Coke commercial comes on. I wonder what a Coke would taste like. Too soon, the credits start to roll and when the hourglass appears on the screen, I flick the television off and shove it back in its hiding spot. Then I stroll out to the garden.

"Hey!" I squat down next to Winky, watching as he pours a bucket of water over the pepper bush. He grunts in response but doesn't look up. "I was afraid you might not be here. How'd you get out of Ascension duties today?"

Winky reaches under his robe and removes a small pair of garden shears from his back pocket. "I was peeling potatoes, but Beatrice said I was too slow. She told me to go away." He struggles to get the words around his tongue, which lolls heavily against his lower lip.

"Oh, Beatrice is an idiot," I say, sitting down carefully on the grass. "She thinks she can boss everyone around because Veronica put her in charge of the Ascension dinner this year. She's impossible. Don't take it personally."

Winky begins snipping off the dead leaves from the pepper bushes. "I don't think she likes looking at me. She gets scared. She always tells me to go." His left eye, which spasms uncontrollably as he talks (and is the reason for his unusual nickname), is moving so fast that I wonder if there is a small engine underneath the lid.

"Well, that's her problem. I can't think of too many people who like looking at her, either, especially with that big ugly mole on her chin." I stand back up. It hurts way too much to sit right now. Plus, while it's nothing new, I still get agitated when I hear about people brushing Winky off, as if he were some kind of subhuman species. It's not his fault that he can't think as quickly as they do, or that his weird older brother who arrived with him ten years ago decided to leave to "pursue other avenues"—without his handicapped younger brother. Most people at Mount Blessing barely give Winky the time of day, and if they do, it's usually because they're complaining about something he didn't do or scolding him for doing it wrong. I know they just take their cues from Emmanuel, who has never bothered to have an actual conversation with Winky about anything, let alone acknowledged his presence. I know for a fact he's never gotten a copy of *The Saints' Way*, and while we've never talked about it, I'd bet my life he's never seen the inside of the Regulation Room. I'm not sure he even knows it exists. Emmanuel would never waste his time trying to "retrain" someone like Winky, who is still "broken." Winky's just . . . here. Kind of like me.

"Wow, this garden is really coming along!" I put my hands on my hips and survey the neat rows of butterfly bushes we planted last night. "It's gonna be huge this year!" This is the time of year when Winky's butterfly garden, which he dug and planted all by himself ten years ago, begins to turn into a carpet of color. The pepper and butterfly bushes will bloom in just a few weeks, small pink, purple, and white flowers that will perfume the air with a wonderful lemony smell. By the end of May, most of the purple phlox, French marigolds, nasturtium, and verbena plants will have opened, and in June the rows of purple coneflowers, scarlet sage, and wild zinnias will take center stage.

Of course, the best part of the garden—and the reason Winky planted it in the first place—is the butterflies it attracts. Winky is obsessed with butterflies. He says that the healthiest environments are the ones that attract lots of butterflies. (Don't think it's any accident that Winky had to actually *build* a butterfly garden himself to get butterflies to come to Mount Blessing, but that's beside the point.) At the height of summer, there will be hundreds, maybe even thousands, of winged visitors to his garden, each one hovering inside its favorite flower. Winky has planted specific flowers for specific butterflies and they love him for it. At times the air seems to hum with the beating of paper-thin wings.

"I don't know," Winky says, twisting his head to look up at the sky. "*Farmers' Almanac* says it's supposed to be a dry summer. It might not do so good this year."

"Well, I'll pray for rain."

Winky snorts. "You? Pray?"

I kick at a loose clod of earth. "Hey, did you hear anything about Emmanuel buying a new car? A Mercedes?"

Winky nods. "I heard Beatrice talking about it. It's for Veronica. Her birthday, I think."

I shake my head. "It's just unbelievable. It really is."

"What, the car?"

"*Yeah*, the car. And the TV and the stereo and the baby grand piano and all the rest of it. I mean, how stupid *is* everyone, just nodding and smiling whenever he brings some other ten-thousand-dollar toy into the place?"

"I think the Mercedes cost a little more than that," Winky says.

"Well, whatever." I reach down and scoop a handful of the dark earth into my palm. It is cool and dry against my skin. "Seriously, Wink, are we the only two people who think it's just *slightly* ludicrous that Emmanuel gets to be the exception to every single one of his rules? I mean, the man is a complete hypocrite! All the way through!" I lob a small stone into the distance. It arcs cleanly over the garden, landing in the field behind it. "And I'll tell you what, one of these days, I'm going to do something about it."

Winky turns around and squints up at me. Even with his

swollen tongue hanging out of his mouth, I can tell the left side of his face is cocked up into a grin. "Oh yeah? You and what army?"

I shrug. "Maybe I don't need an army. Maybe I'll figure out something on my own."

Winky shoves his scissors back into his rear pocket and looks around carefully. "What're you talking about exceptions for, anyway? You know I got a TV under my bed." He acknowledges this with a hoarseness in his voice, as if the guilt is eating him alive.

"Oh, who cares?" I say impatiently. "The thing barely even *works*, Winky. And the only thing you watch is baseball, for crying out loud." I pause. "Unlike me." I mutter this last statement, but Winky jerks his head up and eyes me suspiciously.

"You watching those bad shows again when I'm not around?"

I kick at the ground as the blood rushes to my cheeks. "They're not *bad*, Winky. I told you that. They're just . . ."

He struggles to his feet and cuts me off roughly with a wave of his hand. "I *told* you, Honey!" His face gets red; spit flies out of his mouth. "I told you be*fore!*"

I raise my hands against my chest. "Okay, okay. I'm sorry. I won't do it ever again, okay? I promise."

"You said that last time," Winky says accusingly. His nostrils flare under his wild eyes. "You lied."

I hang my head. "I'm sorry. I really am. I won't do it again." I watch shamefacedly as he drops down again to his knees and begins yanking at a patch of weeds. Minutes tick by in an awkward silence. The only sound is the forceful ripping of roots from the ground. After a while I get down on my knees opposite Winky and start weeding my side of the garden, pretending with every pull that I am wrenching Veronica's head out from between her shoulders.

It feels good.

AGNES

As Benny and I wind our way down the path that leads to the Great House, I catch a glimpse of Nana Pete's green Cadillac parked in the driveway. The Queen Mary.

I stop momentarily, regarding the physical proof of her presence with an inflating sense of happiness. "Wow, it really is her."

"I told you!" Benny says, jumping up and down. "I told you!" He yanks on my hand, nearly dragging me down the rest of the hill. "Hurry up, Ags! She's waiting!" We break into a dead run, but as we approach the Great Door, I reach out and pull Benny back.

"I know. I *know*," he says irritably, shrugging me off.

Weighing close to a hundred pounds, the Great Door is a thing of beauty. Carved from the trunk of a maple tree fifteen years ago by two of the Believers, it is meant to slow whoever approaches with its intricate carvings of suns, moons, and stars. Etched along the top of the top, like an enormous banner, are the words "*Glori Patri,*" which is Latin for "Glory to the Father." Benny and I drop to one knee beneath the watchful phrase, crossing ourselves in a somber genuflection. Then it takes both of us, straining under our full weight, to push open the door. When I lean against it, the scent of old sap fills my nostrils. It creaks and moans and then seals shut with a gasp behind us.

The inside of the Great House is one gigantic, long room.

It is filled with blue-robed Believers sitting at the long wooden table doing any number of things. Because this is Ascension Week, most of the men who work in town are here instead, getting ready for the feast day. Mr. Murphy, Iris's father, is in the corner a few feet away, polishing the life-sized crucifix on the wall. His cloth lingers reverently over the exposed rib cage and the blood-mottled skin. Over in the corner, Beatrice, who is one of the head kitchen women, is giving instructions to other women who are peeling potatoes and onions and chopping celery. Lynn Waters, who paints beautiful portraits of Emmanuel, is in the midst of a deep discussion with four women who are holding hand-painted Ascension banners. Four more men are washing the floor-to-ceiling windows, which line the length of the far wall. Despite the amount of activity, no one speaks above a hushed whisper. Emmanuel himself resides in the rooms at the very back of the Great House and must not—under any circumstances—be disturbed.

"There she is!" Benny points to the left side of the room where three leather couches are arranged neatly around a dead fireplace. Nana Pete's signature braids, pinned tightly across the top of her head, gleam like a silver moon above the soft leather. Mom and Dad are seated on the couch opposite her, their robes fastened tightly under their chins. Mom's face is set tight, the way it always is when she is in the same room as Nana Pete. Dad looks as though he might faint. Although it is forbidden, Benny breaks into a run down the length of the Great House, his sandals slapping the black-and-white checked linoleum floor.

"Benny!" I hiss. *"Walk!"* But he is too fast for me. I watch with dismay as he barrels headfirst into Nana Pete's soft lap.

"Ooof!" She laughs delightedly. "Benny! My *word*, darlin'!" She holds him at arm's length, gazing up and down. "Look at how much you've grown!"

I walk up slowly, my arms tucked into the opposite sleeves of my robe.

"Mouse!" She uses the name she gave me after my nose started doing that wiggling thing. "I was wondering when y'all would get here!"

I close my eyes as she encircles me tightly and inhale the familiar, lovely scent of her: Wrigley's peppermint gum, Nina Ricci perfume, and the slight tang of sweat. But a rustle of material makes me open my eyes again. Mom and Dad stand before us, erect as soldiers, their silk cords swaying from side to side. Loose hairs from Mom's bun cascade softly along her shoulders and there are dark circles under her eyes.

"Sit. Down." Dad's voice is as faint and threatening as thunder. "Both of you." His mustache twitches, and his nostrils flare white. Nana Pete stares up at Dad and then over at us. I wonder how long it is going to take this time for an argument to explode between them.

"Oh, Leonard," my grandmother says, waving her hand. "Don't start on the children. I just got here—"

Mom cuts her off. "Petunia, please lower your voice. And please stop calling him Leonard. You know that's no longer his name."

Nana Pete winces, either at Mom's use of her full name, which she despises, or the fact that three years ago, after Dad was received into Emmanuel's inner spiritual circle, he was rechristened Isaac. Nana Pete's not too happy about it, but this is pretty common at Mount Blessing. Mom's name used to be Samantha, but Emmanuel renamed her Ruth at her inner-circle ceremony. Most of the Believers have new names. It's a symbol of their willingness to shed their old life and start a new one. Someday, if I'm ever so blessed, Emmanuel will bestow a new name upon me, too.

Nana Pete smiles offhandedly at Mom. "Of course," she says, rearranging herself back into the couch. "I remember."

Mom sits back down on the couch next to Dad and shoots Benny and me a look. "Fasten your robe, Benedict," she whispers. "And tie your belt cord. You must remember that you are in a sacred place."

Benny scrambles again to his feet. I help him adjust his robe and cord until they both hang down neatly around him. Nana Pete watches us with a slightly pained expression on her face.

"That's better," Mom says, nodding. "Now sit back down and lower your voices."

I sit carefully, putting my hands on the seat first and then sliding my bottom over them, biting my tongue so that I don't wince.

Nana Pete is watching me. "Is something wrong, Mouse?" she asks.

I look up quickly, as if I have been caught. "No, no," I answer, shaking my head.

Nana Pete's violet eyes crinkle a little the way they do when she knows I am not telling the truth. I stare at Mom's feet, which are encased in brown sandals. Her toenails need to be cut.

"Did Emmanuel call for you and Honey this morning, Agnes?" Mom asks, pulling her feet abruptly under her robe. I nod, keeping my eyes on the space where her feet have disappeared. This is all that needs to be said between us. They know the rest. Later, when we return to our own house, they may ask the reason why I was sent to see Emmanuel; then again, they may not. It is not up to them to discipline me for the major wrongs I commit; that is Emmanuel's job.

Nana Pete looks confused for a moment by the things not being said between my parents and me. She opens her mouth, leans toward Mom, and then closes it again. Putting her arm around me, she pulls me in close. "I'm so glad to see you, darlin'," she murmurs. She squeezes Benny, who is on the other side of her. "And you too, cowboy."

A faint ringing sounds from inside Nana Pete's leather bag. "Pardon me," she says. A muscle in Dad's cheek moves as she begins rummaging through her bag. The ring gets louder as she pulls out a thin silver box. We stare as she flips open the top of it, gazes at something for a moment, and then shuts it again with a *click*. The ringing stops.

"Cool!" Benny breathes, leaning over Nana Pete's lap. "Is that a phone?"

Nana Pete laughs. "Of course it's a phone, Benny!" I watch out of the corner of my eye as she flips the top up again and holds it out for him to see. "It's a cell phone! Haven't you ever seen one of these?"

Benny and I shake our heads. Mom clears her throat.

"Mother." Dad sits forward a little in his seat. "*Please.* Put the phone away. You know things like that are not allowed here. And turn it off so it doesn't ring anymore."

Nana Pete slides the tiny phone back inside her purse and, exchanging a look with Dad, crosses her pink rattleskin-snake boots at the ankle. "Fine. But are you really serious about not leaving here for the rest of the afternoon—even to visit with your old mother?"

Dad sighs and glances apologetically at Mom. "Mother. Keep your voice down, first of all." Nana Pete presses a finger against her lips. Dad closes his eyes briefly, as if searching inside for an untapped source of patience. "As I said before, Ruth and I are in the middle of planning the details of the Ascension March, which is taking place here Thursday evening. It's a very, very big deal, one of the holiest days of the year, and this year Emmanuel has asked me and Ruth to lead all the team meetings."

Mom casts her eyes down at the floor. "To be asked to plan such an event is an enormous honor," she says.

Dad draws his thumb and index finger over the sides of his mustache. "I remember telling you specifically about this whole thing the last time we spoke on the phone, Mother."

"Which would have been when?" Nana Pete asks, reaching under the leg of her pants to scratch her shin. "Eight months ago?"

"Yes, eight months ago. Don't you remember? I explained everything to you then, from start to finish." Dad rubs the tops of his knees, as if to stunt the flush that is creeping up along his neck. "Ascension Thursday is the root of our deepest beliefs here, Mother. I know you know that. And for you to just show up—without warning—and expect us to realign our plans according to your whims is just . . . just incredibly *rude!*" He leans back into the couch, red-faced from his outburst, and wipes his lips. A long silent moment passes as Nana Pete stares at Dad. No one moves.

"Well," she says finally. "You're exactly right, Leonard, come to think of it. I shouldn't have come swooping down on you out of the blue. I've had some things come up unexpectedly over the past few weeks that I thought I would share with you. But you're right. I should have at least called. My needs are no more important than yours. They can wait." She reaches down and tugs at the bottom of her white button-down shirt until the wrinkles disappear. Then she places one palm on my knee and one on Benny's. "I won't stay long. A few days at the most. And while I'm here, I won't get in your way. I promise. But will you give me some time with the children until I leave again?"

Dad's face softens at his mother's conciliatory words. He shifts uncomfortably in his seat. "Of course," he says. "But it *is* Ascension Week, which means the children must stay quiet. No running around the grounds like they usually do with you. You'll have to take them back to the house and visit there until dinnertime."

"Fine," Nana Pete says. She gets up, pulling Dad to his feet, and kisses him hard on the cheek. He looks uneasy. "Have you called Lillian?" she asks in a low voice. "Even just to say hello?"

Mom looks up sharply.

"You just never know when to stop, do you, Mother?" Dad drops Nana Pete's hands. "Let's go, Ruth," he says. "We have work to do."

. . .

Nana Pete takes my hand as we walk out to her car. Benny has already raced on ahead and climbed inside. I run my thumb gently over the raised green veins on the surface of her hand. They are soft as velvet.

"Why do you always bring up Lillian, if you know Dad's just going to get mad?" I ask gently.

Nana Pete tilts her head and studies a turtle-shaped cloud. "Oh," she says finally. "That's just what mothers do."

I don't press her. The only thing I know about Lillian is that she is Dad's younger sister and that there was some kind of falling out between them years ago. To this day, I've never heard Dad talk about her, and for some reason, he has forbidden Nana Pete from discussing her at all with us. Still, I can't remember a single visit where Nana Pete hasn't mentioned Lillian to Dad at least once.

"So why did you come now, instead of in August like you usually do?" I ask.

"Well, I can't come in August, Mouse. My doctor wants to do a few tests on me then, so I won't be able to travel for a little while."

I stop walking. "Tests?" I repeat. "Why? What's wrong?"

Nana Pete laughs. Her teeth are the color of dimes. "Now, don't get yourself in a tizzy, darlin'. I'm not getting any younger, you know. And this is what happens when you get to be my age. My doctor just wants to check out this old body of mine to make sure everything's still ticking."

"Oh. So it's just a checkup, then?"

Nana Pete nods, staring straight ahead. "Exactly right, Mouse. A checkup."

The inside of the Queen Mary smells faintly of onions.

One of Nana Pete's weaknesses is junk food, especially something called Funyuns, which she brings us (secretly) every year. They're puffy little things that taste like onion-flavored air. I like them all right, but I've tried only a few and that was a long time ago, before I started reading *The Saints' Way*. For one thing, they're completely against the rules here. For another thing, saints would never fill their bodies, which are temples of the Holy Spirit, with junk food. But Benny is addicted to them. Now he waits in the backseat, his mouth hanging open like a puppy, until Nana Pete pulls a bag out of the glove compartment.

"Nana Pete," I start. "Please. You know . . ."

She laughs and tosses the bag back into Benny's outstretched hands. "I know. I know, Mouse. But they're not going to kill him. I promise."

I turn and glare at Benny. He already has four of the puffed rings inside his mouth. His jaw freezes as our eyes meet.

Nana Pete reaches out and cups his chin in her hand. "Oh leave him *alone*, darlin'," she says. "Let him enjoy something." She squeezes Benny's chin and, as if on cue, he starts chewing again. I turn back around and stare straight ahead. Nana Pete laughs and then pokes me in the arm. "You don't have to be so serious about everything *all* the time, Mouse."

"Can we go back to the house now so I can lie down for a while?" I ask, not taking my eyes off the windshield. "I'm pretty tired." Nana Pete slides her hands over the white leather wheel. Her fingernails, painted a shiny purple color, glitter under the sun.

"Actually, Mouse, I think that's a fine idea." She starts the engine and revs the gas. The radio turns on immediately, filling the car with pounding drums and a wailing woman's voice: *Sweet dreams are made of these, Who am I to disagree?*

I clap my hands over both ears. "Turn it off!"

Nana Pete leans over quickly and switches off the radio. "I'm sorry, Mouse. I forgot." The tires make a crunching sound beneath us as she backs the car out of the driveway. "Why aren't you two in school?" she asks after a moment, steering the car onto Sanctity Road. "It's Tuesday, isn't it? Is this a holiday?"

"Emmanuel always shuts school down during Ascension Week," Benny says.

"The Ascension," Nana Pete murmurs. "Which one is that again?"

I almost laugh out loud, until I remember that people like Nana Pete who don't know the holy days of obligation, let alone recognize Jesus Christ as the one and only Lord and Savior of the world, are going to end up burning for all eternity in hell. Dad says that Nana Pete is a heathen because she doesn't believe in any kind of religion at all. But when I asked her once about that, she said that believing in God and believing in religion were two different things. Which doesn't make any sense at all.

"It's when Jesus Christ rose up to heaven," I answer.

"Ah." Nana Pete nods her head. "Of course. And what about that march thingie your father was talking about? What is that, exactly?"

I tell her about the annual tradition, the biggest one of the whole year for Believers, when everyone, including the children, dress in snow-white robes (made especially for the occasion) on the evening of the sacred night. Then we will wind our way up a sloped gravelly path until we reach the highest point of the hill where, as a congregation, we will reenact the Ascension itself.

"And let me guess," Nana Pete says dryly. "Emmanuel plays the part of Jesus Christ."

"Well, yeah," I answer. "Of course." Her tone of voice irritates me, but I stay quiet. There's no way my grandmother could ever understand how amazing a thing it is, how last year, as I stood between Christine and Mr. Murphy and stared at Emmanuel, who lifted his arms toward the purple sky and tipped his head back, an energy began to emanate from him. It was like an actual heat began to radiate from his body, and his feet very nearly lifted off the ground. It was incredible, just like the picture of Saint Joseph of Cupertino, who used to float off the ground when he meditated.

There is a pause, the only sound in the car the *pat-pat* of Benny batting his empty Funyuns bag between his hands.

"So have you been staying up late to practice for this Ascension March?" Nana Pete presses. "Is that why you're limping?"

I shake my head as my cheeks flush hot. "I'm not limping."

"Okay." Nana Pete eases the bulky car into the narrow driveway of our house and throws it into park. "Can I ask you another question, then?" I can feel her eyes on me. "What did your mother mean earlier when she asked if Emmanuel had sent for you and Honey? Were you in some kind of trouble?"

My blood runs cold. The batting of the plastic bag behind us stops.

"Did Emmanuel take you guys into the Regulation Room?" Benny asks.

I snap my head around and glower at him. His eyes are as wide as softballs behind his glasses.

"The *what*?" Nana Pete asks, looking at Benny.

"Benedict." My voice feels and sounds like steel. "Shut your mouth. I mean it."

My little brother whimpers and then slumps down behind the backseat, disappearing from view. Nana Pete turns off the car engine.

"What exactly," she asks, staring at me, "is the Regulation Room?" She says the last two words very slowly, as if something bitter has just filled her mouth. My nose starts to wiggle. "Agnes? Talk to me." Nana Pete never calls me Agnes unless something is seriously wrong. I swallow hard and shake my head.

"It's nothing. Really. It's nothing." The sting of tears pinches the back of my throat.

My grandmother reaches out and grabs my hand. "Agnes. Darlin'. Look at me. Please. Don't tell me it's nothing. I know that's not true."

But I just shake my head harder. My nose is going into overdrive thinking about having to tell another lie today, a frantic little knob of a thing that is moving so hard that I am afraid it's going to take flight off my face. I grab the door handle and yank it open.

"Mouse!" Nana Pete pleads.

Slamming the door behind me, I break into a run, ignoring the white-hot burning of my legs, and disappear into the house. It is not until I get into my room that I realize she has not followed me. I listen to the Queen Mary's engine as it revs furiously, like a rabid animal growling, and then fades into the distance.

Slowly I take the stones out of my pocket, lining them up one by one on top of my bed. Then I lie down, trying not to wince as they dig and poke into my back. If Saint Rose could do it, then so can I.

HONEY

Winky's butterfly garden is my favorite place to be. Not only is it beautiful—even in the pale light of winter when the furrowed, frozen earth looks like the surface of the moon—but it is also a complete little world all its own. The butterflies' whole cycle of life—from beginning to end—takes place here. The Believers refer to it only in a patronizing kind of way; I've actually heard some of them call it "Winky's little hobby," which makes me want to scream. Like he's down here digging in the dirt with a spoon or something. They have no clue how complex the whole thing is, or how much work Winky has put into it over the years.

The garden itself is divided into two parts: a weed section and a nectar section. The weed section, which is filled with plants like snapdragons, turtleheads, thistles, wild fennel, mint, sassafras, and violets, is basically one big food source for the caterpillars, which have hatched from eggs the female butterflies have laid earlier. The nectar section consists of flowering plants and bushes, which have been carefully chosen according to the butterfly population in our part of the country. Purple phlox and aster, for example, are some of the Clouded Sulphur butterfly's favorite flowers. Violets and sassafras are favored by the admirals. We have to check the nectar source plant leaves every day when it starts to get warm, because sometimes the caterpillars wander over there and start eating. When we find them, we transfer them back into the weed section so the nectar source plants have a chance to grow big and healthy.

This is what Winky and I do for the next hour, pushing back the leaves of every single nectar source plant—there are at least fifty—searching for caterpillars. We work silently, peeling off the tiny worms one by one and, when our palms are full, transporting them back to the opposite end of the garden. Every so often, I look over at the top of Winky's head, hoping he will raise it again and talk to me, but he stays quiet. I'm not sure which situation he is angrier about: that I have been watching his television without asking, or that I have been watching soap operas again. But I don't want to ask. I'm afraid it might make things worse. Winky has been angry with me before; once we got into an argument and I blurted out that he was an idiot and he refused to talk to me for two days. They were the two longest days of my life. I did not sleep, and for some reason, the ache inside for my mother, which most days I am able to put on a back burner, intensified like a sharp stick poking at me from the inside out.

"Hey, Wink?" I venture now. "You still mad?"

He straightens up, holding a palmful of tiny green worms, and looks directly at me. "Yup."

"How mad?" I watch as he turns and strides toward the weed section. Without his belt cord, which he always removes before working in the garden, his robe flaps open in the middle, exposing his ample belly. I make my voice louder. "Sorta mad or mad like you're not going to talk to me for two days mad?"

Instead of answering, he pushes the worms from his palm onto a sassafras leaf and then leans down, double-checking to make sure none of them have fallen into the dirt. When he is satisfied, he turns, and as if he has all the time in the world, strolls back toward me.

"Sorta mad," he says finally, and then he grins and I know that everything between us is still okay. I smile back at him and then head over toward the weed section with my own worms.

"Why're you walking funny?" Winky asks. "You hurt yourself?"

For an eighth of a second, I wonder what would happen if I broke down and told Winky what Emmanuel and Veronica did to me this morning. But I dismiss the thought just as quickly. What good would telling Winky do? It's not like he'd be able to *do* anything about it. I don't even know if he could comprehend the details. And, oddly enough, the Regulation Room has been Mount Blessing's dirty little secret for so long that talking about it would feel really weird. I mean, even Agnes and I barely talk about it.

"Yeah, I was messing around on my bike the other day," I say. "You know, acting like a goof. I tripped over one of the pedals."

Winky starts to respond, but is interrupted by the squeal of tires. A pale green car shoots into view, coming to a halt alongside the lawn. I stare as Nana Pete opens the door of her car and starts marching across the lawn. Something about the way her mouth is set in a straight line is setting off alarm bells in my head.

"Nana Pete?" I call. "Hi!"

She beckons me forward with one hand. "Honey! Come with me! Now!"

Now the bells are ringing really loudly. Usually there is a hug and kiss, a "How have you *been*, sugar pie? You've gotten so *tall* since I've seen you last!" Maybe even a supersize bag of Funyuns hidden behind her back. There is none of that now. My suspicions sharpen even more when I get a glimpse of Benny sitting in the back of the car, staring out the window.

"What's wrong?" I ask. "Where's Agnes?"

Nana Pete is next to me now, almost out of breath. She leans over and hugs me quickly, as if to get it out of the way.

"Please darlin'. I've been looking for you for over an hour. Please just come with me. I need to talk to you. Right now." She puts her hands on her hips and looks over at Winky, noticing him all at once.

"Winky," she says, extending her hand. "Hello. I don't know what window my manners flew out of on the way up here, but I do apologize."

Winky sticks out a dirty, gloved hand.

Nana Pete grabs it and pumps it up and down. "Your garden looks absolutely lovely," she says, surveying the plants. "The nasturtium especially."

"Thank you," he says, looking pleased.

"You don't mind if I borrow your helper here for a little while, do you?" Nana Pete asks. "I have to talk to her about something."

Winky shakes his head. "Go 'head, Honey. I'll be here till late."

I trot behind Nana Pete down to the car, trying to keep up with her. For an old lady, she can *move* when she wants to.

"Where's Agnes?" I ask again, my hand poised on the handle of the door.

"Just get in the car, Honey," Nana Pete answers. Her voice is terse, almost rude. "And shut the door."

I slide into the front seat next to her, clutching the armrest as she guns the car down Sanctity Road. Glancing over the backseat, I stare at Benny, hoping to discern any bit of information from him, but he has drawn his knees up under his chin and buried his face into the top of them.

Nana Pete finally screeches to a halt, coming so close to the edge of the frog pond that I gasp and rear back. She shuts the engine off and turns sideways, looking at me with wild eyes. Her mascara has started to run and her overly rouged cheeks are shiny with perspiration. She looks like a first-class lunatic.

For the first time, I am frightened. *"What?"*

Nana Pete swallows. "What is the Regulation Room? What is it, where is it, and what happens to you inside there?"

I am so shocked at her barrage of questions that for a moment I am speechless. Then I realize I don't know what to say. Except for a few painful details here and there with Agnes over the years, I have never discussed the Regulation Room. With anyone. Ever.

"How'd you find out about *that?*" I ask finally, struggling to keep my voice from shaking.

"Agnes."

"Agnes?" I repeat.

"Well, sort of," Nana Pete says, glancing over at Benny. She is gripping the top of the seat so hard that the soft leather is indented. "Her parents mentioned something earlier about the two of you having been *sent for* by Emmanuel and well, I don't know, something about that particular choice of words got me thinking. Then I saw her limping and I kept pestering her to tell me what was wrong . . ." Her voice trails off.

"It was my fault!" Benny wails, lifting his head. "I asked about it on accident." His face crumples behind his glasses, as if he has just realized the magnitude of his admission. "I didn't mean to, Honey. I didn't know . . ." He lowers his face again and begins to sob, his little shoulders heaving up and down. Nana Pete reaches out and touches his knee with her fingertips.

"Agnes wouldn't tell me anything," she says. "But the way she bolted out of the car when I pressed her about it makes me think there is a lot to tell." Her hand freezes on Benny's back. "I just want to know if any of you are being hurt, Honey. Please. Tell me the truth."

My heart is hammering inside my chest. The tips of my fingers feel tingly. I realize all at once that if I tell Nana Pete the truth about the Regulation Room, a chain of events will probably be set into motion that I will not be able to stop.

"It's . . . just . . . this room," I say.

"And?"

"And . . . what?" I bite my lip, unsure why I am stalling.

"And where is it?"

"It's . . . um . . . behind Emmanuel's room."

"Behind Emmanuel's room? Like a hidden door or something?"

I shrug. "It's not hidden, really. But there's a door."

"Okay. And what would I see if I opened this door, Honey? Hmmm?"

My mouth tastes bitter, just thinking of it. "A kneeler," I say quietly.

Nana Pete's face blanches. "What's a kneeler?"

"It's a bench thing you kneel on."

"To pray?"

"No," I answer. "Not to pray."

Nana Pete shakes her head slowly. "What's it for, then?"

I stare at the top of Benny's head. The hairs are so white that it is hard to distinguish them from his scalp.

"Honey?" Nana Pete presses. "What's the kneeler for?"

I wince, thinking of this morning. "He makes us kneel on it and then lean forward."

"On your stomach?"

"Yeah."

Nana Pete swallows hard. "Why?"

A picture of me bent over that damn thing, naked from the waist down, flashes through my head. Suddenly I remember where my shoes are. They had been covered with mud and Veronica made me take them off before I went into Emmanuel's room. "I don't want your smelly shoes stinking up the room," she had said. Her lip curled over the top of her teeth. "Get rid of them." I was glad that Agnes and Peter had already left; it was humiliating to have to hide my dirty shoes under the bench, and even more awful to walk back inside in my bare feet, which smelled even worse than my shoes.

"Honey?" Nana Pete says my name so softly that it makes me want to cry. "Honey. What else is in the room?"

I grit my teeth. "Belts." Behind me, Benny's shoulders tighten.

"Belts?"

"A wall of them. He makes us choose which one we want

him to use before we take our robes off and get on the kneeler."

There. It's out. Finally. But instead of relief, my whole body feels rigid, as if I have been shoved into a too-small compartment and am struggling for air.

"And then he hits you?" Nana Pete whispers. "With the belts?"

"Yes."

"Once?"

I almost laugh the question is so ridiculous. "No, not once. Lots of times."

"And this . . . this is where you and Agnes were this morning?" Nana Pete's lips are trembling. I nod. She wipes her forehead with her fingers. "Do Agnes's parents know? Have either of you told them?"

"I'm not sure if they know," I answer slowly. "But it doesn't really matter anyway."

Benny takes a deep breath and sticks his fingers in his ears.

Nana Pete doesn't seem to notice. "Doesn't *matter*?" she repeats. "Of course it matters! Do they know what's happening to you? Do they have—"

"Hey, Benny," I say, pulling one of his hands out of his ears. The base of his neck is turning a mottled shade of crimson. "What're you doing, buddy?"

Without opening his eyes, he says, "Trying to disappear."

"Oh, *sugar*." Nana Pete bats gently at Benny's other hand. "Stop it, sweetie. Look at me." But Benny just squeezes his eyes tighter.

I lean in. "Benedict!" His eyes fly open fearfully. "You don't have to do that," I say softly. "It's okay, Benny. It's just us." A tear slides down the front of his face, behind his glasses. I wipe it from his cheek with the pad of my thumb. "Listen. Why don't you go down to the pond and look for that huge bullfrog we've been trying to catch? Go ahead. And I'll come join you in a few minutes."

Benny is out of the car before I can finish, leaving the door wide open. There is a horrible, awkward silence as Nana Pete and I watch him squat down at the pond's edge and stare out at the water. I can feel her gaze shift back over to me, but I don't turn my head. Not yet.

"So Agnes's parents . . . ," she begins.

"Agnes and Benny's parents know all about the Regulation Room," I say, drawing my finger down a wide crease in the seat. "Emmanuel has taken them in there several times."

Nana Pete's lips curl back over her teeth. "You mean, *they*'ve been whipped, too?"

"Yeah. Most of the Believers have. It's not just for kids. Emmanuel uses it for the retraining of anyone. That's why it's called the Regulation Room."

"Retraining," she murmurs. "My God. What a word. How could Leonard . . ." She shakes her head. "I've got to do something about this. Right now. Right this minute. I'm going to have to call the police. This is unbelievable. You can't continue to live here."

Something inside of me rises like a wave of heat at her words. Can this really be happening? After all this time? Someone coming in and putting a stop to all of it?

And then, with a lurch, I think of something. "You can't call the police," I say.

"What do you mean, I can't? Why not?"

"If the police come and investigate, we might be taken away."

"But that's a *good* thing, Honey! That's the whole point! I don't want you liv—"

"But I—I'll be sent away," I stutter. "Agnes and Benny will get to go with you, probably, but *I'll* be sent to an orphanage or something because I don't have any parents here. I belong to Emmanuel."

Nana Pete gets a strange look on her face. "You don't *belong* to Emmanuel."

"Well, there's no paperwork that says otherwise." A panic is starting to rise within me. "My mother just left me here. With him. And he's the one in charge. He's the only one who gets to say what happens to me. If they take him away, that means I'll have to go, too. And they'll just put me away somewhere until they get it all straightened out, until everything is legal. Which means that I'll probably never see any of you again." I grab on to the sleeve of Nana Pete's blouse. "Please don't call the police, Nana Pete. Please. I just . . . I won't be able to . . . I mean, without Agnes, I don't know if . . ." My throat is getting smaller and smaller, until it is a little pinpoint of pain.

"Honey." Nana Pete's voice is firm and calm. "Calm down. No one is going to put you in any sort of orphanage or take you away from Agnes. I promise. But I have to do something. There's no way I'm going back to Texas now that I know all of this."

"Then take us with you!" I blurt out.

"What?"

"Just take us! Take us! We'll sneak away at night when everyone is at evening prayers or something and just leave!"

"Oh, Honey." Nana Pete's voice is faint. "I can't do that, darlin'. That's kidnapping. I would get arrested, maybe even sent to jail."

"But it's not kidnapping if we *want* to go with you," I plead. "Or if you're taking us out of here because we're being hurt. Please, Nana Pete, it's the only way! Just take us and leave. Then we can all be together, at least until everything gets straightened out."

"But what about Leonard and Samantha?" she asks. It takes me a minute to realize she is talking about Agnes's parents. "They would never come with us. And I don't want to be responsible for breaking up the family . . ."

"The *family*, Nana Pete, is not what it is supposed to be. Emmanuel is the real father here. And Veronica is the mother. Agnes and her parents are complete strangers to one another."

"But *they're* her parents!" Nana Pete says. "Emmanuel isn't . . ."

"Yes, he is." I finish the statement for her. "After all these years of coming to visit us, how can you not see it, Nana Pete? Why do you think all the kids live in the nursery for the first seven years instead of with their real parents?" I breathe in deeply through my nose. "It's so that whole . . . parent-kid thing . . . that bond . . . can be broken. He wants it attached to him. Not them."

Nana Pete is looking at me incredulously. I know what she is thinking. Like Agnes, Mount Blessing is all I have ever known. How is it that I have managed not only to remain unaffected by Emmanuel's ways, but to figure out how deeply everyone else has been? I look out the window again at Benny. He is still crouched down on the edge of the pond, scanning the smooth surface for frog eyes. He looks so small. "I watch TV, okay?" I say suddenly, knowing she is waiting for some sort of explanation. "I know what it's supposed to be like out in the real world."

"*TV*? But I thought you weren't allowed . . ."

I shrug. "Winky has one. It's real tiny and it doesn't work very well. It only has three channels. But I've seen enough things on it to know that this place is a freak show. I know most people don't live like this."

Nana Pete stares at something above my head and shakes her head slowly. "Why haven't you said anything to me before about the Regulation Room, darlin'?"

Her question stops me cold. I'm not sure if I even know the answer. The easy explanation is that it has never come up. There have never been any Regulation Room visits in August, when Nana Pete usually comes to visit. Is that a coincidence? Has it really taken something as simple as Nana Pete dropping in unexpectedly for Emmanuel's ugly secret to be unearthed? Or is it something more complex? Have I been afraid all these years of exposing him? Does Emmanuel really have that kind of power over me? The thought makes me angry.

"I don't know," I answer, kicking the bottom of the dashboard in frustration.

"Hey," Nana Pete says gently. "It's okay. I'm not blaming you, Honey. Don't get angry."

But I *am* angry. I'm livid. And not just at Emmanuel. I'm aware suddenly of a horrible, frightening fury against my mother, who left me here with this monster. When I think about the disgusting word in red marker on my back, the fury transforms into a heavy, choking thing, like a giant sea monster sitting in my belly, reaching up the back of my throat with its long tentacles. Before I can stop myself, my arms and legs begin flailing, kicking, and pounding the inside of the car, the dashboard, the front seat, the floor, the door.

"I hate him!" I scream. "I hate him! I want to kill him! And her, too! I want to scratch her eyes out!" I pound the soft leather and kick the underbelly of the car until, exhausted, I sit limp and dazed, staring at the swollen ridge along the tops of my knuckles. Nana Pete is frozen next to me, her hands pressed tightly over her mouth. But then she opens her arms and pulls me inside them. She is warm and soft and she smells like nail polish and peppermint gum. I cry so hard and for so long that when I am done I feel sick. My nose is running in one big snotty ribbon down the front of Nana Pete's shirt and when I sniff, it makes a gurgling sound. Without a word, Nana Pete reaches over me, extracts one of her handkerchiefs from inside her purse, and presses it against my cheek. I blow hard and then sit up. My ears are ringing.

"You've been waiting for someone to take you out of here for years, darlin', haven't you?" she asks softly. I swallow hard and nod, trying not to cry again. She cups the side of my face with her palm. "Well, you don't have to wait anymore, Honey. I'm going to get you out of here. And Agnes and Benny, too." I lean forward and bury my face against the side of her arm. My whole body feels loose and shaky, as if the bottom of the car has dropped out from under me.

"When?" I whisper.

"As soon as possible," Nana Pete says, smoothing my hair. "Don't you worry." The only sound in the car is the light rasping of her fingers against my braids. "You know, it's amazing," she says. "My doctor just told me he wasn't sure if I'd ever be able to make this trip again."

I sit up. "Why? Are you sick?"

"No, no, sugar. He just wants me to get some tests in August. That's why I came up now, so I wouldn't miss our visit."

I lean back into her soft belly. "Thank God you did."

Nana Pete kisses the top of my head. "I was thinking the same thing."

AGNES

I wake with a start a few hours later and crawl out of bed,
rubbing the deep pockmarks on my back where the rocks
have pressed into my skin. The light outside is deep yellow,
almost orange, and the shadows on the lawn are long. The
blue digits on the clock on my dresser blink 4:45 p.m.
Another hour until dinner. I walk through the house calling
for Nana Pete and Benny, but it's empty. Where could they
have gone? And how could I have fallen asleep?

Walking into the bathroom, I splash cool water on my
face and brush my blond hair. Honey always says I'm the
prettier of the two of us, but I don't think that's true at all.
My lips are ragged and sore from constant gnawing. Violet
half-moons gaze out from under my eyes and there is a new
splash of freckles across the bridge of my nose. I frown. I
hope I don't get as many as Benny. I turn slowly, regarding
my profile. I am finally starting to grow breasts. I'm ashamed
that deep down this fact thrills me. I am becoming a real
woman. But I also know that things like breasts can cause
trouble for a girl who is planning on being chaste for the rest
of her life. Maybe I will bind them with tape, the way Joan of
Arc used to do before going into battle. Something to think
about.

I cut through the kitchen to get to the front door, nearly
tripping over one of the kitchen chairs in my haste. Claudia
Yen, who lives on the second floor just above us with her

brother, Andrew, is standing in front of the stove, watching a grilled-cheese sandwich. Claudia is Mount Blessing's doctor. She takes care of everyone here, from delivering babies to giving us our annual shots.

"Slow *down*," she says irritably. "Andrew is sleeping upstairs."

Andrew sleeps a lot. He is in a wheelchair because of a motorcycle accident he got into before he came to Mount Blessing. Andrew is kind of weird. For one thing, he has blue tattoos all over his upper arms. He also gives Benny a quarter for every frog he catches. Benny says it's because he likes to pull off the legs, fry them up in cornmeal, and eat them for breakfast. It's something I can't even bear to think about.

"Sorry," I say, catching the chair before it topples over completely. I slide it back under the table and resume my path to the front door.

"You all right?" Claudia calls out just as I close the screen door behind me. I stop. In all the years she has lived upstairs, Claudia has never said anything to me aside from "say aaahh" or "this won't hurt a bit."

I turn around, regarding her through the thin mesh screen. "Excuse me?"

Claudia shoves a spatula under the grilled cheese and flips it over. "You're limping. Did you hurt yourself?"

"I'm limping?" I repeat.

Claudia turns the heat off under the pan and slides her sandwich onto a ceramic plate dotted with blue flowers. She picks a dish towel off the counter and wipes her hands with it. "Walk toward me," she commands.

I step out from behind the screen door and take several steps, placing my feet evenly before me.

Claudia watches, a small hand on her hip, and nods. Her dark hair, cut in a blunt bob, swings from side to side. "You're clearly favoring your left side. It might be a pulled hamstring. Do you want me to take a look?"

I shake my head and take a step backward. "It's not . . ." I hang my head. I can't tell another lie. Not today. "I was in the Regulation Room this morning."

Claudia's face changes instantly. "Ah," she says softly, busying herself once again with her sandwich. "Okay."

I turn and push through the door once more. It slams hard behind me, making me jump. I head down the length of Sanctity Road, in the direction of the frog pond, hoping beyond hope that I will find Benny and Nana Pete there. The black pavement stretches out, disappearing around a curve flanked with birch trees. The last time I was on this road I had raced it hard with Honey, who strained and breathed next to me, urging me along. That was two summers ago. My hips ache from the memory. I can feel my steps getting lighter, my walk changing to a bounce. Instinctively, my elbows align themselves on either side of my waist and my shoulders square themselves above my torso. My body, poised and tense, tips forward, and a lightness fills my chest. Suddenly I remember the words of Saint Teresa of Avila: *Everything you do must be done for the greater glorification of God, never for the glorification of yourself.* I put my hands on my hips and take a deep breath, ridding my body of anticipation. Then I reach under my robe and tighten my waist string once again.

. . .

Nana Pete and Benny are *in* the frog pond, knee high in the murky water. Since they are facing away from me, they do not see me as I approach. I sit down on the mossy bank, next to Nana Pete's pink boots, and bring my knees into my chest. Nana Pete is hunched over a part of the water dense with lily pads, her arm around Benny.

"Wait, Benny," she whispers. "Not yet." Her khaki pants are rolled up midthigh; the water is up to her knees. Bobby pins stick out from her unraveling braids like knitting needles. Her cheeks are flushed pink and the front of her shirt is covered with splotches of mud. I don't know if she has ever looked more beautiful.

There is a shout on the other side of the pond, behind the weeping willow.

"Got 'im!" Honey wades out from behind the willow tree's heavy boughs, which hang as thick and as dense as a curtain. A frog the size of a small hamster dangles from her right hand, its pale belly gleaming white.

"Oh, *man!*" Benny yells. "You really did get him!"

I shudder and move back instinctively.

Honey waves to me with her free hand. "Hey, Ags!" Nana Pete and Benny turn as Honey calls my name.

"Mouse!" Nana Pete says. "How long have you been sitting there?" She plods heavily through the water, holding up the cuffed bottoms of her pants.

I shrug. "Few minutes, I guess."

"You get your nap?"

I nod, studying her features carefully. Has she learned anything else about the Regulation Room in my absence?

"It's almost time for dinner, I think," Honey says, dropping the enormous amphibian into a dirty yellow bucket not three feet away from me. I jump to my feet and take another several steps backward.

"Geez, relax!" Honey says, laughing at me. "It's not going to bite you, Ags."

"Just don't let it jump out," I say, eyeing the bucket fearfully. "Please."

"Don't worry," Honey says. She sticks a bare foot into the bucket. "There. He's right under my foot. He's not goin' anywhere." I shudder and cross my arms. Honey looks at Benny. "Tell Andrew I want fifty cents for that one. He's huge. We'll split it, okay?"

"Hold that pose," Nana Pete says, struggling up the grassy back. Her feet make soft sucking sounds as they sink into the mud. "I've got a camera in my purse. I want a picture of the three of you." I sidle in as close as I dare to Honey, keeping my eye on her foot and the bucket. Benny squirms in under my arm. "Say cheese!" Nana Pete says, holding the camera to her eye.

"Cheese!" The Polaroid square slides out of the front of the camera.

"Beautiful!"

"Can I see?" Benny asks, leaning over Nana Pete's shoulder. I look too. Our images, blurred like smoke, appear from beneath a faint brown haze. Nana Pete takes pictures every time she comes up. I never tire of looking at them, especially since we don't have any pictures of our own.

"*Mother!*" I jump as Dad's voice, as sharp as glass, cuts

through the warm air. "Mother! Agnes! Benedict! Are you down here?"

Nana Pete looks up and grimaces. "Aw, rats. We're not supposed to be down here, are we?" She sticks out her arm. "Come on, Benny. We have to go get cleaned up for dinner."

I run toward Dad, who is striding toward us, his jaw clenched tight as a fist. "Hey, Dad," I say softly. "We were just getting ready to—"

"What are you doing down here, Agnes? I told all of you to go down to the house! It is Ascension Week! You know better!"

I nod and gulp over the mound in my throat. "I was, Dad. I mean, I know. I went home just like you said, and laid down for a while. I even fell asleep."

"Did Benny go with you?"

I break into a trot to keep pace with him. "No, he was with Nana Pete down here, I guess. And Honey too."

Dad's eye twitches. "That sounds about right."

I stare down at the ground, thinking about something Honey said to me just a few weeks ago. "Sometimes I think you'd sell your own brother, Agnes, just to save your own soul." A pang of guilt surges over me. I quicken my pace again to catch up with Dad.

"But I don't think they've been here very long, Dad . . . I was only asleep for—"

"*Mother!*" Dad yells, cutting me off again. "*Benedict!*"

They are sitting next to Honey, wiping the mud off their feet with one of Nana Pete's handkerchiefs. Nana Pete lifts her hand, the dirty handkerchief dangling between her fingers like a peace offering.

Dad comes to a halt a few feet from them, his face shiny

with perspiration and rage. "I don't even have time to get into this with you right now, Mother," he says. "You have to come with me immediately and get cleaned up for dinner. During Ascension Week, Emmanuel shares evening meals with everyone in the community and we cannot, under any circumstances, be late."

Benny and I exchange a look. His eyes are wide with fear.

"Okay, okay," Nana Pete says, patting her ankles with the handkerchief. "In a minute, Leonard."

"Mother!" Dad says sharply. He glares at Honey as she stifles a giggle. "We have to go now!"

Nana Pete shoves the handkerchief into her front pocket and stretches out her arm in Dad's direction. He pulls her to her feet and then turns, striding back down the road again. I stare beseechingly at him as I struggle to keep up, hoping that he'll look over and cast me a forgiving look. But he storms ahead of us the whole way back and doesn't turn around once, not even when I trip and fall, cutting my knee on a rock.

Since Emmanuel rarely eats with the general population of Mount Blessing, when he does (usually during a holy week), it's a huge deal. It's also a sign of great disrespect to be late. Stragglers who show up after the six o'clock bell are locked out of the Great House for the rest of the meal. It happened to Dad once a few years back, right around this time. It wasn't his fault—the car he was driving home broke down on the side of the road and he had to wait for someone to pick him up—but Emmanuel didn't want to hear it. Poor Dad had to go back down to the Field House and wait for us to finish eating. I told Benny to shove extra bread in his pockets for him, but Dad didn't want it.

"No, Agnes," he said, shaking his head. "You shouldn't have done that. Emmanuel is right. I deserve to go hungry tonight."

"But it wasn't your fault!" I protested. "The car—"

"Nothing happens by accident," Dad said, putting his hand on my shoulder. "Everything is God's will. And tonight he was testing me. The truth is, I should have tried harder to find another way home so that I wouldn't miss Emmanuel's presence at a meal. But I didn't. I gave up and just waited for someone to come get me."

"But . . ."

"No buts," Dad said firmly. "God helps those who help themselves."

I was so confused that I almost felt angry. Rule or no rule, Dad's explanation just didn't make any sense. *None.* But it had to, I told myself later, retying my waist rope in bed. After all, it was Dad talking. Next to Emmanuel, he was the holiest person I knew.

Tonight there is a low murmuring throughout the Great House, like the inside of a beehive. The room is a sea of blue robes moving in every direction. Mothers are hustling their children into their required seats, while others place baskets of bread on the table. There are green plastic bowls at every place setting, along with a small plate and cup. I follow Mom and Dad and Nana Pete over to our usual table and sit down. Benny settles in next to me and begins to fiddle uneasily with his glasses. I glance around the room, looking for Honey. Usually she is at the table opposite ours, sitting with Winky. I catch sight of Christine, Claudia Yen, and her brother, Andrew, but I don't see Honey anywhere. Where is she? I look up at the clock nervously: 5:57. She has three minutes before the Great Door will close and then lock.

Suddenly a hush descends and, like an enormous wave cresting, the room surges to its feet. Mom and Dad close their eyes and bow their heads, solemn looks on their already solemn faces. Benny hops up next to me, squeezes his eyes shut, and begins tapping the front of his legs with his palms. I look nervously out of the corner of my eye at Nana Pete. She is not standing.

"My children!" the familiar throaty voice calls out. "Good evening! Bless you all on the first sundown of the holiest week of the year."

Dad opens his eyes briefly, frowns, and then pokes Nana Pete in the arm. "Get up," he hisses. But Nana Pete just stares straight ahead.

I turn back around quickly, moving sideways and then forward until I can see Emmanuel through the throng of people. Fear flashes through me for a split second as I get a glimpse of the top of his head. His thick silver hair is meticulously groomed, brushed to one side in a deep swoop. When he talks, his yellow teeth glitter behind his beard, and his eyes seem to settle on every single person in the room. But it is his voice that finally causes me to drop my eyes, a deep baritone so full of assurance and authority that sometimes my knees feel as though they will buckle out from under me.

"Tonight as we begin our evening meal, let us remember

who it was that gave up his own body and his own blood for us so that we might live forever."

"Amen," the room says collectively.

"And let us always be mindful of the fact that we are sinners of the worst kind, unlovable in every way, if not for the love and mercy of our Lord Jesus Christ."

"Amen, alleluia!" the room chants, a little more enthusiastically than before. I bow my head.

"And like Jesus Christ, I love each and every one of you," Emmanuel continues, lowering his arms slowly. "You are all my children, and as your father, I am not only aware of, but understand, your most repulsive weaknesses. Despite that, I love you even more, just the way you are."

I pretend not to hear the low grunting sound behind me over the awed murmuring of the crowd.

"Thank you, Emmanuel!" someone cries.

"Oh, Emmanuel!" says another. "Bless you! God bless you!"

Emmanuel looks over and smiles at Veronica, who is standing next to him. She reaches out and takes his hand. Cords of green veins stand out against her forehead and her pink lips look like a bow on a Christmas present. Even with her robe on, I can see the sharp angles of her collarbone sticking out, and when she lifts her hands to smooth her hair back, one of her heavy gold rings, a gift from Emmanuel, glitters on her fingers. She is so beautiful. I turn back around slowly and put my napkin in my lap, trying not to think about the word she wrote on Honey's back.

Across the table, Dad is whispering angrily in Nana Pete's ear. But she doesn't seem to be paying much attention to whatever it is he is saying. Soon the women who work in the kitchen are moving in and among the rows, spooning ladlefuls of thick yellow broth into our bowls. My heart sinks as I realize that it is one of my favorites, a hearty corn chowder, dense with potatoes, celery, and fresh corn. Slowly, I close my hands over my bowl as the woman lowers her ladle over my shoulder.

Nana Pete frowns as the woman moves on, filling Benny's bowl next to me. "Not eating, Mouse?"

I shake my head. "I've decided to fast for a while," I answer quietly. "For the . . . sins I've committed today."

Dad nods his head slowly and smiles. I wonder if that means I am back on his good side.

Suddenly there is a commotion on the other side of the room.

"I told you, I don't *want* it!" Iris Murphy yells. "I feel sick! If you make me eat it, I'm going to throw up!"

I roll my eyes. Just last week, Iris threw herself on the floor at dinner and screamed about having a headache. Emmanuel hadn't been eating with us, but it had still ended badly, with Emmanuel taking her into the Regulation Room. Why doesn't she learn? All heads turn in her direction.

Mr. Murphy yanks his wild-eyed daughter to her feet. "Shut your mouth!" He is shaking with rage.

Iris tilts her head back and wails. "But you're not listening to me! I just—"

Emmanuel cuts Iris off before she can finish her protest. "Bring her here, Samuel!"

The room is deathly quiet as Mr. Murphy drags the crying girl over to Emmanuel's table. Next to me, Benny's legs stop moving. Iris, who is in his age group, is one of his best friends. As she struggles and twists against her father's grip, his lower lip begins to tremble. I lean over and take his little hand in mine. He knows as well as I do that Emmanuel has no qualms about disciplining someone in public—he says a lesson for one is a lesson for all. Now, as Mr. Murphy and Iris stand quivering, Emmanuel wipes his mouth, pushes back his chair, and stands up.

But as he does, Nana Pete stands up, too. Her movement is so quick and so sudden that she knocks over her bowl of soup. It crashes to the floor with an angry sound, splattering corn and potatoes everywhere. Emmanuel looks over, startled, but Nana Pete meets his gaze over the ocean of heads and doesn't flinch. Her fists are clenched so tightly that I can see the knuckles straining under her skin.

"Why, Petunia," Emmanuel calls out. "No one told me you were here." His eyes flick over toward Dad, who bows his head.

"Yes," Nana Pete answers. Her voice is steady and strong. "I'm here."

For what seems like forever, the two of them stare at each other. My eyes dart back and forth between the two of them, but neither of them blink. What is going on? My stomach churns with dread. Finally Emmanuel turns back around to regard Iris, who is still standing in front of him. Her face is white, and she shrinks under his glowering eyes. I squeeze my eyes shut, bracing my whole body for the imminent sound of her face being slapped. Next to me, Benny puts his fingers in his ears and starts to rock back and forth in his seat.

But there is no slap, no sound of a body collapsing to the

floor, or even a cry. Instead, as I open my eyes slowly, I see Emmanuel putting his hands on Iris's head. He closes his eyes and begins speaking in Latin: "*Gratia vobis et pax a Deo Patre nostro et Dominio Jesu Christo . . .* " It is a prayer said at Sunday sacrament: "The grace and peace of God our Father and the Lord Jesus Christ be with you."

Iris begins to cry quietly as Emmanuel's hands move down from the top of her head to just under her chin.

"Go finish your meal," he says firmly, "and act like the child of God you are."

Iris nods, wide-eyed, and backs away, new tears streaking down her pink face.

Mr. Murphy bows low in front of Emmanuel and then turns, following Iris back to their table.

Emmanuel turns around, too, flicking his eyes briefly in Nana Pete's direction. She is still standing, rigid as a soldier. He smiles thinly at her and then sits back down at his table.

Benny is leaning forward with a strange look on his face. Suddenly all the bread and soup he has just eaten comes pouring out of his mouth. He gags, choking, and then throws up some more. The Believers around us jump to their feet and rush to clean up the mess. Mom gathers Benny in her arms. He is sobbing quietly now, his small body shaking.

"I'm sorry," he whispers.

"It's all right," Mom hushes. "Shh . . ." She takes Benny's soiled robe off him and hands it to me.

"Let me take him back to the house," Nana Pete says, putting her napkin on the table. "He needs to rest."

"We have evening prayers in a few minutes," Dad says. "He can go afterward."

Nana Pete stands up and gives him a look of disgust. "This child has just vomited all over himself." Her voice is way over the Great House decibel range. "I am taking him to bed."

"Is there something else on your mind, Petunia?" Emmanuel's voice comes drifting over to our table. Dad stiffens.

"Not at all." Nana Pete's voice is like ice. "I'm just taking a sick child to bed, where he belongs." She glares at Dad, scoops Benny up in her arms, and strides out of the room.

"Go with her," Mom whispers, putting her arm around my shoulder. "I don't think she knows where any of Benny's nightclothes are. And take Benny's robe with you. I'll wash it out tonight."

Giving Dad a tentative look, I dart from my place at the table, and rush to catch up with Nana Pete.

HONEY

I have every intention of getting cleaned up and going up to the Great House for dinner after Agnes's father finds us all down at the frog pond, but then I run into Winky, who is just finishing up in the garden.

"Hey," he says, peeling off his dirty gloves. "Mr. Schwab says he's got a big ol' pile of compost for me at the farm. You want to come help me bring it back?"

"Absolutely!" I answer. "Let's go!" Pushing all thoughts of the kinds of trouble we could both get into out of my head, I pull the smaller wheelbarrow out of Winky's garden shed. Emmanuel can stretch me out on a rack tonight and torture me, for all I care. As soon as Nana Pete gives the word, we are going to hightail it out of here and nothing is going to change that.

Winky takes one of the back roads down to Mr. Schwab's farm, just in case anyone is out looking for us. He walks quickly, even with his wheelbarrow in front of him, and I have to struggle to keep up. Winky is better acquainted with the woods and outlying boundaries outside of Mount Blessing than I am, since he's always on the hunt for new and interesting plants he can bring back to the garden. Actually, that's how he first met Mr. Schwab, a corn farmer who lives two miles down the road. Winky says Mr. Schwab was a little leery of him at first—not because he was slow, but because he was wearing a heavy blue robe with a silk cord around his waist in the middle of August. Still, they became fast friends after Winky told Mr. Schwab what it was he was looking for. Mr. Schwab's wife, Libby, apparently has a flower garden of her own and knows all about wild plants and shrubs.

Mr. Schwab is one of the nicest guys I've ever met. He's middle-aged, like Agnes's father, but he looks younger. He has black hair and a nice, plain sort of face. It's always tanned because he is outside so much and his teeth are very white. One time he even took me for a ride on Dorothy, his tractor. I got to stand in the little space right behind his seat with my hands on his shoulders and look out over what seemed like miles and miles of hills. I thought I had died and gone to heaven. His wife, Libby, is great too. She invited me into the farmhouse one afternoon while Mr. Schwab and Winky were digging up a milkweed plant, and sat at the kitchen table with me while I ate a piece of her red-raspberry pie. I forked bite after bite into my mouth, swallowing my twinge of guilt about eating red food, and nodded politely as she told me all about her favorite flowers. When I was finished, I asked for another piece.

By the time we reach the edge of the Schwabs' farm, I have a stitch in my side and am panting for breath. The stripes along my back and legs feel as if they were on fire. I am just about to stop and sink to the ground when I see Mr. Schwab. He is sitting on Dorothy, waving to us from the other side of the empty cornfield. Behind him, the sky is a pale charcoal color, tinged orange at the bottom like a slice of cantaloupe.

"Winky! Honey! Over here!" The sight of him gives me renewed vigor and I scramble again to my feet. "I was hoping you'd come tonight," Mr. Schwab says, looking down at me from the tractor seat. My head barely skims the middle of Dorothy's enormous rear wheel. Mr. Schwab is wearing his usual red baseball cap, faded pink from the sun, blue overalls, and a white shirt. The soles of his work boots are caked heavily with dried mud. I wonder if Veronica would make him take them off before he came into Emmanuel's room—not that he ever would.

"Oh yeah?" I ask "Why?"

Mr. Schwab's eyes twinkle. "I thought you might like to take Dorothy for a spin."

I gasp. "You mean *drive* her?"

Mr. Schwab laughs and then nods. "I only have a few rows left in the back of the field over there before I call it a night. It's just tilling, nothing too fast or exciting. Think you're up for it?"

"Yes!" I burst out. "Absolutely!"

Mr. Schwab laughs again. Then he looks at Winky, almost apologetically. "You okay going over to the house by yourself, Winky? Libby's there waiting for you."

Winky nods and waves. "You be careful, Honey."

I've been atop Dorothy before, but only in the tiny space behind the driver's seat. Now, sitting *in* the driver's seat with Mr. Schwab behind me, I feel like a king. Mr. Schwab takes a long time explaining the four pedals on the floor to me. There is something called a clutch on the left, two brake pedals on the right, and the throttle all the way over on the other side. By the time he lets me insert the key into the ignition and start the engine, the sky is a pale purple. My hands are trembling with excitement.

"Just take her real easy," Mr. Schwab says as the engine roars to life. "Dorothy responds best to a nice, gentle touch."

My face burns as the tractor lurches and chokes to a stop under my tentative direction, but Mr. Schwab keeps talking to me in a low, steady voice, and a few minutes later Dorothy is rolling smoothly over the soft dirt.

"Yeah!" I scream. "Look at me! I'm driving a tractor!"

Mr. Schwab throws his head back and laughs. "I'm glad you like it. You're good, too, Honey. A natural. There's still a bit more work to do, though. Can you turn her to the left now?" I follow his instructions as he leads me to the far end of the field. An hour passes like a heartbeat as I lower the sod till in the back and let Dorothy drag it up and down the neat rows. The smell of warm dirt fills the air as the sky around us gets darker and darker. I can't remember ever feeling so happy.

And then Mr. Schwab goes and blows it.

"Boy, if your folks could see you now!" he shouts as I make the final, narrow turn down the field. He looks over at me and raises his eyebrows. "Right?" Mr. Schwab doesn't know anything about my parental situation—or more accurately, my lack of it—and so I know his comment is completely innocent, but something inside of me deflates anyway. I nod quickly and then look away. We drive in silence for a few more minutes until the last row is finished and then I turn around.

"Thanks a lot," I say quietly. "It was fun. Winky and I should be getting back, though. It's almost time for evening prayers."

Mr. Schwab nods his head knowingly. He doesn't ask us very many questions about Mount Blessing, but he knows we have weird rituals like evening prayers and Ascension Marches. "Okay then," he says. "Let's go get Winky and get you guys back."

The walk back is a long one, especially since it is dark and Winky and I are pushing wheelbarrows filled to the brim with Libby's special compost. Although mine feels like it weighs two hundred pounds, the weight in my chest feels heavier. Winky walks alongside me for a little while, watching me out of the corner of his eye. He points out a cluster of White Admiral butterflies flapping around a chokecherry bush, and then two Silvery Checkerspots who seem to be mating atop a budding stalk of purple dragon flower. But his voice sounds far away. I don't answer him. The night air, edged with just the whisper of a chill, makes the hair on my arms stand up. My mouth feels dry. When we come to a fork in the road, Winky turns sharply and I tilt my wheelbarrow too fast, trying to keep up. Suddenly the whole thing tips over, spilling compost in every direction. A horrible smell, like cow manure and rotten eggs, fills the air.

"Shit!" I yell, sitting down hard next to the pile of dirt. George digs into the soft part of my thigh inside my pocket. Furious, I reach inside, pull him out, and throw him as hard as I can into the trees across the road. He lands with a soft *plop* behind a mound of bushes.

Winky stares at me for a minute and then lowers his wheelbarrow. "What'd you go do that for?" he asks. Suddenly I realize what I have just done. Without waiting for an answer, Winky plods across the road.

"Don't bother!" I yell, feeling like a three-year-old, but not caring, either. "Leave him! I don't want him anymore! Just leave him, Winky!"

He ignores me. I watch with dull eyes as he pushes back brambles and tall weeds, sinking to his knees alongside the patch of bushes, pawing the ground with his thick, stubby hands.

"She's probably just as insane as everyone else here," I mutter. "Who in their right mind gives a ceramic cat to an infant right before abandoning her?"

Suddenly Winky stands up straight, holding George triumphantly in his hand. Holding a sob of relief in my chest, I shake my head as he sits down in the road next to me.

"Take him," he says, balancing the tiny figurine carefully on my kneecap. "This here's the only thing you've got of her. So hold on to him, even if you don't know what it means. Then when you find her someday, you can ask her." He is looking directly at me, something he rarely does when we talk.

"You think I'll find her someday?" I ask.

Winky nods. "Yup."

"Why?"

Winky struggles to his feet. "'Cause you want to. It's a fire thing inside you. And when you got something burning like that inside, nothing else really matters till you find a way to put it out."

I pick George back up with two fingers. The top half of his left ear is missing. I rub my finger over it tenderly and then insert him back into my pocket, pushing him down deep until he reaches his usual place against the curve of my thigh.

"Come on, now," Winky says. "Let's clean up this mess.

We're gonna be late for prayers." He looks over his shoulder as I get to my feet. "And no more pouting."

The Great House doors are unlocked, which means that dinner is over, but evening prayers have begun. Winky and I slip in quietly and kneel down at the very back of the room. The service is interminable, as always, and I soon stop chanting and begin looking around for Agnes and Benny. I strain to the right and then to the left, looking around the throng of robed bodies, but I don't see either of them anywhere. Mr. and Mrs. Little are kneeling in front, right behind Emmanuel and Veronica, counting off the prayers on their consecration beads, but the space next to them is empty.

Emmanuel completes the service by standing in front of everyone and making the sign of the cross over our heads.

"In nomine Patris . . . ," he intones.

I hate your guts, I think to myself.

". . . et Filii . . ."

You big phony. You monster.

". . . et Spiritus Sancti."

In a little while, you're never going to see me again.

"Amen."

All around me, people bow their heads, murmuring "amen" under Emmanuel's raised arms. They do not move until he recedes from view, head lowered over his folded hands, and disappears into his room at the back of the house. I angle my way through the crowd, sidling carefully over to the bench outside his door and reach under it for my shoes. They're there. I feel a weird sort of tenderness toward them as I pull them back out, as if they have been lonely without me.

Now I head over to Mrs. Little so that I can ask her about Agnes, but someone has already gotten hold of her and is steering her toward the kitchen. That leaves Mr. Little. I swallow hard and walk up to him.

"Do you know where Agnes is?" I ask.

Mr. Little looks down at me as if regarding a bug on the sidewalk. "Excuse me?" He takes a step backward the way he always does, as if I have cooties or something.

"I said, do you know where Agnes is? I didn't see her during prayers."

Mr. Little inserts his arms, one at a time, into the billowing sleeves of his robe and fixes his gaze at a spot in the middle of my forehead. He has a buzz cut and it makes his head look pointed on top. "Agnes and my mother took Benedict down to the Field House. Benedict got ill during dinner and had to go to bed."

"Oh. Okay. Thanks."

"You're not to go down there," Mr. Little says. "I mean it."

A sour taste fills my mouth. "I'm not going to *do* anything. I just want to check on Benny. And say good night to Agnes."

Mr. Little doesn't blink. "Benny doesn't need checking. And Agnes will be fine for one night without a good-night from you." His eyes squint at the corners, exposing a fan of wrinkles. "Actually, maybe it will do her some good. Whenever you're around, Agnes gives in to all sorts of temptation and sin. She becomes like jelly around you. She thinks nothing of disobeying orders, which is exactly why she ended up in the Regulation Room this morning . . ."

Other Believers within hearing distance are looking over at us. I stare at the floor and bite my lower lip.

". . . and why I found her at the frog pond this afternoon," Mr. Little continues, "instead of at the house, as I ordered. As far as I'm concerned, the less time you spend with my daughter—especially during this holy time—the better." His eyes move from my forehead directly to the center of my eyes. It feels as though he is shooting lasers into my pupils. "For all of us."

The weight of his words feels like a stone on my chest. I've known for years that the man didn't like me, but this, *this* feels like hate. Suddenly a hand drops on my shoulder.

"Come on, Honey," Winky says. "Let's go."

I follow him somberly down the hill, past the lilac bushes and along the length of Sanctity Road until we get to the Milk House. A little farther down, through the pine trees, I can make out the edge of the Field House, where Agnes is.

"I'm going down there," I say, striding past Winky toward the Field House. "He's not my father. He can't tell me what to do."

But Winky grabs my arm. "Don't." His eye is twitching terribly. "He'll ask her t'night if you came, and you know she won't lie. And then she'll have t'pay for it."

I stop and then whirl around, furious. "God, Winky, do you have to have *all* the answers tonight?"

His eye slows down a little as he lowers his voice. "C'mon. It's already ten. The game's prob'ly half over by now."

"Who're they playing tonight?" I ask grudgingly.

"Cleveland. And they're good this year."

I arrange myself at the foot of his bed as Winky pulls out the TV and adjusts the wire antenna on top. In thirty seconds, there is a fuzzy picture of the Cleveland pitcher throwing a ball to the catcher. A Yankee strides up to the plate. Winky pulls nervously on his bottom lip. "C'mon, buddy," he mutters. "Let's get a move on."

I pull out my butterfly journal from Winky's bookshelf and page slowly through the sketches and information I've collected over the years. So far I've recorded seeing one hundred and forty Spangled Fritillaries (the most common butterfly in these parts), sixty-four Clouded Sulphurs, ninety-two Northern Cloudywings, sixteen whirlabouts (they prefer ocean air, which we're not close to), twenty-nine Spicebush Swallowtails, two hundred ten American Coppers, nineteen Spring Azures, and twenty-seven Silvery Blues. I've got a rough sketch of each species, including the caterpillar stages. Tonight I mark down the Yellow Fritillary I saw in the field today with Agnes and then the two White Admirals Winky pointed out to me on the way back from the farm.

Next I pull out *The Encyclopedia of Butterflies*. I always open it to the same page and stare at the same butterfly, which Winky pointed out to me a few years ago. It's called a Zebra Longwing and it is so beautiful, with its white-and-black-striped wings and long, teardrop shape. Winky says he's seen only one in all the years he's had his garden, and that when he did, it was one of the best days of his life.

I'd like to have one of those days.

My eyes feel heavy as I close the book and look up at the TV screen. Cleveland is up by two. "I'm going to bed," I say. "I'm tired."

"Okay," Winky says. "Night."

I climb the steps to my loft, pull the heavy drape across the front, and put on my pajamas. With George in one hand, I crawl into bed and count to ten, but it doesn't do any good. My little heart night-light burned out years ago and I haven't wanted to ask Christine for a new bulb. She doesn't need to know that I'm still afraid of the dark.

"Wink?" I call out after a few minutes.

"Yup," he says, getting up and clicking on the tiny lamp atop his dresser. The light makes a soft halo on the ceiling. "Sorry. I forgot."

AGNES

It's almost ten thirty by the time Mom and Dad get back from the Great House. Benny has been asleep for hours, but I am still awake, trying to find a bearable position atop the layer of rocks under my sheet. Lying on my back again is impossible, but I discover that if I lay perfectly still on my belly, it is not quite so bad. I prick my ears as Dad and Nana Pete start arguing in the next room.

"But you said I could see them until I leave again," Nana Pete says. "You said it wouldn't be a problem."

"And when I explained the sacredness of this week to you, *you* said you would take them down to the house and do something quiet," Dad retorts. "Half an hour later, I find you stuck in the mud with a frog in your hand."

Nana Pete clears her throat. "Well, we certainly won't do that again. I promise."

"I'm sorry, Mother, but the children need to be in their groups tomorrow," Dad insists. "They are making all the banners for the march, as well as new robes this year. There is a lot of work still to be done and it's not fair that they get to be excused."

"Leonard—"

"*Isaac,*" Dad interrupts. "It's Isaac, Mother, okay?"

Nana Pete takes a deep breath. "Isaac. Please. I'm only staying a few days. Please just let me take them for the day tomorrow. I won't ask for any more time after that. Please."

I can hear Dad hesitate. I squeeze my eyes shut and hold my breath, praying silently to Saint Jude, who is the patron saint of lost causes.

"The afternoon only," Dad says finally. "They must attend all prayer services and work on their banners and robes in the morning. After lunch you can take them." He pauses. "Back here, to the house. *Only* the house, Mother. Nowhere else."

"Okay." Nana Pete sounds disappointed, but I smile in the dark.

"Oh," I hear Dad say. "Veronica approached me after prayers this evening. She said that Emmanuel would like you to join them for breakfast tomorrow, after morning prayers. Ruth and I have been invited, too."

"Why?" Nana Pete sounds perplexed.

"What do you mean, *why*? Because he knows you just drove nine hundred miles and he wants to share a meal with you. He's a gentleman." Nana Pete coughs lightly. No one says anything for a moment. "All right?" I hear Dad say finally. "Mother?"

"Okay," Nana Pete says. But her voice sounds faint. "All right, then. Fine. I'll be ready."

The next morning, Nana Pete is in the kitchen, dressed in a clean pink shirt and freshly ironed blue pants. Her hair has been brushed, braided, and pinned back up around her head, and she has put on a coat of pink lipstick.

"What are *you* doing up?" Benny asks sleepily.

Nana Pete grabs him and plants a kiss on his cheek. "Good morning to you, too, darlin'." She looks over at me. "I'm going up to morning prayers with y'all and then on to breakfast with Emmanuel." I glance over at Dad, barely able to contain my happiness. He nods and grimaces.

During morning prayers, Honey nudges me and then nods her head in Benny's direction. I watch as he puts his hand under his robe and pushes something down in his pants pocket. There is a muffled croak as he jams his hand down again, harder this time. Honey giggles. "The frog," she mouths. "From yesterday. He still has it."

I can feel the blood run out of my face. Pressing my lips together, I sneak a look behind me, wondering if any of the Believers kneeling on all sides of us have noticed Benny's squirming. Claudia is a little ways off to the right, but she and all the other adults have their eyes shut tightly, lost in prayer. I transfer my gaze again to the cross on the wall and try to do the same.

"*Pater noster, qui es in caelis, sanctificetur nomen tuum. Adveniat regnum tuum. Fiat voluntas tua, sicut in caelo et in terra . . .*"

"I get y'all after lunch," Nana Pete says, putting her arms around the three of us after prayers have ended. "And I have some really fun stuff planned for us to do." Dad gives her a sidelong glance. "At the house, of course." She kisses us each on the forehead. "I'll see you after lunch."

"Come on, Mother." Dad looks jittery and pale as Mom takes his hand. "We don't want to keep him waiting."

"Where're they going?" Honey asks as we watch them walk away.

"Emmanuel invited Nana Pete into his room for breakfast. Mom and Dad got to go, too."

Honey's face pales a little. "He did? And she's going?"

I glance at her sharply. "Yes, she's *going*. Why wouldn't

she? Emmanuel's just trying to be nice after her long trip. He's a gentleman."

At the other end of the room, Christine is herding all the kids around the first table, where we will eat breakfast. I pull on Honey's arm, but she doesn't take her eyes off Nana Pete, who has just disappeared around the corner. "Come on, Honey. It's time to eat."

Breakfast, like every other meal this week, is lean. Still, the slice of toast set before me and the tiny glass of apple juice look as good as any five-course meal. I am so hungry I feel like I could eat my arm. The yellow scent of butter wafts inside my nostrils, making my head spin. Honey, who always eats as if she is starving, inhales her toast and then looks over at me. "You gonna eat that?"

I shake my head miserably and slide it over in her direction.

"Man," she says, snatching it before I can blink, "I wonder what they're talking about in there."

"Who?"

"Nana Pete and Emmanuel." A vein at the corner of her eye pulses as she talks. "God," she says. "I can't stand it."

I glance at Amanda, who is sitting across from us, but she is talking to her little sister, oblivious to our conversation. Christine is still busy at the other end of the table, pouring juice into more cups. Honey crams the rest of the toast into her mouth and looks around the table wildly, as if another piece might magically appear. "They could be talking about anything, you know?"

"What are you so nervous about?" I ask.

Honey looks at me and then drops her eyes. "Me? Nothing. I'm not nervous. I was just wondering, is all."

"She was arguing about it with my dad last night," I say, against my better judgment. Honey loves to hear stories about Nana Pete getting into it with my dad, especially when Emmanuel is concerned. I hate that. I always feel like I have to take sides and no matter whose I pick, I always lose.

"About going to breakfast?"

"Yeah. She didn't want to go for some reason."

Honey grins at me. "That's 'cause she wants to keep her food down."

Christine raps the end of the table with her knuckles. "Time to go down to the East House," she says quietly. "Everyone please get in single file behind the Great Door."

I grab Benny's hand and lead him over to the line. His pocket is still wiggling.

"Get in the back of the line with me," I whisper. "And as soon as we get out of the Great House, you are letting that frog go."

"No!" Benny protests. "It's for Andrew! He told me to bring it up this morning, but I haven't seen him yet. He's gonna give me fifty cents. I'm splitting it with Honey."

"You're letting it go, Benny," I say, looking straight ahead. "Don't argue with me."

Benny's shoulders slump as the line begins to move. I pull him along as everyone heads out the door, but he hangs back, dragging his feet, and after a minute I let go.

"Fine, be a pain," I hiss into his ear. "But when you get called into the Regulation Room, don't expect me to go in there with you."

At the mention of the Regulation Room, my little

brother's face pales. He whimpers and runs to catch up with me, but I am already out the door.

"Agnes!" he pleads. I turn slightly when I hear him shout, just in time to see the frog, in one last effort at freedom, leap from his pocket back inside the Great House. Halfway between the closing door, Benny turns and as he does, the door slams shut. There is a split-second pause before a noise unlike anything I have ever heard before comes from the other side. It is a wild, animalistic sound, a howling so pure in its pain that it makes the inside of my mouth turn cold. I stand rooted to the spot, but Honey turns and throws herself against the door. It creaks open again slowly.

"Oh my God," she wails. Just under her slumped form, I can see the outline of Benny lying on the floor. There is a blur of movement as Christine pushes past me. She sinks to her knees next to Honey and then picks up my little brother in her arms.

"Someone help!" she screams, running into the foyer of the Great House. "Help us, please!" My legs begin to move with a mind of their own, and I follow, struggling to keep Benny in sight.

Claudia meets us halfway inside the foyer, her blue robe flapping behind her like a pair of enormous wings. "What is it? What happened?"

"His hand!" Christine yells. "It got caught in the door!"

I avert my gaze from the top of Benny's head down to his hand, which is dangling like a gutted fish over Christine's arms.

"Oh, Jesus," Claudia says, bending over Benny, who

has begun to moan desperately. "The fingers are almost completely severed. We're going to have to call an ambulance."

Honey has backed off to the side, but I squirm and claw my way between Claudia and Christine. "Benny! Are you all right? Let me see! Let me *see!*" There is a bright flash of blood as Christine transfers Benny into Claudia's arms, but they are both moving so fast I can't tell where it's coming from. Is he hurt somewhere else? "Benny!" I scream.

Claudia is moving toward the middle of the room, yelling at Mr. Murphy, who is still eating breakfast, to clear off a table. By now Benny has begun to scream. Claudia lays him down and then starts barking orders.

"I need to make a tourniquet, Samuel. Go to the kitchen and get me a rag or dish towel, anything! Just so I can stop the blood from flowing!" Mr. Murphy turns and runs.

Claudia looks over at Mrs. Winspear, who is in charge of answering the communal phone. "Martha! Call 911! Tell them we need an ambulance right away!"

Mrs. Winspear's small eyes open wide inside her doughy face and her two chins tremble. She starts dialing the phone. Mr. Murphy reappears, holding a fistful of rubber bands, wet washcloths, and a beat-up-looking roll of gauze. I grab on to the back of Claudia's shirt as she snatches a rag. She doesn't seem to notice. Out of the corner of my eye, I glimpse Honey running down the length of the Great House, toward Emmanuel's room. In the background, Mrs. Winspear is yelling into the telephone.

"Yes, that's right, Mount Blessing! Right off of Sanctity Road. Yes, yes, the commune! There's been a terrible accident!

Please hurry!" Her voice, shrill as glass, cuts through me. Benny shrieks and kicks on the table, flailing his arms and legs wildly.

"Hold him down!" Claudia yells.

Christine and Mr. Murphy each take hold of Benny as Claudia begins tearing the washcloth into strips. Christine is crying—great, gulping sounds, like a child who has had a bad dream. Benny's eyes are rolling around in their sockets and strange, grunting sounds are coming out of his mouth. I squeeze in next to Claudia and move in close to his face. Beads of sweat glisten above his pale eyebrows.

"Benny," I whisper. "Benny, it's Ags. I'm here, Benny. It's gonna be okay. They called the ambulance, sweetie, and you're gonna be all right. Don't worry, Benny. I'm here." He lurches, screaming again, as Claudia does something to his injured hand.

"It's all right, Benny," Claudia says firmly, her eyes wide with concentration. "I need you to be brave. Two of your fingers are hurt really bad and I need to wrap them up so that you don't keep losing blood." She gives Mr. Murphy a curt nod. "Hold him down, Samuel. He's not going to like this."

I sob along with Benny as he wails and arches his back under Claudia's tight, rapid movements. Christine's cries get louder. Suddenly, out of nowhere, Mom, Dad, and Nana Pete rush forward, trying to get through the throngs of other Believers who have gathered around the table.

"Isaac!" Christine takes a step back, nearly knocking me over. "Oh, Isaac, I'm sorry! It was an accident! I didn't even see him go back in!" Dad looks confused for a moment as he stares down at Benny.

"It's his hand?" Nana Pete shouts, trying to squeeze past Mr. Murphy. "Is that where he's hurt?"

Suddenly the crowd begins to shift and separate. People move back and then fall silent as Emmanuel and Veronica walk through their midst. Claudia, who is still working like crazy, doesn't notice as Emmanuel stands a few inches from my little brother, surveying the damage, but Dad looks up instantly. His face pales.

"Stop what you are doing," Emmanuel says. He is eerily calm.

Claudia looks up. "Emmanuel." She sounds stunned.

Emmanuel nods in Mrs. Winspear's direction. "Call the ambulance back, Martha, and tell them it was a false alarm."

Now it's Mrs. Winspear's turn to look confused. She brings her fat hands up to the sides of her face and presses them against her cheeks, looking first at Claudia and then back at Emmanuel.

Veronica takes a step forward and purses her lips. "*Now*, Martha." Mrs. Winspear turns and starts to redial the phone.

Claudia stands up. "What are you—"

"Bring him into my room," Emmanuel says. His voice is grave, mysterious.

"Oh no," Claudia says, shaking her head. "With all due respect, this child doesn't have time right now for a prayer service. He should get to the hospital immediately before he loses any more blood."

"There's not going to be a prayer service," Emmanuel says. He leans over, lifting Benny from the table. "I am going to heal him."

The crowd gasps.

Claudia's face turns pale. "*Heal* him? How?"

Emmanuel's voice booms over the upturned sea of Believer faces. "'For truly I say to you, if you have faith like a grain of mustard seed, you will say to this mountain, "Move from here to there," and it will move, and nothing will be impossible for you.'"

Claudia is aghast. "This child needs a *surgeon*! Faith can come later! There are bones in these fingers that are probably broken, tendons and nerves that must be reattached! There is nothing you can do here, Emmanuel! You have no medical training!"

But Emmanuel turns his back on Claudia's pleas, still holding Benny, who is whimpering like a little puppy. His voice reverberates through the Great House as he walks through the stunned crowd. "And so I say to you, 'Whoever does not doubt in his heart, but believes that what he says will come to pass, it will be done for him.'"

"Please, let the hospital—," Claudia begins.

But Veronica cuts her off with flashing eyes. "Hold your tongue! Do you realize who you are talking to?" Claudia steps back and presses her hand tightly against her lips. Nana Pete grabs Dad's arm.

"Don't be a fool, Leonard!" Her voice is breaking. "Don't let him go! Benny might die if he doesn't get the right medical care!"

I can tell by the momentary shift of panic in Dad's eyes that he is considering Nana Pete's words. But then he blinks and the look of panic disappears.

"The only fools in this world, Mother," he says slowly, "are the ones who refuse to believe. That is why we are Believers."

He takes Mom's hand in his and begins to walk alongside Veronica toward Emmanuel's room. "'Blessed are the ones who have not seen and yet still believe,'" he says. Listening to him, the crowd now surges behind, individually murmuring their own verses of faith and belief.

"'Then Jesus said, "Did I not tell you that if you believed, you would see the glory of God?"'"

"'Put your trust in the light while you have it, so that you may become sons of light.'"

I stop as a familiar voice echoes in my ears. "'He took up our infirmities and carried our diseases!'"

It's mine.

HONEY

Nana Pete, Agnes, and I keep watch, sitting on one of the couches just outside Emmanuel's door, but the hours tick by and no one emerges from Emmanuel's room. There is no way to tell what is going on in there, since the three of us have been forbidden to enter. Even when I stand up and press my ear against the door, I can detect no sound at all from inside. All around us, the rest of the Believers buzz silently, cleaning and sweeping and washing the windows, as if nothing has happened. Mr. Murphy even goes back to finishing his breakfast. When the phone rings, Mrs. Winspear picks it up and blinks, saying the same thing she always does: "Hello and God bless you! How can I help you today?" as if a little six-year-old kid is not clinging to life just fifty feet away from her. These people make me want to mess someone up.

Nana Pete does not look at anyone or say anything as the morning light fades outside the windows. She just stares into the ashy mouth of the dead fireplace across the room with a vacant expression on her face. Every once in a while, she reaches into her purse, pulls out a pink handkerchief, and pats her upper lip. Agnes, who is sitting on the other side of her, rocks back and forth in her seat, reciting Bible verses about faith and ticking off the beads on her consecration beads. I feel like I'm going to start screaming. Instead, I get up and start walking toward the bathrooms.

I almost miss Benny's glasses, which are lying in a heap

just inside the Great Door, forgotten amid all the excitement. Picking them up, I stare for a moment at a tiny drop of blood on the left frame. Fear grips me as I think of Claudia's words: "He should get to the hospital before he loses any more blood!" How much blood has he lost? Is it too late? I wipe the glasses gently with the hem of my robe, fold the stems, and insert them back inside the robe's wide sleeves. Then I go back and sit down on the couch next to Nana Pete and wait.

Finally, after four and a half hours, Mr. and Mrs. Little emerge from Emmanuel's room. All the Believers in the room rush over, surrounding them like a horde of bees. Benny is in Mr. Little's arms. His eyes are closed and his mouth is hanging open slightly. Nana Pete and Agnes and I have to struggle to get through the crowd.

"Is he dead?" Agnes cries. Mrs. Little's face is a weird bluish color, as if all the blood has gone out of it. She reaches out and puts an arm around her daughter.

"Of course not, Agnes. He's just sleeping." She reaches around and lifts Benny's bandaged hand gently. "And you should see his fingers." Now she is addressing the crowd. "They're as good as new. Emmanuel sewed them both back on, inch by inch. He's going to be just fine. As good as new."

"He *sewed* them back on?" Nana Pete says, but her voice is drowned out by the crowd.

"It's a miracle!" someone says.

"He's more than a healer," says another, clearly awestruck. "He's a miracle worker! We are so blessed!"

Dad nods, beaming, and then starts walking toward the

exit. "Let's get back to work!" he says over his shoulder. "The excitement is over and we still have much to do." The crowd begins to disperse accordingly.

Nana Pete presses her fingers against her lips and rushes up alongside Mr. Little, as Agnes falls into step next to her mother. "Leonard, did he really *sew* them back on? How is that possible? There's no way he could have done it correctly!" I walk behind the two of them closely.

Mr. Little looks at his mother out of the corner of his eye. "We're going down to the Field House to put Benny to bed, Mother. He's probably going to sleep through the night, which will be incredibly convenient, since we still have a lot of work to do for the Ascension March."

"The *march*?" Nana Pete repeats. "Y'all are going ahead with the march, with all of this going on?"

Mr. Little looks genuinely perplexed. "Of course we are. Why wouldn't we? Things are fine now. Everything's back to normal."

"Things aren't back to *nor*mal, Leonard! Listen to me, please! At least just take him to the hospital to be checked out!" I follow behind Agnes and her mother, trying to keep out of Mr. Little's line of vision. "What if he needs medicine, Leonard?" Nana Pete pleads. "Antibiotics, so he doesn't get an infection?"

Mr. Little shakes his head, as if a fly is buzzing around it. "There is no need to take him to any hospital, Mother. When Benedict wakes up and starts to feel better, I'll take the bandages off so you can see for yourself what kind of miracle Emmanuel performed."

"Miracle?" Nana Pete shouts. She stops walking. "Leonard, you've lost your mind! You're not thinking clearly!"

Now Mr. Little stops walking. *"Enough!"* His eyes are flashing. Nana Pete stares back at him, her face a pained question mark. "If you insist on continually questioning our choices as Believers, I am going to ask you to leave. *Now*." And with that, he turns and continues walking down the hill. Mrs. Little hurries to catch up with him.

I watch as Agnes stares uncertainly at her parents, and then back again at Nana Pete. I take a step closer to Nana Pete, pressing myself against her side, and will her with my eyes to do the same.

"Come along, Agnes," Mrs. Little calls suddenly, turning around. "It looks like you're going to have to take care of Benny by yourself this afternoon."

Agnes walks obediently behind her mother, but as they near the bottom of the hill, just past the lilac bushes, she turns her head and looks back at me. Her eyes are empty.

Nana Pete blots her face again with her handkerchief. She is sweating profusely.

"Are you all right?" I ask. She nods and then looks around the empty grounds. There is no one in sight.

"Change of plans, darlin'. We're not going to wait for the Ascension March tomorrow night. We're leaving in the next hour, as soon as Leonard and Samantha go back up to the Great House. We've got to get Benny looked at in a real hospital and we might as well split for good while we're at it. Go get packed and meet me at the bottom of the hill in thirty minutes."

I hold her gaze for a full moment before I realize she is dead serious. "What are you going to tell Agnes?"

Nana Pete looks away for a second. "You let me worry about that," she says. "Now go."

I'm in a dead run, halfway up the side of the hill leading to the Milk House before I realize that I'll probably never see Winky or the butterfly garden again. The thought brings me to a screeching halt, as if someone has just yanked me backward with a length of cord. For a brief second, I consider turning back around and telling Nana Pete to go ahead without me, that I can't do it. But that's crazy. I've never wanted anything more than this in my life. There's no way I'm turning back now.

Still, when I come over the rise and see Winky's outline hunched over the butterfly bush, I feel like I might faint. There's no way I can face him. Instead, I sneak back down the other side of the hill so I can get inside the house from the opposite side. I try to move quickly, but my legs feel stiff, like wood. I don't have any kind of suitcase or carrying case, so I just empty the trash can and cram as many clothes as I can fit inside the liner bag. George and my butterfly notebook are the last two things to go in. I stuff George inside the toe of my sneaker and push my notebook all the way to the very bottom of my bag, where it won't get crinkled or ripped. There. Done.

I tiptoe over to the window and press myself flat against the wall, leaning over just a bit until I can see Winky. His back is to me, and he is on his hands and knees, tamping down more of the new compost from Mr. Schwab under the butterfly bushes. My head races with possibilities. Should I tell him the truth? Or maybe just part of it, that we're taking Benny to the hospital, but that we'll be back? If I told him everything, would he tell someone eventually? I close my eyes. Oh my God. What should I do? Maybe I'll just go out and pretend like nothing's going on at all. He'd ask about the garbage bag full of clothes probably, but I could toss that on the side of the house so he wouldn't see it and then go back for it afterward. I glance down at my watch. Only ten minutes left. I can't afford to waste any more time.

And then, all at once, I know what to do.

Reaching into my bag, I pull out my butterfly notebook, sit down on the edge of my bed, and start to write.

When I'm finished, I tiptoe back downstairs, creep over to Winky's bed, and stick the note underneath his TV. My eyes sweep the inside of the house slowly, taking in every last detail. I know this will probably be the last time I am ever inside it.

"I love you, Winky," I whisper.

Then I turn and run.

"We can't just *leave*," I hear Agnes saying as I creep back inside the Field House. Her voice is trembling. "Believers aren't allowed to leave the grounds unless they work in town. And Benny's sleeping. Mom and Dad said that I was in charge of him for the rest of the night. I have to—" She stops as I push my way into the room and then looks at me, annoyed. "What, you know about this?" I nod.

"We'll be back in a few hours, Agnes," Nana Pete says, pulling a cardigan sweater off the back of a chair. "No one will even notice that we're gone. But I'm taking your brother to a real hospital to be looked at by a real doctor. God only knows what kind of damage Emmanuel did to his poor fingers."

"But Dad said he healed him," Agnes protests. "He said it was a miracle."

"Agnes." I take a step toward her, trying to keep my voice calm. "Listen to yourself. This is the real world we're talking about, not some martyr story out of your saint book. Your brother could really be in trouble." She cuts her eyes at me.

"Actually, darlin'," Nana Pete says, moving around the room now with startling speed, "the only miracle here is going to be if your brother survives through the night without losing his hand altogether."

"It's true," a voice behind us says. Claudia is standing in the doorway, her dark hair framing lips white and thin as paper. "And when you get him to the hospital, make sure to let the doctors know that Emmanuel used ether to knock Benny out. They'll need to check his blood count."

Nana Pete claps her hand over her mouth. *"Ether!* Where in God's name did he get his hands on a bottle of ether?"

Claudia shakes her head. "I don't know where he got it. Ether hasn't been commercially available for years. But what really worries me is how much he may have used. I don't know too much about the effects of it on children, but it's not something I would fool around with." Claudia looks at Agnes steadily for a moment. "Your brother might never be able to use his hand again, Agnes, if he doesn't get real medical attention. Listen to your grandmother. She knows what she's doing." Agnes has a skeptical look on her face.

"This isn't about anything except Benny, Agnes," I say,

taking her hand. "Claudia's a doctor, for God's sake! She knows what she's talking about."

But Agnes pulls away from me and goes over to the bed to sit next to Benny. We watch her in silence as she takes his good hand in her own. "We'll just be gone for an hour?" she asks. Nana Pete and I exchange glances.

"Definitely," I answer. "Just a little while, Ags. Just so he can get checked out."

Agnes runs her fingers over the top of Benny's hand. "And I can stay with him the whole time?"

"Of course," Nana Pete says.

Claudia steps forward. "You'd better get going, Petunia. I really don't think you have much time to waste."

Nana Pete looks at Claudia beseechingly. "Please don't let on that you know we're leaving."

Claudia squeezes Nana Pete's hands. "I just came back here to get a change of clothes for Andrew." She looks Nana Pete directly in the eye. "I didn't see a thing."

Part II

AGNES

I stare at the space of windshield between Nana Pete and Honey from the backseat of the Queen Mary, where I am sitting with Benny's head on my lap. The sky is a pale, underwater blue. In the rearview mirror, I can see the ball of sun turning golden and then orange. The clock on Nana Pete's dashboard is broken, but I know it must be close to six. We have been driving for over an hour and Nana Pete is showing no signs of slowing down anytime soon. Twenty minutes ago, when we passed the sign for the Fairfield hospital, I asked her why she wasn't stopping.

She tightened her hands on the wheel and stepped down harder on the gas pedal. "We're going to a different hospital," she said. "Claudia told me about one a little ways from here that has surgeons who specialize in amputations."

I shift carefully in my seat, so as not to disturb Benny, who is still out cold. "Where *is* the other hospital?"

Nana Pete glances into her side mirror and swerves, passing a car on her left. "We're almost there. Try to relax, Mouse."

But I can't relax. Every nerve ending in my body is standing on end, like split wires. I am so nauseous from fear that every time Nana Pete changes lanes, I have to choke back the bile rising in my throat. All I can think about is the amount of trouble we are going to get into when we get back. It is nearly unfathomable. Forget leaving Mount Blessing without permission, which, aside from defectors, no Believer has ever done. The real crime is our obvious lack of faith in Emmanuel. Taking Benny to a hospital to be checked out by "real" doctors after Emmanuel spent four and a half hours performing a miracle on him is like spitting in his face. No one believed Saint Bernadette either, I think to myself, when the Blessed Virgin appeared to her. People even laughed when she told them of the miraculous spring of water the Virgin told her to dig out from the ground. But it turned out to be true. Later, these same disbelievers had brought their sickest relatives to the spring to be healed. And the miracles—countless numbers of them—had begun.

"Please, Nana Pete, let's just turn around, okay?" I ask for maybe the hundredth time. "Please? We'll get back before Mom and Dad's meeting ends, and I bet we can even convince them to take Benny to the hospital in the morning."

But Nana Pete shakes her head. "No can do, Mouse. You heard what Claudia said about the ether and Benny not being able to use his hand again. We've got to get him checked out. Right now."

I look down at Benny. His face is very, very white, like snow in winter. The edges of his lips are tinged blue and under his eyelids I can see his eyeballs moving back and forth, as if he is having a bad dream. I try to not to think about the last thing I said to him before he got hurt, but it echoes in the back of my head: *Fine, be a pain. But when you get called into the Regulation Room, don't expect me to go in there with you.* My eyes fill with tears. How could I have said such a thing? I don't even know where to begin to atone for this sin, it's so big.

Honey, who has been unusually quiet until now, turns around. She looks down at my little brother with a serious expression. "I have his glasses," she says. "Just so you know."

Her statement startles me. How could I have forgotten about Benny's glasses?

"Where were they?"

"Right inside the Great Door. On the floor. I guess they fell off when . . . when everything happened." She reaches over the back of the seat and brushes her fingertips gently over the front of Benny's shirt. "He *looks* okay," she says. "Don't you think?"

As if on cue, Benny's lashes flutter and his lids slide open heavily.

"Hey," I whisper, leaning over him. "Hey, Benny. It's me." Benny blinks several times without seeing anything, and then, disoriented and frightened, starts to scream. He thrashes violently until he slides off my lap onto the floor of the car.

"Benny!" I screech.

"Oh my God." Nana Pete nearly swerves off the road. "Get in the back, Honey! Help Mouse get him off the floor before he hurts his hand even more!"

Honey is over the seat in a flash and in ten seconds my brother is stretched out tightly between us. I have both of his arms pinned carefully to his sides, and Honey is hanging on to his legs, which are still flailing.

"It's okay, Benny!" I shout, trying to make myself heard above his still-piercing shrieks. "We're going to the hospital! You're going to be all right!" I start to cry along with him. I'd give anything to take the pain for him. Anything at all.

"We're almost there," Nana Pete says grimly, eyeing the three of us in the rearview mirror. "Hang in, guys." She gives the car another surge of gas. "Hang in."

The Queen Mary finally screeches to a halt in front of a wide blue building with EMERGENCY glowing above the doors. Nana Pete rushes inside, carrying Benny, who is still wailing. Honey and I are close at her heels. Within seconds, a flurry of white-clad medical personnel appear, as if from the woodwork. The next moment, they vanish into a small room behind a glass door and stretch Benny out on a silver table.

Somehow Honey and I manage to slip into the room behind everyone. We hover at the room's periphery, trying to stay out of the way as nurses run in and out. Suddenly a tall man dressed all in blue strides into the room, snapping on a pair of thin rubber gloves.

"The injury is to the extremities, is that correct?" He has a deep, rumbling sort of voice and a neatly trimmed white beard. A pin on the front of his shirt identifies him as Dr. Pannetta.

"His right hand, Dr. Pannetta!" The nurse has to shout over Benny to be heard. She has a silver ring in her nose. "Second and third digits!"

Dr. Pannetta slides a gloved hand under Benny's wrist and then leans in to get a closer view. He grimaces, as if he has just come into contact with a horrible smell. "What the hell is this?" The other nurse, who is shorter than me, leans up on her tiptoes, looks over at Benny's fingers, and gasps. Dr. Pannetta looks at Nana Pete. "What *is* this?" he asks again. "What happened here? Did someone try to sew these fingers back on?" Nana Pete drops her eyes, as if searching for the right words somewhere on the floor.

Out of nowhere, I step forward. "It was Emmanuel! He healed him! My father said it was a miracle!"

Dr. Pannetta is staring hard at me. His eyes rove across my robe, as if seeing it for the first time. Honey and Benny do not have their robes on. I feel self-conscious suddenly, as if I am naked. "Who the hell is *Emmanuel*?"

"He's the leader of the Believers," I say without thinking. "At Mount Blessing. Where we—" The look that crosses Dr. Pannetta's face makes me stop talking.

Nana Pete comes to my rescue, gesturing loosely with her hands. "Actually, he's . . . he's just . . . someone we know."

There is a pause as Dr. Pannetta's eyes sweep back over Benny's fingers.

"Well, whoever he is, he's certainly no doctor," he says. He looks over at me, still holding Benny's injured hand. "I hate to burst your bubble, sweetheart, but this is no miracle. This is just about the worst hatchet job I've ever seen. This Emmanuel, whoever he is, has put this kid at serious risk of losing his fingers for good, not to mention the possibility of contracting a blood infection." My stomach flip-flops inside of me.

Dr. Pannetta, all business again, addresses the two nurses. "Let's prep him and take him up to Operating Room 3. And page Dr. Francis and Dr. Stella." I stand back, dazed, as the nurses wheel Benny out of the room. Dr. Pannetta follows and then pauses at the doorway, as if remembering the three of us still standing there.

"I'm going to have to undo everything that Emmanuel

guy did," he says, talking directly to Nana Pete. "And then I will try to salvage what is left and reattach those fingers the right way." He grimaces. "It's going to be a complicated surgery, but you came to the right place. I know what I'm doing. Try to get some rest in the waiting room, and I'll come down afterward to let you know how he's progressing." Nana Pete nods gratefully. Dr. Pannetta gives her shoulder a light tap and strides from the room.

"Wait!" I plead, rushing out into the hall.

Dr. Pannetta turns. He is so tall that when I look up, I see his Adam's apple first and then his face. "Yes?" he asks.

My nose starts to wiggle, but I need to know.

More than anything, I need to know.

"Emmanuel didn't heal him? There was no miracle?"

Dr. Pannetta gazes curiously at me for a long moment. His eyes are gray with little specks of blue in them. "No," he says gently. "There was no miracle."

And then he is gone. The two words reverberate through my head.

No miracle. No miracle. No miracle.

Behind me, Honey's hand descends lightly on my shoulder. It feels like a thousand pounds.

"Don't touch me," I say, shrugging her off. "I mean it. Don't *touch* me."

HONEY

Nana Pete leads both of us into a small waiting room filled with dark blue chairs. The walls of the room are the same color as the chairs and the rug and it feels as if the heat has been turned on. Very cavelike. Maybe they want people to fall asleep in here. Except for a television mounted on the wall and a green plastic tree in the corner, the room is empty. When Nana Pete and I take a seat, Agnes moves purposefully to the other side of the room and, with her back to us, kneels down on the floor and stretches out her arms. I roll my eyes as she begins to whisper the familiar Latin chants and stand up.

"I'm gonna go outside."

Nana Pete looks over at me. "I don't think—"

"Just to get some fresh air," I say. "Don't worry. I'll be back in a few minutes." I walk for a while along the white halls of the hospital, reading signs that say things like PEDIATRIC UNIT, THIRD FLOOR, and VISITING HOURS WILL BE ENFORCED. I can't believe how big it is! Long, immaculate corridors filled with closed doors stretch out like pearly highways and then disappear around a curve. Every few minutes I jump as a female electronic voice fills the air, informing people that visiting hours are almost over. Then, when I turn a corner just beyond a door marked SCRUBS, a horrible shrieking sound fills my ears. A large blue sign on the opposite wall indicates that I am at the PEDIATRIC BURN UNIT. Suddenly a woman with a paper mask over her mouth rushes past me, toward the room where the screaming is coming from.

"How'd you get in here?" she barks. "You're not sterile! You have to leave!" She pushes open the door to the room. The horrible screaming gets louder, the sound of someone being tortured. Sounds I've heard before. I turn around and run in the other direction. A hundred yards down the opposite hallway are the front doors to the hospital. I make my way toward them and stop in surprise as the wide glass frames slide open automatically. I've seen these kinds of doors on *Days of Our Lives* lots of times. Someone is always rushing through them just as the music swells and the picture fades. Turning back around, I walk up to the doors again so I can see them yawn wide, like magic. I do it once more. And a fourth time.

"Those doors aren't for playing around with, young lady."

Startled, I turn around to see a woman frowning at me over a pair of pale blue glasses. She is sitting at a desk with INFORMATION in gold on the front, tapping a pen against the bottom of her chin.

"Sorry. It's just . . . I've never seen . . . I mean, I've never gotten to use doors like that before."

"You don't get out much, do you?" the woman asks dryly. Her lips are painted a bright orange color and she has pale, watery eyes. Coils of long blond hair are piled so high on top of her head that it looks as if they have exploded straight out of her skull. She unwraps a roll of red circular candies and holds the tube out in my direction. The silver paper on the outside reads CHERRY LIFE SAVERS. "You want one?" Red food. Forbidden.

"Why do they have a hole in the middle?" I ask, popping one into my mouth.

The lady sucks on hers and studies me for a minute. "Where're you from, *Mars?*"

I look up at her, suddenly aware of how stupid I must sound. We're out here now. In the real world. I've got to get a grip. Quit asking so many dumb questions. Taking a step backward, I give her a small laugh. "Yeah, Mars," I say nervously. "Next stop is Pluto." I wave. "Thanks for the candy. And stuff. Bye."

The cool air hits my face as I step outside and slump down on an empty wooden bench. It feels good against my sweaty skin and I sit for a minute, letting it wash over my face. The cherry candy makes a sour pocket on the back of my tongue, but it tastes good, like it's waking me up. I reach inside my pocket and take George out.

"Hey, buddy." I stroke his broken ear gently. "How you doing? You okay?" George blinks and then gives me a little nod of his head. I take a deep breath. "We're out of there, George. For real. Mount Blessing and Emmanuel and all the rest of the Believer freaks are history." I close my fingers around his tiny shape. "I'm not gonna tell anyone else this, George, but I'm a little scared. I really am. I don't know what's going to happen or even what we're gonna do next. I don't want Nana Pete to get in any kind of trouble. I was thinking on the car ride here that, you know, if anything happens, like Emmanuel coming to get us, or Agnes's parents finding us and dragging us back, that I'm just gonna run away. I can't go back there, George. Not ever. As scary as it is out here, it's ten thousand times worse back there. I've gotta go my own way now."

Without warning, a man and a woman burst out of the

automatic doors and run down the cement path. I shove George back into my pocket.

The woman, who is about my height but heavier, is running ahead of the man. She is wearing a white skirt with yellow tulips along the bottom, a white sweater buttoned up to her chin. She is laughing and making whooping sounds. The man, dressed in a light green coat and blue jeans, follows her. Suddenly the woman stops and, turning, throws her arms around him. When she kisses him, her hands move around toward the back of his head, through his dark hair. He kisses her back deeply.

Something stirs deep inside me, watching them. This, *this* is what Emmanuel almost beat me to death for doing? When they break apart, the man puts his arm around the woman and draws her in close against his chest. Together they walk down the rest of the path. I stare after them as long as I can, hoping they will stop and kiss one more time. If it was *Days of Our Lives*, they would still be kissing and music would be playing in the background. But just as quickly as they appeared, they turn a corner and disappear from sight.

I stand up and start walking around the outside of the hospital, looking at the sea of cars in the parking lot, the crest of hills in the distance. Halfway past the emergency room, I'm distracted by several peony bushes, some of which have already started to bloom, and a small cluster of Clouded Sulphurs, which are fluttering around one especially large flower. Leaning in, I study the butterflies, examining their delicate antennae, already heavy with nectar, and their pale yellow wings, which are the color of the sky just before a winter sunset. I count the butterflies silently. There are six of them. I will make a note of it later in my butterfly notebook.

I wonder if Winky found my note yet. The moon is just peeking out from behind a few wispy clouds in the sky, which means that the Yankees are probably already on. What will he do when he reads it? Anything? Nothing? I miss him already and it's been only a few hours. I try hard to push him from my mind as I head back inside.

Nana Pete is sitting alone inside the waiting room, staring at a television set with the sound turned off. Some guy is on the screen, pointing at a toaster oven and waving his arms around like a nut. She starts as I come into the room and I realize I have woken her.

"Where's Agnes?" I ask as she rubs her eyes.

She points at another room across the hall. "In there. She said she needed privacy."

I peek across the hall. Agnes is facedown on the floor, her arms spread out on either side of her. God Almighty. When does this stuff end?

A faint ringing sound comes from somewhere on the floor. I look over at Nana Pete's purse. She freezes as it rings again.

"What's that?"

"My phone," she answers. It rings again, a high, fluted sound. I lean over and watch as she flips open the top. It rings one more time as the words UNKNOWN NUMBER blink on the tiny screen. "Damn it," she says, holding the phone away from her.

"What's wrong?" I ask. "Who is it?"

"It's an unlisted number, which means it's probably

Leonard." She rubs her nose. "I forgot that I gave this number to him." It rings again.

"Just ignore it," I say. "Put it back in your purse."

But Nana Pete shakes her head. "He'll just keep calling." She looks out toward the other waiting room, where Agnes is. "Shut the door, will you?"

I close the door softly as she flips open the phone again, pushes a small red button, and holds the instrument to her ear. I can hear a voice, frantic and furious, on the other end.

"Mother?" Nana Pete winces and holds the phone away from her. "Mother? Is that you? Please answer me. Mother? Hello?"

Nana Pete closes her eyes and starts to bring the phone again to her ear. But I catch her arm, angling myself so that I can hear what he is saying. She takes a deep breath. "I'm here, Leonard."

"Mother! Where are you? Where are the children? What have you done?"

Nana Pete gets up from her seat and begins to pace. I follow, still holding her arm down so that I can hear what is being said. Here we go.

"They're here, Leonard. They're right here. They're safe. Benny's hand is being operated on—"

"Operated? *Operated!* What are you talking about, Mother? Where are you? What are you doing?"

"The surgeon here said Benny would've lost his hand if I hadn't brought him in," Nana Pete says firmly.

There is no response from the other end of the phone. Then: "Okay, Mother. Okay, fine. Just tell me where you are and I'll come get you."

Nana Pete inhales through her nose, her breath a single tremble. "They're not coming back, Leonard. I'm taking them with me."

"What do you mean, you're taking them with you? Have you lost your mind? You can't take them! They're my children! Tell me where you are, Mother! Tell me right now or so help me, I'll call—"

"No police!" I hear faintly in the background. Agnes's mother. She's crying. "No police, Isaac! Please! Remember what Emmanuel said about calling the police!"

I close my eyes, remembering what Mrs. Little is referring to. Three years ago, there was a slight uproar when a young woman named Anna Storm told Emmanuel she was calling the police after he took her into the Regulation Room. True to her word, two police officers arrived a few hours later. One of them, an Officer Marantino, informed Emmanuel that he was conducting a "thorough investigation regarding Anna's abuse allegations." He stayed for nearly eight hours, interviewing first Emmanuel, then Veronica, and finally numerous random adult Believers. No one admitted to ever receiving any kind of abuse by Emmanuel. Worse, after Officer Marantino asked to see the Regulation Room, he came out of it scratching his head.

"I can't imagine what Ms. Storm is talking about," he said. "That there is one of the nicest TV rooms I've ever been in." He shook hands heartily with Emmanuel, nodded politely at Veronica, and left the grounds with his partner, shaking his head. No charges of any kind were filed and the abuse accusation was eventually erased from the record. Within minutes of Officer Marantino leaving the grounds, however, Emmanuel called for a mandatory meeting of all the Believers, including the children. His face was purple with rage and when he talked, spit flew from the corners of his mouth.

"If any Believer *dares* to call the police department to investigate my actions again, he or she will discover the real consequences of my wrath," he roared. "Get out if you are not happy here! I am warning you! Get *out*!"

"Just tell us where you are, Mother." Mr. Little pleads now. "Please. We're not going to get the police involved, and Emmanuel doesn't even have to know about it. Please, just let us come get the kids and we can forget any of this ever happened."

Nana Pete shakes her head. "No one's going to forget anything, Leonard. I know all about the Regulation Room." There is a dead silence on the other end of the line. Nana Pete swallows hard and I can tell she is blinking back tears. "How could you let this go on, Leonard? How? They're children! They're my grandchildren!"

"Mother." Mr. Little's voice is shaky and light. "Just wait a minute, all right? Just hold on. Before you jump to any kind of conclusions, just let me explain . . ."

"Nothing you say to me right now, Leonard, could possibly explain what you have been putting your children through. Nothing."

"Mother!"

But Nana Pete clicks the phone shut again and turns the ringer off.

"Wow," I say softly. "That was great. You were really strong." But she is trembling. "Hey, it's all right." I put my arm around her and lead her over to the chair. "C'mere. Sit down. You're gonna fall over."

She sits down heavily and puts her purse on her lap. I keep my mouth shut, just in case I end up saying the wrong thing. After a few minutes, she turns and looks at me. Her eyes are sort of glassy-looking. "This is probably the hardest thing I've ever done in my life, Honey. And I don't even know what we're going to do next."

"It's okay," I say. "We have to get Benny fixed up and then we'll just start driving to Texas. Okay? Just like we talked about." Nana Pete swallows and nods her head, but I don't know if she's really listening. She's getting scared; I can tell. Quickly I grab hold of her arm. "You know what else? You should probably take some pictures of my back with that camera you brought."

Nana Pete looks at me, bewildered. "Your back?"

"Yeah." I nod, pushing back the dread that is beginning to rise in the back of my throat. "I have belt marks on my back from the Regulation Room. Maybe you should take a picture in case we have to show anyone. You know, later, if we have to prove our case." Nana Pete starts fanning herself with her handkerchief.

"You okay?" I ask.

She nods, moving the handkerchief faster. "Little light-headed all of a sudden. I'll be okay in a minute." After a few minutes, she drops her handkerchief back inside her purse and pulls out the camera. "Okay." Her voice is shaking. "Let's do this."

I turn around and, before I lose my nerve, lift up my shirt and lean against the wall. Nana Pete gasps. I stare at a groove in the blue wall, try to imagine myself sliding into it, disappearing completely.

"That word," she whispers. "Why did he write that word on you?"

The soft part behind my eyes burns, like I have a fever. Why does it feel that Emmanuel has, after all this time, managed to take a little part of me? "I kissed a boy," I murmur. "Please. Just take the picture."

I can hear Nana Pete bring the camera up to her face. She clicks once, twice, three times. The camera makes a whirring sound as each picture slides out. I pull my shirt down and sit in one of the blue chairs. Nana Pete puts the photos in her bag and sits next to me.

"Honey," she whispers, drawing the backs of her knuckles against my arm. "We are doing the right thing." I nod and keep my head down low, hoping she doesn't notice the splash of tears that dampen the front of my pants. When she takes my hand in hers, I lean in a little so my head rests against the top of her arm.

After a while I close my eyes.

AGNES

To doubt is human. Even Saint Thomas the Apostle, after Jesus himself appeared to him and allowed him to place his hands in his crucifixion wounds, refused to believe that it was the actual risen Christ.

No miracle.

Was the devil speaking through Dr. Pannetta, trying to get me to doubt the validity of Emmanuel's work? It's entirely possible. Emmanuel says that the devil has a tendency to be more clever than God, since he has to work so much harder to get people to listen to him. I think of one of my favorite saint stories, Saint Juliana of Nicodema, who was tormented mercilessly by the devil. He tried to trick her, appearing as an angel dressed in white robes surrounded by light. Disguising even his voice, he tried to convince her to worship the stone idols and to turn away from Christ. If the devil could disguise himself as a messenger angel, I think to myself, why couldn't he conceal himself as a doctor?

No miracle.

"Lord God," I whisper. "Suffer me not to be lost, but of thy grace show me the way and the truth." I wait facedown on the scratchy surface for what feels like hours. No voice comes out of the sky, the way God did for Juliana, telling her to turn away from the diabolical angel. No shimmering light appears, like the Virgin did for Bernadette. Why can't someone up there just show me? Just once? I am not strong enough to know on my own. It is too hard. I cannot even detect who is telling the truth, deep in my chest, the way it sometimes feels. Closing my eyes, all I can see are a thousand exploding pinpoints of light. I wonder if my brain is actually disintegrating behind my eyes. Everything else around me is falling apart; why shouldn't my brain? A parade of images perforates my mind's eye, marching before me in a kaleidoscope of color: HARLOT, Benny running to us in the field with news of Nana Pete's arrival, the frog pond, Claudia screaming for tape and bandages, the look on Benny's face when he woke up in the back of the car . . . My eyes swell with tears.

"No crying," Emmanuel said to me once inside the Regulation Room. "If you cry, I will start over and keep going again until you stop."

Wiggle, wiggle.

I reach up and hold on to the consecration beads around my neck.

Wiggle, wiggle. Getting up on my knees, I hold my arms out on either side and start to chant evening prayers. "*Credo in Deum Patrem omnipotentem . . .*" The block of pain does not lessen inside my chest, but I can feel my breathing start to slow as the familiar words flow through my lips.

Wiggle, wiggle, wiggle.

Nana Pete pokes her head into the room. "Mouse?" I keep praying. "Mouse? The nurse said Benny just got out of surgery. We can go see him now, darlin'."

Benny's room is all white with blue and pink curtains hanging over a single window. For some reason, it smells like mashed potatoes and gravy. A television floats from an angled metal arm above the bed, and a small picture of orange marigolds hangs on the wall. Benny is in the middle of the bed. He looks terribly small. Green plastic tubes snake out of his nostrils. His hand, which is wrapped in gauze all the way up to the elbow, reminds me of a butterfly cocoon Honey showed me once.

I stare at him for a minute, thinking back to the day last year when he came out of Emmanuel's room wearing his glasses for the first time. They were much too big, and although Emmanuel had fashioned an elastic strap that anchored them around the back of his head, they still slipped forward along the bridge of his nose.

"They're horrible, Ags," he'd said, staring down at his shoes. "All the kids are gonna make fun of me. I hate them."

I got down on one knee. "They're a little big. But they're not horrible, Benny. You'll grow into them. And you let Honey know about any kids that make fun of you, okay? She'll take care of them."

Benny looked at me. "And you too?"

I nodded, although I knew very well I would do nothing of the sort. Getting into physical altercations with the bullies of the playground was not saint-wannabe behavior. Now I take his little hand in mine. Why haven't I been a better sister? What is wrong with me?

Nana Pete steps inside the room, rubbing the sides of her arms. "I just talked to Dr. Pannetta. He said the surgery went better than expected and that he was very pleased. He expects Benny to gain full use of his fingers again in another month or so."

"When will he wake up?" I ask.

"Probably in a few hours. At least that's what the nurses said." She looks at me. "He's okay, Mouse. Really. It's just from the anesthesia. He'll wake up soon."

"Well, we should call home," I say. "Let Mom and Dad know where we are. They're probably worried sick." Nana Pete and Honey look at each other and then back down at the floor. "What? We've got to at least tell them when we'll be back."

"We're not going back," Nana Pete says quietly. From the windowsill, I can feel Honey staring at me. I know that look. It's the look she always gives me just before we are about to go into Emmanuel's room to be questioned for something we've done wrong, a look so full of willpower and stubbornness that it can't help but penetrate my fear. Usually I wait for it, like a talisman that I can glimpse and then rub before the ordeal begins. Now it makes me nervous.

"What are you talking about?" I laugh lightly. "Of course we're going back. Benny has to get back home so he can get better. And we have—"

"We're leaving, Agnes," Honey says evenly. "All of us. We're going back to Texas with Nana Pete. To live."

The floor beneath me feels as loose as quicksand. I steady myself on the edge of the bed. "What? Why?"

Nana Pete steps forward. "Because I cannot, in all consciousness, allow you to stay in a place like that anymore."

"A place like what?" I am aghast. "Like Mount Blessing?" Nana Pete nods. I look over at Honey. "Honey!" I plead. "Tell her! It's fine. There's nothing wrong with Mount Blessing."

Honey bites her lip and then shakes her head. "No, Agnes."

I look at Nana Pete again. "But you've been coming up to Mount Blessing for years! Why all of a sudden do you want to take us away from it?"

Nana Pete clears her throat. "Because I didn't know about the Regulation Room before." When she starts talking again, her voice is stronger. "That in itself is reason enough to burn that place down to the ground. It's sick, Agnes. Sadistic. No one should ever have to undergo what y'all have been through in that room. And then, with Benny's accident and Emmanuel sewing his fingers back on . . ." She pauses, shaking her head. "Maybe I've had blinders on all these years, but I just had no idea. I've never seen anything like it. This is not the way normal people live, darlin'. Emmanuel belongs in a mental institution. Or jail."

"*Jail?* What are you talking about? Emmanuel doesn't belong in jail! He's in charge of us. He's the holiest person I know. He'll never let you—"

"Emmanuel is not in charge of us," Honey asserts. "And he is not holy. He just thinks he is and he's made everyone else in that place think he is, too. He's a monster, Agnes."

I blink, trying to separate the words I am hearing from something shifting in my heart. "What about Mom and Dad? They're not monsters, Nana Pete. I know you don't get along and everything, but . . ." I struggle to hold back the tears. "But you can't do this to him. We're his kids, Nana Pete, whether you like it or not."

Nana Pete blinks. "I know, Mouse. And that is the hardest part of all of this." She drags her hands slowly down the sides of her face. "But what is happening to you is called child abuse. Do you know what that is, Agnes?"

I take a step backward. "We're not being abused! We deserve it! Emmanuel has to do it for the retraining of—"

Nana Pete grabs my hands, hard. "It's abuse, Agnes. There's no other way around it. And there is no such thing as retraining people, okay, darlin'? People are free to make up their own minds, not be trained to think and act like seals. If the police found out what was going on in that room, Emmanuel would be hauled off to jail so fast it would make your head spin." I wince under her grip and try to pull away. She just holds on more tightly. "It's not your fault, Agnes. It's not your fault that you don't understand this or that you think its okay. Emmanuel has you and your parents convinced that all of you deserve such . . . such . . ." She stops, unable to go on, and then gestures toward Benny's hand. "And now he thinks Emmanuel performed a *miracle* on Benny's fingers! I mean, if we hadn't brought him here . . ."

I stifle a sob, thinking again of Dr. Pannetta's words. *No miracle. No miracle.*

"Agnes," Honey says, stepping forward. "Listen to what Nana Pete is saying. Please."

With one final tug, I wrench free of Nana Pete's grasp and hold on tightly to the edge of Benny's bed. The edges of the room are beginning to swim. Could the devil, disguised as Honey and Nana Pete, be speaking? Of course he could. The devil can disguise himself any way he wants.

"Listen?" I spit out. "You think I'm going to listen to you two, who think you can decide for the rest of us what's best? How about considering my feelings? Did it ever occur to you to ask me my opinion about all of this?"

"Of course we did," Honey says matter-of-factly. "And we decided not to because we knew you would do exactly what you're doing now."

"Which is what?"

"Freak out."

"I am not freaking out," I say evenly. "Just because I happen to disagree with an insane idea the two of you cooked up does not mean I am losing my mind."

"Then listen to what we're saying!" Honey yells. "For once, Agnes! Even if you don't understand it! Open your ears and listen! We can go with Nana Pete down to Texas and have a whole new life for ourselves. No Emmanuel, no Veronica, no Regulation Room ever again." She pauses. "We'll be free for the first time in our lives, Ags. *Free*. We can go places, do things. Watch TV. Not be afraid all the time. Be normal kids, just like everyone else, living a normal life."

"Who wants to be normal?" I yell. "We're Believers! We're better than normal!"

"Better than normal is still abnormal, Agnes." Honey's voice is stoic. Her eyes glitter enticingly, reminding me of a story Dad told me once about Saint Thomas Aquinas. To see if they could tempt him from his chosen life of abstinence and virtue, some evil men sent a naked woman to his room. When St. Thomas opened the door and saw the woman standing there, he grabbed an iron poker out of the fireplace and chased her, screaming, down the hall.

"All men are tempted," Dad had said after the story, "but only the saints refuse to succumb." I glance around the room quickly. The only thing resembling an iron poker is the thin metal pole that is connected to some kind of machine next to Benny. There's no way I can pick that up.

"I'm not listening to you," I say through clenched teeth. "You wouldn't understand anyway." Honey opens her mouth, but I shake my head and point my finger at her. "Stay away from me, Honey. I mean it! I'm through with you and all your talk against Emmanuel." I look over at Nana Pete. "And you, too, Nana Pete. You're both heathens!"

Without warning, the nurse with the teddy bear jacket pops her head inside the door. "Everything okay in here?" A silver stethoscope is draped like a necklace along her chest. For a moment I think of screaming out that Nana Pete is trying to kidnap us. But something holds me back. For the life of me, I cannot get the words out.

Nana Pete smiles brightly. "Oh yes. Everything's fine. Thank you."

The nurse nods and then looks at Benny. "Careful not to wake him too soon. Rest is the best thing for him now." I look back down at my little brother, envying his obliviousness. But I am fighting for him, too, I realize. Maybe for the first time in his life. And I won't let him down again. The nurse shuts the door behind her and Nana Pete takes advantage of the sudden privacy to touch me on the shoulder.

I jerk away from her. "Don't touch me!"

Nana Pete withdraws her hand but stays put. "The life you have been leading at Mount Blessing is all you know, Agnes, which is why you can't possibly understand that what I am trying to do is for your own good."

Blah, blah, blah, I think, shoving two of my fingers in

my ears. *Yammer, yammer, yammer.* Nana Pete's mouth stops moving.

I feel a surge of courage as I drop my hands from my ears. "You know what? You two can talk until you're blue in the face. But I'm not going to Texas. And Benny's not going to Texas, either. You can't make us. That's kidnapping."

"I'm not going to kidnap you or force you to do anything against your will, Mouse. I mean it." Nana Pete grabs my hand again and points her finger between the pink curtains. "Look out the window. You see that bus terminal across the street?" I glance at the array of blue and silver buses, lined like up like sleek fish in front of a low building. "If you want to go back to Mount Blessing, I'll put you on a bus right now and pay your fare."

"Okay," I say instantly. "Then put me on a bus. With Benny. Now."

Honey steps forward as Nana Pete drops my hand. "She said you. Just you, Agnes. Not Benny. Benny and I are leaving with Nana Pete." Her words feel like needles going into the softest parts of my belly. There is a rushing sound in my ears. A bitter taste pools in my throat.

"You can't take Benny." My voice cracks like ice around the words. "He's my brother. I won't let you."

"He's my grandson, too," Nana Pete says. The tone in her voice is the same one she uses with Dad whenever she has an argument with him and knows she's right. "I have just as much of a responsibility to protect him as you do, Mouse." The silence in the room is deafening, the *beep beep* of the machine next to Benny's bed the only distraction.

"Why are you doing this to me?" I whisper.

"Because there isn't any other way," Nana Pete says. "There just isn't." The skin around her nose is getting red and blotchy. She stretches her arms out again. "Let me take you somewhere safe, Agnes. Let me take you to a place where no one will ever hurt you like this again."

Honey is staring at me through the little space between Nana Pete's arm and her waist. "Please," she mouths. "Please, Agnes."

For a moment I wonder if maybe I am in limbo, that place between heaven and hell where movement of any kind is impossible. Can't go up, can't go down. You just have to wait until someone prays hard enough to convince God that you really do deserve to go to heaven after all. Until then, you're suspended, hanging out on a cloud maybe, or sitting on the moon, staring at possibility.

Emmanuel always warned us of the physical sensation that accompanies the act of sin, a stomachache perhaps, or a sour taste in the mouth. What, I wonder, does the feeling of being on fire mean?

"I'll go for Benny," I hear myself saying. "He's going to need me when he wakes up and finds out what you're doing to us. He won't be strong enough to save himself." I try to keep my voice steady as I raise my eyes to meet Nana Pete's and Honey's. "But let's just make one thing perfectly clear right off the bat. You two can say whatever you want or take us wherever you think you should, but Benny and I will always be Believers." I pause. "No matter what."

HONEY

Benny wakes up just as the sun starts coming in through the window. By then Agnes has decided, against all odds, to come with us. I don't care if she considers it some kind of martyr journey, or if she feels she has to protect Benny from Nana Pete's and my evil clutches. Whatever it takes to get her on the road is fine with me. We can deal with the rest of it later. Benny's eyes are a little swollen for some reason, and when he opens them they look like two little blueberries staring out from under a fat piecrust. Agnes rushes to his side and tries to get him talking, but his head just lolls heavily on the pillow. Nana Pete runs out of the room and returns with the nurse, who takes off her stethoscope and listens to Benny's heart and checks his eyes and feels his forehead and wrist. After a moment she stands back and smiles.

"He's doing wonderfully," she says, looking at Agnes. "What a little trouper. I'll call Dr. Pannetta and let him know he's awake."

As soon as the nurse leaves the room, Nana Pete springs into action, folding blankets, shoving small paper packages of gauze into her purse, emptying the side drawer of a dresser next to Benny's bed, and folding Benny's clothes. Agnes and I just stand there dumbly for a moment, watching her.

"Let's go, girls," she says in a low, conspiratorial voice. "We can't waste any more time. We've got to leave now before they make me sign any more paperwork and start asking real questions."

But the nurses at the front desk freak out when Nana Pete comes out of Benny's room, holding him in her arms.

"Where do you think you're going?" one of them asks. She's dressed in a white short-sleeved tunic and has braces on her teeth. The one with the teddy bear jacket is eating a blueberry muffin.

"Please," Nana Pete says. "We have to go."

"Go?" the nurse repeats. She laughs, as if Nana Pete has just told her a joke. "This little boy has just gotten out of surgery! You're not *going* anywhere!"

"Actually," Nana Pete says, taking a few more steps, "we are."

Suddenly Dr. Pannetta appears with a cup of coffee in his hands. He looks different than the night before, dressed in navy blue pressed pants, a white button-down shirt, and a yellow tie with blue stripes. His shoes, brown and glossy, make a clicking sound when he walks, and his white hair, which is still damp, has been combed neatly.

"Does Benny have a sudden craving for a Big Mac?" he asks, striding toward us. "Or are you thinking of leaving the hospital with him?"

"She's trying to leave!" the nurse with the braces yells frantically. "I've been trying to explain things to her, but she won't listen!"

Agnes and I stay close to Nana Pete as she shifts Benny in her arms. She beckons Dr. Pannetta out of earshot, and moves close to the opposite wall. Agnes and I follow.

"I do appreciate all you've done, fixing my grandson's hand. I'm sure you saved his life and I will never be able to tell you what that means to me." She takes a deep breath. "But please don't prevent us from leaving now. I know the whole situation seems pretty bizarre, but we really do have to get moving." She nods toward the nurses' station on her left. "They have all my forwarding information. You can just send me the bill."

Dr. Pannetta gives her a quick, tight smile. "This is a hospital, ma'am, not a jail. And we're not wardens. You're free to come and go at your discretion. I do have to warn you, however, that considering the rather—" He breaks off, upending his palms. "Well, to use your word—*bizarre*—circumstances in this case, we're under a legal obligation to report the situation to Children's Services."

My stomach plummets when he says these words. I'm not sure what they are or what they do, but nothing about the words Children's Services sounds good. We've got to get out of here now or we'll all end up separated, placed in different homes. Maybe for good.

Nana Pete nods. "Yes, of course. I understand. And I appreciate your concern. But we really do have to go."

Dr. Pannetta touches the edges of his beard with two fingers, as if deliberating this last statement, and then glances over at the nurses. The one with the braces nods. "Actually, I believe someone from Children's Services has already been called," he says, glancing down at the wide silver watch on his wrist. "They should be here in less than an hour, tops. Why don't you wait until they come? They'll ask you and the children some questions and when they're done, I'll sign you out." He shrugs lightly. "Then you can leave. No big deal."

I hold my breath, count to ten.

"I'm sorry," Nana Pete says, turning away. "But we don't have time to wait. We have to go now. Come on, girls."

Dr. Pannetta reaches out and grabs her arm. "Just a minute, please!"

Nana Pete looks down at his hand. "I thought you said you weren't a warden."

"Yes." Dr. Pannetta's voice is tight, clipped, as he releases her arm again. He studies Nana Pete for a moment and then holds up his hand. "If you'll just wait two minutes, I will give you Benny's antibiotics."

Nana Pete's face turns white. "Oh. Well. Yes. Of course."

We watch tentatively as Dr. Pannetta strides over to the nurses' station, scribbles something inside a chart, and fills a small plastic bag with three or four bottles of pills. Handing the bag to Nana Pete, he takes Benny gently out of her arms and leads us down the hall.

"I had no choice but to sign you out AMA," he says. "Against medical advice. That's to cover our end of things. And I have to warn you it may not work to your advantage if anyone comes around later, asking questions." He shifts Benny in his arms. "This little guy's going to be just fine, as long as you make sure to give him his medicine regularly and bring him to someone *professional* to check his progress in a few days. A week at the most."

"Thank you," Nana Pete whispers. "I'll make sure to do that."

By now we are at the front entrance, a few feet away from the wall of sliding-glass doors. The Life Saver lady looks up from behind the information desk. She smiles at me and I smile back.

Dr. Pannetta hands Benny back to Nana Pete. "You take good care of him now," he says. "I worked hard on those fingers."

Nana Pete nods. "I promise I will."

Dr. Pannetta looks over at Agnes and me. "And you make sure his hand doesn't get stuck in any more doors, okay?" We nod. He walks toward the rubber mat in front of the glass doors. Agnes jumps back a little as they slide open.

"It's okay, Ags," I say, grabbing her hand. "They're just automatic doors. They won't hurt you." But I have to pull her to get her all the way through. She keeps her hands up close to her mouth and walks on leaden feet. When we get outside, I glance back once. Dr. Pannetta is resting his arm on the front of the information desk, watching us. The Life Saver lady's face is level with his elbow. I wave good-bye. The two of them raise their hands briefly in my direction, their faces clouded with bewilderment.

Agnes gets a little spooked out again when we reach the Queen Mary.

"Oh," she says. "Oh, I can't. I can't. We're going to burn in hell for this. Please let's go back. Please."

"Get in, Mouse," Nana Pete says. Her voice is stern and sharp. "Right now."

Agnes gives her a blank stare and then gets in the back, biting the inside of her cheek. We get Benny arranged carefully on her lap and then Nana Pete peels out of the hospital parking lot. The next thing I know, the Queen Mary is flying along a road called Route 81 South, going so fast that the trees seem to blur. I don't say anything, but I get the feeling that we're not in Connecticut anymore.

No one talks for what seems like a very long time. I am, maybe for one of the first times in my life, at a complete loss for words. It feels sort of like we are riding along inside a soap bubble, a thin, transparent little thing that might pop at any second if the wind blows too hard or I breathe too loudly. And so I hunch down in the front seat of the car and just stay still. For a while, I stare out the window. To tell you the truth, I'm a little disappointed. Maybe it's because we're on a highway, or maybe the excitement of being out here for the first time is starting to wear off, but the outside world—at least from this vantage point—is pretty boring. All the commercials I've seen on TV have shown hot-air balloons soaring over wide green fields, shiny cars racing along winding roads, people running toward the ocean or sailing on huge boats. But all I can see, as far as I look, are trees and more trees. Mostly maple and oak, with the occasional scrubby pine. A field here and there breaks up the line of forestry, but even they are flat and full of dull, wilted-looking grass. I try to keep my eyes peeled for butterflies, but it's nearly impossible with Nana Pete whizzing along like she is. We've passed five or six signs already that have indicated that the speed limit is sixty-five miles per hour, but she's going at least eighty. At least.

After about an hour, however, I catch a glimpse of some houses. And although they are set back against the highway and not in a neighborhood, they still have yards and flowers in the front and in the back of one, a kid swinging on a tire. I crane my neck as we pass the kid on the swing and I want to ask Nana Pete to stop so I can get out and ask the kid his name and where he goes to school and how he likes living where he does, but of course I can't. Then there are some big buildings—a tan one with bright red letters that spell out SHOP RITE, and a smaller one that reads RITE AID. People are hurrying in and out of both stores, their arms full of packages. I wonder what sorts of things they have purchased, and how much money they spent. What do things like toothpaste or soap cost, anyway? Finally we pass a whole line of stores, all connected together in one straight line. I read as fast as I can, but they pass by in a blur and the only one I can make out is ROY'S PIZZA. I sit back in my seat, feeling impatient and hungry.

"Nana Pete?" I ask finally.

"Yes, sugar?"

"What does a Big Mac taste like?"

"A Big—" Nana Pete looks confused.

"Dr. Pannetta said something about Benny having a craving for a Big Mac," I press. "Are they that good?"

"Oh my Lord, darlin', you've never had a Big Mac, have you?" She looks into the rearview mirror. "How 'bout you, Mouse?" I glance back at Agnes. She doesn't move. "No, of course you wouldn't have if Honey here hasn't." Nana Pete smacks both of her hands against the steering wheel. "Well, that, my fellow travelers, is the first business of the day." She veers widely off the road, toward a green sign that says HARRISBURG. In a few minutes, we are sitting behind four other cars in a line outside a brown, squat building with a gigantic yellow M on the roof. "This here is called the McDonald's drive-through," Nana Pete says, looking more excited than I've seen her in days. "McDonald's is the official home of the Big Mac."

"What is it, exactly?" I ask. "A Big Mac, I mean?"

Nana Pete rubs her hands together. "A Big Mac, darlin', is

just about one of the worst things you can put into your body. It's also one of the most delicious, which is why I make it a point to have at least three a month." She sighs. "Two greasy hamburgers layered between three hamburger buns, slathered with ketchup and cheese and special sauce. Oh Lord, when you wash it all down with some french fries and an icy cold Coca-Cola, you'll think you died and went to heaven."

My stomach gurgles with excitement. "Man," I breathe. "It sounds amazing. Can I get two?"

"Of course!" Nana Pete claps her hands together. "Get three if you want! It's your first Big Mac!" She looks over the seat at Agnes. "How 'bout you, Mouse? You want to try one?" Agnes bites her lip and stares out the window. The car in front of Nana Pete finally drives away and she pulls up in front of a flat board covered with pictures of hamburgers. Then she starts talking into it! I almost fall out of the car when a girl's voice shoots back at her, repeating her order.

"Holy cow, Agnes, can you see this?" She cuts her eyes at me and looks away again. I glance down at Benny, who is still drifting in and out of a light sleep. I feel sorry that he is missing all of this. Nana Pete pulls up to a window, where another girl is waiting to give her our food, and then places the brown, oily bags in the front, between us.

The immediate aroma when I open the bag hits me like a fist. A combination of salt and warm cheese fills the car as I unwrap a small, dense package sitting on top.

It's better than I could have imagined, warm and slightly peppery with the tang of cheese in the background. I think I can taste a pickle, too, and maybe mustard. I close my eyes as I chew.

"*Eh?*" Nana Pete says, watching me. "Didn't I tell you?"

"Mmmm," I answer. "Even better than I thought it would be." I turn around, placing the bag on the floor next to Agnes and raise my eyebrows. "You gotta try this, Ags. Don't let it get cold."

But she only turns her head, affixing her gaze to another blurry patch of green outside, and reaches up around her throat for her consecration beads.

Nana Pete makes her way through a sandwich quickly, while I start on my second Big Mac. We share an enormous red paper sleeve of french fries and a gigantic Coke, and by the time I sip the last of it, I'm about ready to pass out.

"You must have a tapeworm in there, Honey," Nana Pete laughs. She says that on every visit, surprised all over again that I eat so much. "Boy, you can eat a *lot*."

"Actually, I don't feel so good," I say, unbuttoning the top of my jeans.

Nana Pete laughs. "That's the thing about McDonald's. The joy of it is so fleeting and then you have to pay the price."

"Just like sin," says Agnes from the back.

I start to turn around and then think better of it. She's going to be like this for a while.

We're just going to have to wait it out.

AGNES

I try hard to make Benny as comfortable as possible, arranging the blankets around him tightly and putting his head on my lap, but he doesn't seem to notice. He just sleeps. The nervous feeling in my stomach isn't letting up. I still can't believe I allowed Nana Pete and Honey to talk me into this madness. And all because of the Regulation Room. What did Nana Pete call it? Child abuse! How absurd is that? She doesn't understand. Well, of course she wouldn't. She's not a Believer. She doesn't get how much we all *need* that kind of discipline, or the type of people we would turn into without it. We'd be . . . well, heathens.

The sun is low in the sky, which means morning prayers have probably just ended. I am too frightened to look out the window at everything. It's too big, too scary. Instead, I pull on my consecration beads around my neck, close my eyes, and start chanting. The next thing I know, Honey's talking about something called a Big Mac. I will my stomach pangs to go away, offering up each growl and twist in my groin for the horrible way I treated Benny, as the two of them slobber away at their food up front. It is no easy task, as the faint odor of the Big Macs lingers long afterward inside the car. It smells delicious and nauseating at the same time. When I'm sure Honey and Nana Pete aren't looking, I tighten my waist belt one more time in an attempt to constrict my hunger, but the only thing it seems to be doing is making it harder to breathe.

Then, just as we pass a sign for Gettysburg, Honey asks Nana Pete if she can turn on the radio.

"Sure you can." Nana Pete leans forward to click on the silver dial. "You just fiddle with those knobs down there until you find something you like."

I know Honey can feel my eyes boring into the back of her neck as she starts pushing the buttons, but she just purses her lips and keeps pushing. Finally she stops as a woman's voice comes over the radio. It is the strangest voice I have ever heard, simple and unadorned, but the words she is singing, about God being a slob like the rest of us, are shocking.

"Turn it off!" I scream. "Turn it off, Honey, before we go to hell!"

Honey jumps forward in the seat, clearly startled, but blocks the silver buttons with her hand, as if I have already reached over the seat and am trying to turn it off. "No!" she says. "I want to listen to it!"

I lean over and stuff two of my fingers into Benny's ears. He doesn't move. "This is exactly why we're not allowed to listen to music!" I scream. "It's blasphemy! Turn it off! Now!"

Nana Pete is watching me carefully in the mirror. She leans over and touches Honey's wrist. "Turn it off," she says softly. "Just for now, darlin'."

Honey gives me a dark look and punches the off button hard with her index finger. "Happy now?" I don't answer. She turns to look at me. "Blasphemy? You seriously think God's going to send us to hell if we listen to music?"

"That lady was saying God was a slob!" I shake my head side to side, as if trying to empty the words out. "It's as bad as breaking the third commandment!"

"Which one is that again?" Nana Pete asks.

"Thou shalt not take the name of the Lord thy God in vain," Honey recites scornfully.

"It's true!" I yell. "God could never be a slob! He's perfect!"

"What's interesting to me," Nana Pete says, "is that your idea of perfect seems so off-kilter."

I blink twice. "No, it's not."

"But it is," Nana Pete says gently. "If God was perfect in every way, as you say he is, then that must mean that he is all loving and forgiving, right?" I nod carefully. "So how could he send people to hell for listening to music?" she asks. "Wouldn't that go against everything that love and forgiveness are all about?"

I open my mouth and then shut it. "He's not gonna send the people who listen to *good* music to hell," I finally reply.

"And what's good music?" Nana Pete asks. I don't answer. "Tell me, Mouse."

"Stuff that, you know, gives glory to him. Like the music Emmanuel plays on the piano."

Honey groans and bangs her head off the seat. "Agnes. If the only music people were allowed to listen to in this world is that boring, horrible stuff he plays, people would go nuts!"

"People who are writing stuff about God being a slob are already nuts," I retort.

"And doomed, I guess," Honey says, rolling her eyes.

"Yes. They're definitely doomed."

No one says anything for a minute. Then Honey turns around, as if someone has flipped a switch in her back. "Do you really want to go through the rest of your life thinking like a robot?"

I turn my head. "No," I say calmly. "I want to go through the rest of my life thinking like a saint."

"But you're not a saint!" Honey roars. "Even the saints, when they were alive, busy leading their lives, weren't saints, you moron! And you have to be *dead* for at least a hundred years before you can even *be* a saint! Is that what you want, Agnes? You want to live a life full of restrictions and punishments and whippings so that when you die—a *hundred* years after you die—someone will call you a *saint*?"

I stare at the cuticles on Benny's good fingers, white and curved like small crescent moons. "If that's what God requires of us, I do." My voice is shaky. "It's not up to us to question his ways."

Honey's face, bright with perspiration, deflates like a pink balloon. "Man, you sound just like Emmanuel," she says, turning back around slowly.

I stare at the back of her neck. "Thank you. I'll take that as a compliment."

"Well, then you're an idiot. It was meant to be an insult."

My mouth feels cold. "I don't even remember asking for your opinion."

"Don't worry," she says. "I won't be offering it anymore."

Just outside of Emmitsburg, Maryland, Nana Pete pulls into a wide parking lot and parks the car in front of a building that says WAL-MART.

"What're we doing?" Honey asks. Nana Pete opens the door and stretches.

"Y'all are going to need a few necessities for the rest of the trip. And there ain't nothin' you can't find in a Wal-Mart."

Wal-Mart is so big inside that for a moment when we step through yet another set of automatic doors, I wonder if it is an actual city disguised as a store. The smell of stale popcorn hangs in the air and people are everywhere, pushing carts filled with blue jeans and coffee and sneakers across the shiny white floor. We arrange Benny in the back of one of the carts, piled on top of his blankets, and push him through the aisles.

"This place is awesome!" Honey says.

Nana Pete leads us down an aisle filled with backpacks and chooses three of them in different colors. "Fill 'em up," she says, handing me a dark blue one edged in silver. "Toothpaste, soap, hairbrushes, whatever. Throw in anything you see that you think you might need in the next few days or so." She points to a larger section of the store behind the backpacks, filled with shoes. "I'm going to go look at some sneakers. Right over there. Come over when you're done."

I push Benny down the large aisle across from the backpacks while Honey walks in front of us. One side is filled with hundreds of different types of toothpaste; the other is a sea of multicolored toothbrushes.

"I guess we'll need toothpaste," I say quietly.

Honey scans the shelves quickly and grabs a box of Orange Mango Anticavity Fluoride paste. She grabs a neon-yellow toothbrush and tosses it carelessly in her bag. "I'll be in the next aisle," she says over her shoulder. "We need shampoo."

I take my time, deliberating for a while between two

toothpastes called Vanilla Mint, and Superwhitening. The Vanilla Mint is bound to taste better, but will the Superwhitening make my teeth look better? Are my teeth not white enough? I can't decide. Finally, I hold them both up in front of Benny. "Which one, Benny?"

Benny points to the Vanilla Mint with a shaky finger.

I smile. "Good. That's the one I wanted, too."

We do the same thing with several toothbrushes before settling on a light purple one with blue stripes running down the bristles for me and a blue one with a lightning bolt across the stem for Benny. I didn't know toothbrushes came in colors other than white. Benny points and nods his head again, instead of answering. I wonder if the anesthesia in the hospital has made it hard for him to talk.

The next aisle has so many different kinds of shampoos that I start to feel light-headed looking at all of them. There are bright green bottles with names like Clarifying Fruit Acid Rinse and square purple ones called Coconut-Freesia Detangler. Honey has already thrown two bottles in her bag.

"I'll be right over there with Nana Pete," she says, pointing. Nana Pete is in view at the end of the aisle, trying to cram her feet into a pair of blue shoes. Honey looks back over her shoulder. "There's hair ties and stuff, too, at the end of the aisle. Make sure you get a few."

Benny stares through the slats of the shopping cart, examining the rows of hair ornaments, while I start uncapping and smelling the different shampoos. I am beginning to feel as giddy as a bumblebee flying from flower to flower. They all smell so delicious! I settle finally on a bottle of Mandarin-Mint Deep Conditioning Shampoo for dry, undernourished hair.

It has promised to transform my dull, lackluster locks into a shiny, bouncy head of hair. I am just about to put it in the cart when, at the very bottom of the shelf, I notice a small, clear bottle filled with orange liquid. As I kneel down to look more closely, the inside of my lungs compress, as if filling with water. The little teardrop sticker says Johnson & Johnson baby shampoo. It's the only shampoo we have ever used at Mount Blessing. My heart pangs for Mom, who, just two weeks earlier, soaped up my hair in the sink when I was too sick to take a shower.

Suddenly I notice that Benny is pointing at something outside of the cart. "What is it, Benny?" He points toward the wall of hair ornaments. I extract a beautiful barrette, as thin as an emery board, with tiny, tentacle-like decorations coming from the center of it. Each pink feeler is secured at the tip with a small silver bead. It looks like a gorgeous flower. "This?" Benny nods his head vigorously and then points at me. "It's beautiful," I whisper. Benny points to my head. "You think it would look good on *me*?" He nods, his eyes wide as I hold it against the side of my head. "Yeah? Really?"

Next to the barrettes is a small selection of handheld mirrors. With the barrette firmly in place, I walk over and stand in front of one until I can see myself. It's so pretty! And it looks just right in my hair, not too large, not too small, just the right shade of pink against my skin. I turn to look at Benny, full of excitement, and then—

And then I remember number two of the Big Four: *Clothe the body. Adorn the soul.* How many times have I heard Emmanuel say that during Sunday services? *Do not concern yourself with the outer trappings for the body. They mean nothing in the eyes of God. Our bodies will die. Souls live forever. Spend your time on this earth clothing your soul.*

Slowly, I put the pink barrette back on the shelf. Benny kicks his foot against the inside of the cart and points angrily at the barrette.

I shake my head. "It's okay, Benny. Really. I don't need it. Actually, we shouldn't be spending any time at all in this dumb store. We don't need anything in here."

Benny stares at the barrette forlornly as I push the cart back down the aisle.

I pull out the bottle of fancy shampoo and put it back on the shelf. In goes the Johnson & Johnson. "This is all we need, buddy. Okay?"

He stares at the floor through the small silver squares of the cart and sticks his lower lip out. Just as I turn the cart around, I catch sight of Honey. She is standing at the end of the aisle, watching me.

"It's okay to get something you *really* want, you know," she says, walking toward us. She pulls the pink barrette back off the shelf and throws it inside the cart. "Benny's right. It looks great on you."

I lean back over and extract the barrette. "You get the things you need, Honey," I say evenly, "and I'll get the things I need." Hanging the barrette back on the hook, I push the cart firmly past her and make my way to the front of the store.

Nana Pete pays for everything with a credit card, swiping the paper-thin rectangle through a little silver machine and signing her name with an odd-looking pen. The cashier is a tall, lanky boy with pale arms and pimply skin. For some reason, the lights behind him look very bright. I stare at his T-shirt with a picture of Jesus on the front. The bearded image blurs, comes back into focus, and then blurs once more. I squint hard, trying to make out the words underneath Jesus's face.

I DIED FOR YOUR SINS, it reads, AND ALL I GOT WAS THIS LOUSY T-SHIRT?

I turn around to make sure Benny doesn't catch sight of it, but the whole room starts to undulate, as if I am riding a wave. I reach out blindly for something to hold, but the floor comes rushing up at me.

And then, blackness.

HONEY

Nana Pete freaks when Agnes faints in Wal-Mart. Luckily, I am standing right behind her and so when she goes down—like a ton of bricks—I catch her just before she hits the floor. Nana Pete shrieks so loud that people in the other aisles start rushing over. That dork of a cashier kid looks over the conveyer belt with a stupid expression on his face.

"Uh, what happened?" he asks. "Should I call an ambulance?"

Benny grips the sides of the shopping cart, looking out at us with huge eyes.

Adjusting her carefully on the floor, I lean in and put my ear to Agnes's mouth. "She's breathing," I announce to the worried stare of onlookers. "I think she just fainted."

A second later, Agnes's eyes flit open.

"Yeah." I nod. "She's okay. She just needs to eat something."

Nana Pete falls to her knees next to us.

"I don't think she's eaten for a few days," I say in a low voice. "She does this sometimes."

"Does what?" Nana Pete asks, bewildered.

"Fasts. You know, like the saints. To atone for any sins she's committed."

Agnes tries to sit up, but Nana Pete stops her. "Don't, darlin'. There's a hotel right across the street. We're going to go there now, get you something to eat, and put you to bed."

"We are?" I ask.

Nana Pete nods. She is clutching the front of her shirt with one hand. "It's been a long two days. No one's slept at all in the past twenty-four hours. We're all running on fumes. A good night's sleep is what everyone needs."

Nana Pete takes Benny's hand and I wrap my arm around Agnes so she can lean on me as we make our way inside our room at the hotel.

"I'm okay," she whispers hoarsely, trying to wriggle out from under me.

I tighten my hold on her. "Just relax. It's not a sin to let someone help you after you've just become personally acquainted with the floor."

The room itself is not very large, but it's clean and smells like pine needles. A large window at the opposite end looks out directly on the front lawn. There are two beds in the middle, draped with orange and brown comforters, one long bureau against the wall, and a gigantic black television set.

"Let's put Benny and Agnes in that one," Nana Pete says, pointing to the bed closest to the wall. "And you and I will share this one."

I help Agnes under the covers as Nana Pete gives Benny one of his pills from Dr. Pannetta.

"Hey," I say, taking her hand. "Nana Pete just bought us new pajamas. Let me help you change so you're more comfortable." Agnes shakes her head and lays her head weakly on the pillow.

"I don't need anything," she whispers.

I pull my hand out from hers. "Would you stop acting like a martyr for two seconds and just let me help you?"

Agnes's face scrunches up like she might cry.

Nana Pete rushes over and puts her hand on my shoulder. "Honey. Please. Be kind."

I shake my head, defeated, and plop down on the other bed next to Benny.

"Agnes," Nana Pete says, using her no-nonsense voice. "You must get into some comfortable pajamas. No arguments, darlin'. Now, let me help you."

Agnes blinks and then brings her arms up weakly alongside her ears. Nana Pete helps her out of her robe and then her shirt as Agnes sinks back into the pillow, arms crossed over her chest. There is a sudden, audible gasp.

"What's wrong?" I ask.

Nana Pete points to the string around Agnes's waist, which is barely discernable among the bruised folds of skin. "No wonder you fainted!" she says, trying to pull the string off. Agnes cries aloud. "My God, Agnes, you can barely breathe with this thing on! Honey, go out to the front desk and ask the man there for a pair of scissors."

I don't move. "What's that, another penance thing?" I can barely hide the rage in my voice. "You get that from *The Saints' Way,* too?" Agnes just stares at the floor. I turn away, disgusted, and march out the door.

The skin around Agnes's waist looks even worse after the string comes off. It's so raw that it's actually slimy, and sections of it are tinged with blood. Nana Pete rushes back over to Wal-Mart and returns with two bottles of hydrogen peroxide, bacitracin ointment, and white gauze. I keep Benny occupied on the other side of the room, playing with the new deck of cards Nana Pete got us, as she wipes down Agnes's wounds. Agnes makes tiny, muted cries as the peroxide and then the ointment is rubbed into her skin.

"Promise me you won't do something like this to yourself again," Nana Pete says, as she wraps the last of the gauze around Agnes's middle. Agnes just looks away from her. "There's no need for it. God already knows what a wonderful person you are, Mouse. You don't have to try to convince him." Agnes closes her eyes.

Later, Nana Pete orders something called room service, which is almost as cool as the McDonald's drive-through, except that it takes way too long to arrive. Benny and I get grilled-cheese sandwich platters with french fries, coleslaw, and baked beans, and Nana Pete orders a taco salad with beef chili and sour cream. She spends a long time trying to convince Agnes to pick something from the menu, but Agnes won't talk.

"Just order her a turkey sandwich," I say exasperatedly. "I'll shove it down her throat if I have to." Agnes presses her lips together tightly.

But when the food comes, it's a different story. Agnes's meal turns out to be a soup-and-sandwich combo, and when Nana Pete takes the lid off the bowl of chicken-corn chowder and passes it under Agnes's nose, her eyes actually fill up with tears.

"Eat it," Nana Pete says gently, pushing the bowl into Agnes's hands. "Please."

She takes a tentative spoonful, sliding the utensil between

her teeth, and when she swallows, her whole face relaxes. In three minutes, the soup is gone. Ten minutes later, her sandwich, side of potato chips, and three pickle spears have vanished as well.

"Thank God," Nana Pete whispers, after Agnes finally falls asleep. Next to his sister, Benny is curled up like a little puppy, his face nestled in tightly alongside her ribs. "Maybe now she'll start feeling normal again."

I roll my eyes. "Don't bet on it."

But Nana Pete isn't listening to me. She's punching numbers on her cell phone.

"Who're you calling?" I ask.

"Lillian." She puts the phone to her ear.

"Lillian?" I repeat. "I think I heard Agnes mention her once, a long time ago. Is she your daughter?"

Nana Pete nods. "My only daughter and Leonard's only sibling." She holds up an index finger. "Hold on. It's the machine. I have to leave a message." She pauses and then speaks into the phone. "Lillian, darlin', it's me. Call me on the cell phone. We need to talk." She clicks it shut and leans back heavily against the headboard, closing her eyes.

"You okay?" I ask.

She nods. "Just tired."

"You know, Agnes told me she's never met Lillian. Is that true?"

Nana Pete rubs the deep wrinkles above her eyebrows with two fingers. "Leonard and Lillian had a falling out just before Agnes was born. She didn't like where he was living and, well, Lillian had her own set of problems that Leonard didn't—or wouldn't—tolerate. They haven't spoken since. One of the rules I had to abide by so I could come visit my grandchildren was that I never talk about her."

"So in order to come to Mount Blessing, you had to promise Mr. Little that you would never talk about your own daughter?" Nana Pete nods. "That's mean," I say. "That's actually kind of horrible, when you think about it. He just erased Lillian completely from Agnes's life. Like she never even existed."

"Yes," Nana Pete answers softly. A strange, faraway look comes into her eyes. "Yes, you're absolutely right, Honey."

I stay still, waiting for her to say more, but she doesn't. Instead she hands me a black rectangular piece of plastic. "Why don't you watch some TV?" she asks. "I'm going to take a shower and then hit the hay."

I pick up the instrument. It's very light. "What is this?"

Nana Pete smiles at me and takes it back. Pointing it at the TV, she pushes a button. Instantly, the screen blazes to life.

I jump back. "Wow! It's color!"

"Of course it's color, silly." Nana Pete tosses me the black rectangle again. "Here. This is called a remote control. You use this to change the channels."

I study the multitude of colored buttons on the front of the rectangle and then turn it over. Nothing on the back. I don't know if I've ever seen anything so cool. Winky would *love* this. After a minute, Nana Pete disappears into the bathroom. I have just started to flip through the hundreds of channels when Nana Pete's phone rings.

I grab it and run toward the bathroom. "Nana Pete!" I strain to keep my voice low. "It's your phone!" There is a brief pause and then the door opens just a crack.

Nana Pete's wet hand snakes through. "Thank you, darlin'."

I head back over to the bed. But instead of picking up the remote again, I start to prowl around the room. The mirrored closet has just four wire hangers hanging on a bar inside. I flip up the bottoms of the comforters and peek under. Nothing. I wonder how dark the room will be when all the lights are off.

"Lord," Nana Pete says, coming out of the bathroom and collapsing on the bed. Her long powder blue robe is buttoned up to her chin, and a white towel is wrapped around her head. "I'm tuckered clear to the bone."

"Was that Lillian on the phone?" I ask.

She nods. "She's going to meet us halfway. Just outside of Raleigh, North Carolina." I am just about to ask why when she points to her purse sitting on the bureau. "Honey, get me my purse, would you?" I remember something all at once and hold my breath as I bring the bag over to her.

Chewing my bottom lip, I watch as Nana Pete extricates a plastic bottle from inside the bowels of her purse. "Aha! Here you are, you little bugger!" She unscrews the top, palms a large green pill, and then tosses it into her mouth.

"What's that for?" I ask.

Nana Pete waves her hand and leans back against one of the pillows. "Just vitamins." She throws the bottle back inside and hands me her purse once more. I place it back on the bureau, breathing a sigh of relief. When I turn back around, Nana Pete has just removed the towel from her head. I try not to gasp. Her gray hair, damp and tangled, hangs down past her elbows. It is so thin on top that I can see the pale pink of her scalp. She looks so . . . old.

"Wow," I say when I find my voice again. "You look so

different. I've never seen you without your hair pinned up in those braids." Nana Pete grimaces as the comb gets caught in a snarl. Wiry strands catch between the plastic teeth like little bits of Brillo.

"It's not my best look," she says with a grin. "Don't tell anyone." She rebraids her hair as I hold out the tiny blue rubber bands for her to secure the ends. Even without a mirror, she pins each braid back up expertly along each side of her head.

"All right?" she asks, cocking her head. "Do I look halfway decent again?"

I smile and nod.

She leans back wearily against the pillow again and closes her eyes. In less than a minute, she is asleep.

As soon as I hear a snore push out from her nose, I lean over and grab her purse again, shoving my hand inside frantically. But the purse is like a bottomless cavern and no matter how much I push things aside, I can't find what I am looking for. Carefully, I turn the whole thing over in my hands and dump the contents on the bed. The exotic pink barrette falls out last. Its delicate tendrils are a little bent at the ends and a lone bobby pin has lodged its way somehow into the center of it. I pull it out and straighten the little feelers until it looks new again. Up until a few moments ago, I had forgotten all about taking the barrette off the Wal-Mart shelf and sliding it inside Nana Pete's purse when she wasn't looking. Now I open my new backpack and throw it on top of my new sneakers.

Replacing the contents of Nana Pete's purse takes a while. There is her camera, her cell phone, an unzipped rose-colored makeup bag filled with a mirrored compact, a gold tube of pink lipstick, two packages of tissues, at least twenty hairpins, and a small white tube of eucalyptus-scented body lotion. There is also a faded pair of ivory gloves stained yellow at the fingertips, a small, leather-bound folder, secured tightly with a blue rubber band, Benny's antibiotics, and two more bottles of those vitamins she took earlier, called Lisinopril. I pick up one of the vitamin bottles and turn it over. Why, if they are vitamins, are they called Lisinopril? I wonder. Or is that what old-people vitamins are called? I get a bad feeling all of a sudden as I remember the discussion we had yesterday at the frog pond.

My doctor just told me he wasn't sure if I'd ever be able to make this trip again.

Are you sick?

No, no, sugar. He just wants me to get some tests in August.

I place the vitamin bottle back in her bag and lie down as close to Nana Pete as I can. She smells like chili and the sweet, lemony perfume she always wears. I move closer, until my ear is just above her chest, and then lean in as near as I dare. Even under the slippery orange comforter and the top sheet, I can hear the lopsided rhythm of her heart beating. *Buh-hum, buh-bum.* Suddenly, for a split second, nothing. I hold my breath. Above me, Nana Pete gasps and exhales loudly through her nose. *Buh-hum, buh-bum, buh-bum.* Her breathing returns to normal again. I press my face along her robe and cry soundlessly in the dark, pushing the blanket into my mouth when my sobs start to overtake me, shaking with fear and love.

Agnes

I wake all at once the next morning, sitting up with a gasp, as if someone has thrown a bucket of cold water over me. It takes me a full minute to remember where we are. My brain races through the events that have occurred over the past two days. Benny's fingers. Leaving Mount Blessing. Dr. Pannetta. Wal-Mart. I feel sick and dizzy, trying to piece it all back together. Benny is sound asleep next to me; Nana Pete and Honey are snoring lightly in the other bed. I can't stop thinking about Mom and Dad. Have they come looking for us? Have they tried to call anyone? Has Emmanuel let them leave to come find us? And if he hasn't, what could they possibly be doing?

Across the room, a flash of light gleams between the heavy curtains. Getting out of bed slowly, I push the curtains back and stare through the dull glass. The sun has just risen over the peak of hills in the distance. Another flash of light, brighter this time, forces me to squint and then shade my eyes. I stare for a moment, unsure if I am really seeing what I think I am seeing. Ten seconds later, as the sun rises another inch or so, the glare disappears and there, in all her glory, is the Blessed Virgin Mary, standing on top of the mountain before me.

I fall to my knees, trembling, but not daring to look away from her. She is dressed all in gold, from the top of her head to her toes. Her arms are stretched out before her, just like on the cover of *The Saints' Way*, as if waiting for a child to leap into them. I make the sign of the cross and stare, overwhelmed, at the vision of loveliness. It is my first apparition. I musn't be frightened. I will stay quiet and wait to see what she asks of me. There is no question it is her, but from this distance, I cannot make out any of her beautiful features, and if she is trying to tell me something, there is no way I will be able to hear her words. The minutes tick by, but she doesn't move, not even when the sun moves higher in the sky, throwing a shadow across the heavy folds in her robe. My knees feel as if they are grinding into a knotted pile of wood, but I do not take my eyes off her golden aura. Maybe there will be no message today; maybe the first apparition will just be a test of my faith, to see if I will stay or run away.

"I will never run away," I whisper. "I will always be here, waiting and listening."

"Listening for what?" The voice behind me comes so suddenly that I nearly fall over with fright. I whirl around to see Nana Pete standing next to the bed, watching me with a peculiar expression on her face. "Who are you talking to, Mouse?"

She won't be able to see her, I think quickly. *Only visionaries are able to see the apparitions.*

"Oh!" Nana Pete says, pointing through the curtains. "You found the statue of Our Lady of the Mountain!" My eyebrows narrow. "But of course! I forgot we were so close to Mount St. Mary's Seminary! Isn't she lovely? I think she used to be on top of a church that burned to the ground. She was the only thing that wasn't destroyed in the fire. Would you like to drive up and see her?"

My brain is racing. Statue? Church? Mount St. Mary's? *Statue?*

"Mouse?" Nana Pete presses. "Would you like to drive over so that you can see her for yourself? She's even prettier up close. She looks almost human."

I stand up and brush invisible crumbs off the front of my pajamas. My knees are throbbing. "No." I hope Nana Pete doesn't notice the flush that has begun to creep alongside my face. "No, actually, I wouldn't." I push past her. "I'm going to take a shower."

I lock the bathroom door and then sag against it, letting my forehead sink against my knees. What were the details in the Saint Catherine Laboure story, when the Blessed Virgin appeared to her? I grab *The Saints' Way* and read it over again. A small child, dressed all in white, had come into Catherine's room at the convent one night and told her to follow him. He led her down a dark hallway and into the chapel. Although it was the middle of the night, every single candle in the chapel was lit. Then, as the church bells tolled midnight, Catherine heard the rustle of a silk dress. Suddenly a beautiful woman surrounded by a blaze of light stood before her. The child, who was still standing next to Catherine, said, "Behold, here is the Blessed Virgin!"

I close the book and go over the details: A rustle of silk. Burning candles. A blaze of white light. My heart sinks, remembering the golden shimmer cascading down the green mountain. I could have sworn . . .

I'm just looking too hard, I decide at last. Trying to see something that is not there. Or maybe my head is still just a little clouded from the fainting episode. Or maybe . . . maybe I am just too much of a sinner for Jesus or the Virgin to ever consider appearing to me. Maybe it won't ever happen. I put my head down again between my knees as I remember the lie I told to Christine and what I said to Benny before he got hurt. Who am I kidding?

Eventually I decide to take a shower, something I can't remember doing recently, and count to a hundred and twenty as I soap myself up under the running water. At Mount Blessing, showers are limited to three minutes tops, since hot water is so expensive. This morning I will limit it to two minutes. The line my waist string has left behind is deep red, almost purple. I make a note to find another one as soon as possible.

After the shower, I brush my teeth for a long time, guiltily relishing the taste of the Vanilla Mint toothpaste. I slide into a clean pair of underwear, a new peach bra Nana Pete insisted on buying for me, my old jeans, a long-sleeved black T-shirt, and then, finally, my robe. I press my face into the sleeves of the robe and inhale. The material has a familiar smell to it, like shoe polish. I have to get back home.

Still squeezing the water from my hair, I come out of the bathroom to find Honey seated on the floor. She has the TV on. Three guys dressed only in wide white pants are dancing on the screen, as loud, thumping music pulses in the background. A girl wearing a black bra and shorts is writhing around on the ground like she has poison ivy.

Honey gives me a quick glance and then looks away again.

"You don't have to wear that robe out here, you know," she says, flipping the channel.

"I know," I answer, heading over toward Benny, whose eyes are glued to the television. "I want to."

"Hey, check this out!" Honey says. I sit down on the bed, directly in front of Benny's line of vision. "I think this guy just made a glass of zucchini juice!" Benny grunts and moves to the side.

"Don't look, Benny," I order. "It's a sin to watch TV. Just close your eyes." But Benny doesn't listen. He struggles to sit up in the bed, pushing me away from him with his good hand.

Honey turns around. "Oh, for crying out loud, let him look. It's just some idiot making juice."

I ignore her. "Benny. Come on. Let's go in the bathroom and get washed up." But he continues to angle his way around me, even elbowing me so hard in the ribs that I lose my breath. "Ow!" I yell. "Benedict *Little*!" I can see Honey put her hand over her mouth, stifling a laugh. It's a good thing, too, because I turn on her then, all fury.

"Turn. Off. The. TV." Honey giggles again behind her hand. "I mean it, Honey."

She opens her mouth to object and then seems to decide against it. Pointing the remote at the TV, she flicks off the screen. A snorting sound comes out of her nose.

"Go ahead and make fun," I say, stuffing my dirty clothes back inside my backpack. "You won't be laughing in the end."

Honey gets up slowly from the floor. "What's that supposed to mean?"

"Think about it." I turn so that she is talking to my shoulder.

Honey grabs my arm and spins me around. "Hey." Her voice, low and steady, frightens me all of a sudden. "You listen to me, Agnes, because I'm only going to say this once. I don't ever want to hear again—or even listen to you insinuate—that I am going to hell because of stuff like watching TV. Or because of anything I do, for that matter. You got it?"

I stare into her glowering eyes. "Just because we've left Mount Blessing doesn't mean you have to throw everything about it away. It's like you don't even care, Honey."

"I care, Agnes," Honey says. "I care more than you will ever know."

"About what?"

"About the things that matter. About you. About Benny and Nana Pete." She pauses. "You're so freaked out all the time about all the little things that might be tripping you up on this path of yours to heaven that you forget to stop and look around once in a while at the things that count."

"Oh, like what, listening to stupid songs on the radio? Or watching that garbage on TV?"

Honey's eyes flash black. "Like taking the time to realize that your grandmother over there is putting her *life* on the line for us."

I toss my head. "Well, no one asked her to. Especially not me."

Honey takes a step away from me. Even I can't believe how awful that just sounded. I turn away so that I don't have to face her anymore, but I can feel her eyes burning into my back. Just then, Nana Pete comes out of the bathroom.

"Onward, tr—" She stops midsentence, noticing Honey and me. "Everything okay here?" I hear a swishing sound as Honey snatches something off the floor.

"Everything's fine," she says. "Let's just get out of here."

HONEY

Nana Pete turns back on 15 South. We drive until we see signs for Washington, D.C., and Virginia and then hit a road called I-270, which we stay on for hours. She starts off strong, driving as if possessed, trying to make up for all the missed miles from yesterday. Staring down her own tunnel of vision, she taps her thumbs along the top of the steering wheel, hearing a beat all her own. A few hours later, though, she seems to have fallen into some sort of trance. She doesn't hear me when I ask her if she's hungry, and when I ask her a few minutes later if she's tired, she just gives me a strange look and shakes her head.

Maybe I'm worrying too much. I pull out my butterfly notebook and try to draw one of the Clouded Sulphurs I saw outside of the hospital, but Nana Pete keeps swerving in and out of traffic so sharply that my pencil darts all over the page. Her doggedness at not letting the speedometer fall under eighty-five is really starting to freak me out. I am just about to say something when I notice that her shoulders are sagging like two weighted logs in a pond. Her skin is a pale, ashy color and tiny beads of sweat, like pearls, have broken out along her forehead.

"Hey, Nana Pete?" I say gently.

Her head jerks at the sound of my voice, and she licks her lips. "I'm trying to make it to Raleigh before it gets dark, but I can't drive another minute, darlin'. Do you think you could give it a try?"

Agnes sits up straight in the back. "Wait, you mean *Honey* drive?" she asks. It's the first thing she's said all day. "The *car*? She can't drive!"

Nana Pete looks over at me. Her face is a map of deep lines and shaded circles. I've never seen her so tired.

"It's okay, Ags," I say. "I've driven Mr. Schwab's tractor before. It can't be much different." My voice sounds confident, but as Nana Pete pulls over and I switch places with her in the front seat, I'm shaking like a leaf. Will it be much harder than driving Dorothy? I put my head down and listen as carefully as I can to what Nana Pete is telling me.

"Now, the Queen Mary is an automatic, sugar, which means you don't have to do much of anything except steer once you put her in drive." Nana Pete points at the two pedals just under my feet. "Just use your right foot when you want to speed up or slow down, all right? Let your left one sit off to the side. Think of it as just being along for the ride. It's not going to do anything." I run the insides of my hands up and down the smooth ridges of the steering wheel. It's much smaller than Dorothy's wheel. And there is no clutch, thank God. That was the hardest thing to learn with Dorothy. "Keep your foot down hard enough on the gas so that this little red stick"— Nana Pete leans over and points to the speed gauge—"stays around sixty-five. Don't go past seventy, no matter what. The last thing we need is to get pulled over by the police. Keep it level. You'll get the hang of it."

"What if I have to turn?" I ask.

Nana Pete shakes her head. "We've only got another hour on this highway," she says. "Straight through to Raleigh. No turns."

"Okay." I take a deep breath. "I can do this."

And I really believe I can.

As I step on the gas, my breath collects itself into a pocket at the top of my lungs and sits there like a balloon waiting to be released. My hands grip the steering wheel with white fingers, swerving the car nervously to the left and then to the right and then back again. I try not to think about the fact that Dorothy doesn't go any faster than twenty-five miles per hour and I am traveling now at almost three times that speed. But after a while, my fingers loosen and my hunched shoulders relax.

"Beautiful," Nana Pete says approvingly. "Just beautiful. You're a pro, Honey. I knew you could do it." Her words relax me even more, and soon I can feel my lower back sinking into the seat. The muscles in my legs begin to unknot themselves and my breathing goes back to normal. Even when I glance over at Nana Pete, whose head is lolling heavily on her chest, I don't panic. I'm driving a car. I'm doing it!

"Ags!" I whisper, sitting up a little so that I can see her in the rearview mirror. "Look at me! I'm *driving!*"

Agnes looks away, but Benny, who is curled up against her like a puppy, looks up and grins.

"Hey, Benny boy! How 'bout this? Huh?"

He nods and smiles. I look back over at Agnes. Her face is set like stone.

"You better watch the road," she says, still looking out the window. "You've only been doing this for about thirty minutes, you know. Don't get smug."

I bounce up and down in the seat a little. "I think I got it figured it out, though! It's not too hard once you sit back and relax a little. Take in a little of the scenery, even, instead of staring at the little yellow squares in the middle of the road."

Agnes rolls her eyes. "Now you're a pro all of a sudden?"

I giggle. "Yeah. How about that?"

Agnes's jaw tightens. "When were you at Mr. Schwab's?"

I stop bouncing. "Oh, you know. Just a couple times with Winky when he had to go over and get stuff for the garden."

She's holding my gaze. "And he let you drive his tractor?"

I nod, looking back between her and the road.

"You know that's forbidden," she says. "Going off the grounds like that."

I shrug. "Yeah, well I guess it doesn't really matter now, does it?"

She turns away when I say that, as if I have reminded her of something painful.

I try to change the subject, but she won't look at me. And while I know we're miles away from being on the same page, for some reason right at this moment, I'm desperate for her to talk to me. "Hey," I whisper. "You want to know a secret?"

Agnes's eyes flit to a spot away from the middle of the window, but she doesn't turn her head.

"We're on our way to see your aunt Lillian. Right now."

Agnes's head whips around on her neck like a spring. *"What?"*

I nod. "I don't know all the details, but Nana Pete said she's meeting us halfway. I guess so she can help out with the trip and all." I pause. "She's the one you've never met, right?" I talk quickly, hoping my words will overtake the shadow that is crossing Agnes's face. But it's not working. She glares at the back of Nana Pete's head with hateful eyes and then sits back in the seat.

Her lips are trembling. "Now, don't get all worked up," I say. "I know you're not supposed to talk about her or anything, but—"

"We're not supposed to have *any*thing to do with that woman." Agnes says the words through clenched teeth. "My father forbids it."

"But she's your aunt! You guys are blood relatives! Aren't you even the least bit curious about what she *looks* like? What she might have to—"

"No," Agnes interrupts. "I'm not curious in the least. My father told me that she was full of sinful behavior. That's why he gets upset whenever Nana Pete even mentions her name."

"What sort of sinful behavior?"

"I don't know," Agnes says. "He didn't tell me. But it was bad."

"Why was it bad? Because your dad thinks it was bad?" Agnes nods. I roll my eyes. "For all you know, Agnes, Lillian's 'sinful behavior' could have been using a curse word. Or eating a strawberry."

"No, I'm sure it was a lot more serious than that," she says. "Besides, what she *did* is not the point. The point is that Nana Pete is breaking a major rule by letting us see her—and she's making us break the rule, too. Against our will, I might add. Dad's going to be furious when he finds out."

"How's your dad gonna find out anything, Agnes?" I say. "He's history, remember? We're leaving him and—" I stop as Agnes's eyes get wide in the rearview mirror. "I mean . . . he doesn't have to find out . . . ," I stammer, trying to repair the damage I have just created. But Agnes isn't listening. She's withdrawn completely inside herself, staring out the window again, chanting her prayers.

I drive for a long time after that without saying anything. I guess I've said more than enough. I glance back once or twice, just to see if Agnes is okay, but her forehead is pressed against the window, and she seems lost in thought. I feel so sad all of a sudden, so lonely, as if the darkness settling down around us is going to swallow me up. A little while later, as the sun sinks completely behind the low green hills and the light disappears, I start to get nervous. The road is harder to see in the dark and I don't like it. I elbow Nana Pete.

"Huh!" She sits straight up, as if someone has just pinched her.

"It's getting dark, Nana Pete. And we just passed a sign that says Raleigh is twenty miles away."

Nana Pete looks out the side window and rubs her eyes. "Lord Almighty, Honey, you did it. I think you can do just about anything you put your mind to." She points to a motel billboard up ahead. "That's where we'll stay tonight. It won't be fancy, but all we need are a few comfortable beds. We'll get a good night's sleep and then hit the road tomorrow, nice and refreshed."

She pulls out her phone and dials a number.

"Hi, darlin'," she says into the mouthpiece. "Yes, we're here."

AGNES

Lillian is prettier than I imagined she would be. She has curly strawberry blond hair, cut close to her head. Seven silver hoops run along the edge of her left ear, but there is nothing at all in her right one. Her nose is long, but not too long, and she has very small, square teeth, exactly like Dad's. Her slight, graceful build is accentuated by a pair of lemon-colored corduroy pants and a white T-shirt. I try hard not to look at her for too long—(I will tell Dad later how I avoided her at all costs)—keeping my eyes on her shoes when she walks over and stands in front of us. Brown leather ankle boots with lug soles. The one on the left has a torn shoelace.

"You must be Agnes and Benny," she says. "I've heard so much about you." Her voice is soft, barely above a whisper. "And Honey." Her voice cracks on the word "Honey," which is what finally makes me look up. When I do, she looks away from Honey and gives me this great big fake smile. "I'm your aunt Lillian." She extends her hand. I drop my eyes again until she lowers her arm. But then Benny steps forward, his good hand stretched out just a few inches. Lillian drops to one knee. "Benny." She studies his face for a few seconds. "You look just like your dad." I sidle a glance over at my little brother, whose hand Lillian is now gripping, and resist the urge to push his hand away from hers. He doesn't know any better.

Benny reaches out and runs his finger along the display

of silver lining Lillian's ear. She doesn't move. "You like those?" she asks after a minute. Benny nods. "I got one put in every year after I turned twenty-five." She grins. "Helps keep me young. I hope." I do a mental math check in my head. Seven hoops. She's thirty-two.

"Well, let's go inside," Nana Pete says, running her hands up and down the sides of her arms. "I'm freezing." Lillian stands back up and looks at her mother.

"Freezing? It's at least sixty degrees out here, Ma." She takes a step toward her. "You look a little shaky. Are you feeling okay?"

"Oh yeah," Nana Pete says. "But lying down for a while wouldn't kill me, either."

"You sure you don't wanna play, Agnes?" Lillian asks me. "Final round? Double or nothing." I look up from my book that I am pretending to read and shake my head for the third time. Lillian, Honey, and Benny are sitting on the floor between the two beds, playing gin rummy. Lillian's back is pressed up against the side of my mattress. Nana Pete is in the other bed, sleeping like a log.

"Don't ask her again," Honey says. "She's doesn't do anything fun anymore."

Lillian turns around to look at me. "Is that true, Agnes? You don't like to have fun?"

I roll my eyes and turn over on my other side.

"See?" Honey says. "I told you. All she ever wants to do is read that ridiculous book."

"Don't talk about me like I'm not here." I'm talking to the wall, but I know Honey can hear me.

"Don't tell me what to do. You're not my mother." Honey's voice is edged with a meanness that I don't recognize. It makes my heart jump a little. I lower my head and stare down again at the picture of Saint Germaine, who was treated like a slave by her own family for most of her life, forced to sleep in a barn, nearly starved to death, and beaten regularly. She had offered everything up for the glory of God, refusing to succumb to her earthly torment. If only I could do the same.

"So, Lillian," I hear Honey ask. "What was it like growing up with Agnes's dad?" She's using her fishing voice, trying to extract information that isn't any of her business. "You guys just don't seem to be anything alike. I wouldn't even guess you two were related." I grit my teeth and roll back over soundlessly, holding the book in front of my face.

Lillian doesn't say anything for a minute. Then she clears her throat. "Actually, I used to be a lot like my brother. Or at least I wanted to be. He was smart and funny and a great athlete. You know, just an all-around wonderful guy. When we were growing up, I followed him around like a puppy dog. He never made me feel bad about it, either. He let me come along when he played basketball with his friends or whenever he went out for a hamburger at the Friendly's on the corner."

I feel a twinge, thinking of how often I have told Benny to scram when he comes around Honey and me. But it fades again as Lillian keeps talking.

"When he went away to college in Iowa, I thought I was going to die from loneliness. I was still in the same high school we had gone to together, but it felt like being in jail or something without him there. Not being able to see him when I walked down the halls or listen to my friends scream his name when he lined up for a foul shot on the basketball court just really tore me up inside. I literally counted down the days until he came home for his first break. All I wanted to do was go down to the hamburger place and sit in one of the booths and talk with him." She pauses. The cards snap and flutter under her fingers.

"And?" Honey asks. I lower my book slightly so I can see the top of Lillian's head.

"Well, the first few times he came home things were all right. I remember during fall break of his sophomore year, he brought home a girl he was seeing. I think her name was Fern. Or maybe it was Bernie. Something like that. Anyway, he took me along for just about everything he and Fern did together that weekend. The three of us went out to the movies, we hung around the house, we even went horseback riding."

"I bet ol' Fern loved you," Honey says.

Lillian grins a little. "Yeah, she wasn't too happy about it. She made it a point to tell Lenny in front of me that the next time they were going to go to her house—so they could be alone."

"Ha!" Honey laughs. "Good for her."

Lillian starts dealing the cards again slowly, placing each one on the carpet until two neat piles form. "But then in his third year," she says, "when he came home for Thanksgiving he was . . . different." I lower the book some more.

"What do you mean, different?" Honey asks.

"He just wasn't the same Leonard I knew. It was like he had turned inward, away from all of us. Away from me, anyway. And definitely from Ma. He spent the whole time just locked in his room. He didn't even come down for Thanksgiving dinner, even when Ma cried."

I listen intently, my eyes fixed on a weird curlicue shape in the yellow wallpaper.

"And then in the spring, a year before he was supposed to graduate, he started talking about this man that he had met named Emmanuel. You would have thought it was Jesus himself the way he talked about his prayer and healing services, the meetings he held at this little house of his off campus. Ma and I asked him questions about it and tried to seem interested, but it was kind of strange."

"How so?" Honey asks.

"Well, we'd just never seen him like that before. Ma actually used the word 'mesmerized.' And that's what he was. He was just completely obsessed with everything about Emmanuel."

"Yeah," Honey says. "That sounds about right." I press my lips together hard. Why can't she just be *quiet*?

"He disappeared pretty soon after that," Lillian says. "It took us a year to find out that he had moved to the East Coast and was living with the Believers at Mount Blessing."

Honey makes a *hmm* sound between her lips. I can tell she wants to ask more, probably something about how much my Dad has changed over the years, but she is guarding her words in front of Benny and me. "Do you miss him?" she asks eventually.

Lillian looks up in surprise at the question. "I do," she

says, placing a card down flat on the floor. There is a pause. "Gin," she says. "I win."

A few hours later, after Honey has disappeared into the shower and Benny has fallen asleep, I get under the covers and start my evening prayers, counting my consecration beads as I go. Lillian is in the corner with her back to me, undressing hurriedly. I close my eyes, trying to concentrate on the prayers and the beads. When I open them again Lillian is kneeling next to me on the floor, dressed in old sweats and a long blue T-shirt.

"What are you doing?" she whispers. "Saying night prayers?"

I am so startled by her presence that I just nod.

"Okay. I don't mean to interrupt, but I just wanted to ask you a question." My fingers are frozen around one of the beads, my eyes fixed on the arch of her red eyebrow. I'm not telling her anything about Dad, no matter how much she begs me. "Who has Honey been living with all these years?"

I narrow my eyebrows. "What?"

"I mean . . ." She stammers, trying to find the words. "She lived in the nursery with you for a long time, right?"

I nod slowly. "Until we were seven."

"Right, until you were seven. And then you went to live with your parents, right? In the house they lived in?" I nod again. Her forehead creases. "Ma told me that Honey went to live with a guy named Winky. Do you know anything about him?"

"Not really," I answer. "He's kind of . . . slow. They live in the Milk House."

"Do you know anything else about him?" Lillian presses. "Is he a good guy?"

I stare blankly at her for a moment. Why is she asking me this? And why would Nana Pete be talking to Lillian about Honey?

The running water from the shower shuts off suddenly. I sit up. "Why are you asking about—" But Lillian stands up, cutting me off with a shake of her head.

"Never mind," she says, walking back over to her side of the room. Her voice sounds garbled, like a small bird trapped inside her throat. "Good night, Agnes." I watch as she slides under the covers next to Nana Pete and pulls the blankets over her head.

"Good night," I whisper, not loud enough for her to hear.

HONEY

Sleep feels as far away right now as Mount Blessing. I turn on the TV, putting the volume on mute so as not to disturb anyone, but pretty soon my mind starts to drift. For some reason, I can't get Lillian out of my head. I like her. She's sort of sloppy, or at least it seems like she doesn't really care all that much about her appearance, and she says things the way they are, even if what she's saying doesn't make her look all that good. I like that in a person. I'm so sick of all this striving toward perfection I could puke. After we were done playing cards, I was so disappointed when she stretched and then told us that she was going to bed.

"But it's only eleven o'clock," I said, trying to hide the disappointment in my voice. She looked at me—and let me tell you something, she has this funny way of looking at you—and smiled.

"Don't worry," she said. "We'll have lots of time to talk tomorrow."

"But I want to talk *now*," I say aloud to no one. Throwing back the covers, I climb out of bed, unzip my knapsack, and pull out my sneakers.

The main lobby is bright with lights. A man is sitting behind the front desk, reading the funny pages on the back of a newspaper.

He looks up as I pad along the floor. "Everything okay?"

"Yeah," I say, pointing to the door. "I'm just going outside for some fresh air."

The night air is sharp and cool. I inhale deeply, filling my lungs as I look around in the dark. It's *really* dark. Just as I am about to turn back around and go inside again, I notice the Queen Mary parked a few cars away. I streak toward it, open the front door with a trembling hand, and scoot inside. Reaching under the front seat, I feel around until my fingers come in contact with Nana Pete's keys. I turn on the engine, and then switch on the front beams until I can see the shrubs on the side of the motel. Okay. Much better.

I open my hand carefully and stare down at George lying in the middle of my palm. I have been clutching him so tightly that I am afraid he is broken. The chips in his tail and ear are still there, and everything else seems to be in place.

"Hey, George," I whisper softly. "How are you, buddy? What's new?"

There is a rapping sound on the side window. My head jerks around so suddenly that I pull a muscle inside my neck. "Agnes!" With only a sliver of light illuminating her wide face and her bare legs sticking out from under Nana Pete's long brown cardigan, she looks like she is about three years old. I wrap George up tight again in my hand, roll down the window, and lean out toward her.

"God, you scared me!"

She cocks her head and pulls the edges of Nana Pete's sweater under her chin. "What are you doing out here? It's freezing. Do you know what time it is?"

I shake my head. "I just needed some air. It's not that cold."

She studies me, waiting for me to say something more, but I don't. "Were you going to run away?" Her voice is wobbly.

"What? No!" I open the door and get out of the car. "I wouldn't do that, Agnes. I promise. I wouldn't leave you. Ever."

She stares at the thick yarn weaving in and out of the cardigan sleeves. "You were ready to back at the hospital."

"Oh, that's just what I *said*. But I didn't mean it. Not really."

"Can I ask you something?" she asks.

I nod. "Yeah, anything."

"Did Winky ever do anything to you? Like hurt you at all? I mean, since you've been in the Milk House?"

I take a step back. "What? *No!* Never! Why would you even ask me that?"

Her body shudders, trying to hold back the tears. "I don't know. I just . . ." She shakes her head. "I've been thinking . . . ," her voice trails off softly. "Things have just . . . gotten so crazy all of a sudden." She brushes her fingers across her eyes. "I don't know what to think anymore. It's so confusing." She presses the edges of the sweater against her face. "I just want to do the right thing, Honey! I just want to be good!"

I wrap both of my arms around her and bury my nose in her hair. "You're already good, Agnes," I say after a moment. "Why can't you believe that?"

She shakes her head. "I'm not good! I'm weak! I was terrible to Benny and I am always tempted to sin, especially out here, where everything is weird and freaky."

"Have you ever tried to trust yourself to do the right thing?" I ask. "Instead of always waiting for some sign or trying to figure out what Emmanuel thinks is right for you?"

She raises her tear-stained face. "I couldn't do that. I'm not strong enough. I need Emmanuel to tell me what's right. We all do."

I shrug. "I don't."

"But that's because you don't care about being good!" Agnes wails. She looks at me intently. "Why don't you want to be good? Why, Honey? Why?"

"I care about being good. I just—"

"Then what's this?" Agnes pulls the pink flower barrette out from under the cardigan and shoves it at me.

I stare at her, speechless. "Where'd you find—"

"In your backpack," she says sadly. "I noticed it sitting open by the door, just before I came out here. The barrette was right on top." She shakes her head. "Why would you steal, Honey? Why? You broke a commandment!"

I shrug. "I just . . . I saw you looking at it in the store and . . . and then you went and put it back and . . . I know it's wrong to steal, but . . . I just wanted you to have it, Ags." I look into her blue eyes. "I just wanted you to have something for yourself for once. To feel pretty, instead of always trying to make yourself ugly with all those freaky penances you do. It's not a sin to feel pretty, Agnes! It's not!"

Agnes's eyes blur with tears as I talk and when she blinks, they roll down her cheeks. "We're not supposed to clothe the body," she whispers. "Just the soul."

"That's garbage," I answer. "God wouldn't't've given us bodies if he didn't want us to take care of them."

Agnes doesn't say anything for a minute. Then she looks at me again. "I'm scared," she whispers. "Everything's changing."

I take her hand in mine. "I know." The words hang between us, heavy as stones. Out of nowhere, a drop of rain hits the side of my face. I squint and look up. Two more drops splash my cheeks and then all at once, as if God has shaken a wet blanket in the heavens, thousands of drops scatter and fall around us. Agnes pulls the cardigan over her head.

"Get back in the car!" I yell, throwing open the door.

We sit there for a while, watching the rain run in soaking rivulets along the windshield. It's coming down so hard that even with the lights on, I can't make out the shrubs anymore. The glass looks like the inside of a thick piece of ice.

"Hey," I say, grabbing Agnes's sleeve. "Let's run."

Agnes looks at me like I'm crazy. "Run where?"

"Just run! *Race!* Like we used to! In the rain!" Something inside me starts jumping around, thinking about it.

But Agnes just stares down at her wet legs. After a moment, she curls them up under her. "I can't."

"Oh, why not?" I reach out and punch her softly in the arm. "Come on, Agnes, you know you w—"

"No, I can't, Honey. I mean it."

I sit back against the seat and pout for a minute. "Is it because you're good at it? Is that why?" Silence. "It is, isn't it? It's just like the 'pretty' thing." I sit up straight again and turn toward her. "Agnes, you know, I've been trying for a while to figure you out since this saint-wannabe thing kicked in. You used to be this really great, funny best friend of mine. Remember how hard you could make me laugh? So that I practically peed in my pants? Remember?" I nudge her a little with my elbow, but she doesn't look up. "I can *kind* of understand the whole penance deal and praying all the time and all that. I really can. I know you want to be good. But this, this I don't understand at all. You're a really good runner. I mean it. And I know you enjoy doing it. And now, because you think that being good at something must mean you're taking glory away from him or . . . or whatever the hell it is . . ."

"Would you *stop* using that word?"

"What word? Hell?"

Agnes flinches and then nods.

"Okay. I'll try." I take a deep breath. "I just . . . God, you already give up so much. You wear strings around your waist that practically cut you in half, and you barely eat, and you probably even sleep on the floor at night when you're in your own room. Why do you have to give this up, too? I mean . . . it's not necessary. I really don't think God means for us to offer up everything, Agnes. I really don't."

She turns her head to look at me and for just a second I can see that clear, liquid light behind her eyes.

"Let's run," I whisper. "Come on, Ags. Just once. It'll feel great."

I switch Nana Pete's beams to high. The bright lights slice through the rain like razors. It's the only light we have to illuminate the length of the parking lot, but it'll have to do. We line up at the far end of the lot, just past the hotel front door. Agnes is tipped forward, the way she used to in the old bicycle ring, her fingertips spread flat against the pavement, her rear end high in the air. She has taken off Nana Pete's cardigan, and her new shorty pajamas are so wet they are practically transparent. I imitate her racer's stance and then look over through my dripping strands of hair.

"Just one," Agnes says, staring nervously ahead. "That's it."

"Ready . . . ," I say, dragging the word out slowly. Her

fingertips tense beneath her. "Set . . ." Her butt lifts up an inch more. *"Go!"*

She doesn't notice when I stop halfway across the lot. The rain is coming down so hard that I can barely see.

"Go," I whisper, watching her run through the downpour, her elbows pumping alongside her hips, hair streaming behind her in thin ropes. "Go, Agnes."

AGNES

The first thing I feel the next morning is the muscles in my calves aching. Although we ran just a single length of the parking lot, my legs had stretched and strained themselves, as if waking from hibernation. In the shower afterward, I massaged them gently, to avoid charley horse cramps. Now I lean up on my tiptoes to ease the tightness behind them and then relax again. I was shocked at how good it felt to run again—even better than I remember. There is something about moving that fast in the rain—it makes my heart beat faster, my legs stretch longer, my breath quicken in my lungs. I can't think of a single thing to compare it to.

"Agnes!" Nana Pete calls. "Are you ready?" Sliding my arms back into my robe, I pin my hair back quickly into a knot and look in the mirror. I feel a little shaky inside, but at least I still look like a Believer.

Lillian wants to get back on the road right away, but Nana Pete says she's not doing anything without her coffee first. We head across the street to a place called Perkins and slide into a green booth. Everything's going along fine until Lillian orders pancakes with strawberries and whipped cream.

"I'm gonna have the same thing," Honey says.

Then Benny points to the picture of the strawberries and pancakes and nods his head up and down.

I give him a little elbow in the ribs. "Strawberries," I say, shaking my head. "You can't."

"Is Benny allergic to strawberries?" Lillian asks. I press my lips together and study the blue rim of Nana Pete's coffee cup.

"No," Honey says finally. "He's not. But Believers aren't allowed to eat red food at Mount Blessing." I can feel Lillian and Nana Pete exchange a look.

"Oh," Lillian says. "Right. I forgot about that one." She pauses and then looks over at me. "But we're not at Mount Blessing anymore, Agnes. I'm pretty sure you and Benny can eat whatev—"

"No, we *can't* eat whatever we want. Just because we're not on the grounds of Mount Blessing, does not mean we have thrown away everything that makes us Believers!" I glare at Honey.

Honey's face darkens. "Don't start with your snippy little—"

"All right," Nana Pete interjects. "I know both of you have a lot on your minds. And I also understand that emotions are running high, and sometimes words will be said." She flicks her eyes between Honey and me as she talks. "But we have to support one another as much as we can right now, not tear one another apart." She takes a sip of coffee and pats her upper lip with her handkerchief. "You know, when Leonard and Lillian were little and they used to fight, I wouldn't let them leave the room until they had apologized to each other."

"'A divided house always falls,'" Lillian says, smiling at her mother.

Nana Pete nods. "Which means, girls, that we've got to stay on the same team if we want to make it. Okay?"

"But we're not on the same team," I say, pushing my

plate away. "Remember? Benny and I are still Believers. You and Honey aren't."

Honey looks at me, confused.

Nana Pete puts her palm over the top of my hand. "You're still my granddaughter, Agnes Little, and Benny is my grandson. That puts us on the same team." Her eyes shimmer as she talks. "Okay?"

Just then our waitress reappears, her pad poised in her hand.

"You look so *nice!*" she says, staring at my blue robe. "Did you sing in the choir at church this morning, honey?"

I gasp, horrified, and stare at Nana Pete. "What day is today?"

"It's . . . Sunday, I think," Nana Pete answers. "Yes, it's Sunday. Why?"

I clap my hand against my forehead. "We have to go to Sunday services!"

Nana Pete looks up at the waitress and smiles. "We'll need just a minute," she says sweetly.

"Sure thing," the woman says. "You holler when you're ready."

"You don't understand." I jab my finger against the glossy green tabletop to emphasize my point. "I *cannot* miss a Sunday service, Nana Pete, and neither can Benny. We just *can't.*"

"Get ahold of yourself, Agnes," Honey says. "We're traveling across the country, for crying out loud. What are we supposed to do?"

Nana Pete nods her head. "I do think there's something called traveler's dispensation, Mouse, which kind of clears you from going to church when you're on the road."

"Kind of?" I repeat. "Kind of isn't going to cut it when the sun goes down tonight, Nana Pete!" My nose starts to wiggle. "We have to go to Sunday service! We have to!"

Across from me, Honey clenches a fist. "You know, I've bailed on tons of Sunday services, Agnes, and I have yet to disintegrate into a pile of ashes at sundown."

I look away from her and shake my head. How could I have let her talk me into running last night? What is wrong with me?

Lillian stares at Honey, trying to comprehend her words, and then over at me. "Disintegrate into a pile of ashes?" she repeats. "Is that what Emmanuel told you would happen if you missed services?"

My breathing, which is dangerously on the edge of hyperventilation, slows down. "I know all of you think everything Emmanuel ever taught us is wacky, but I don't." I stab at the center of my chest with my index finger. "*I* still happen to believe in some things. And Sunday service is one of them."

"Okay, Mouse," Nana Pete says gently. She reaches out and pats my hand. "Okay. Just relax, darlin'. We'll find you a Sunday service somewhere."

Mount Olive Southern Baptist Church, recommended to us by the cashier at Perkins, is a tiny brick building with a narrow white steeple and wide red doors, just five miles outside of Raleigh. From the front, it barely looks big enough to hold the five us. As we climb the front steps, I hear loud, strange singing coming from the inside. I stop and hold my breath, wondering if I should tell Nana Pete that this is a mistake.

For starters, I've never been inside an actual church. All Sunday sacrament services at Mount Blessing are always held in the Great House, after the long tables have been cleared away and the benches rearranged into neat rows of pews. Second, when Nana Pete asked me what kind of service I wanted to attend, I hadn't known how to respond. In fact, up until that moment, I didn't realize any options outside of the Believers even existed.

"Would a Baptist service be all right?" she'd asked. "Or maybe a Methodist one? Lutheran? Catholic?" The words were foreign to me; I stared blankly at her.

Honey rolled her eyes. "I think anything involving Jesus and God will be fine," she said.

And so here we are, standing outside a Baptist church in the middle of Greenville, North Carolina, where not only am I unsure we will have room to kneel and stretch out our arms, but the sound of singing is coming through the walls. Before I can open my mouth to say anything, the door opens. A thin black man in a neatly pressed suit beckons us inside with a low bow. We nod and take our seats in the very last pew. I am surprised at how much room there is inside. The ceiling is wide and high and there are at least twenty pews on each side of the church, each filled to capacity. The floor is covered with thin red carpet and all along the walls are wooden engravings of Jesus at different stages of his life. But the only thing I can look at is the black woman up on the altar.

She has wild, curly hair and gold bracelets on her wrists. Her shiny purple robe sways with her as she moves back and forth, her eyes closed, holding her hands up to the ceiling.

She is singing a slow, slow song that draws murmurs from the congregation and makes my heart ache.

I'm troubled

I'm troubled

I'm troubled in mind

If Jesus don't help me I surely will die.

She sings six separate verses, all by herself. Each one is about being in the dark, about trying to find the light. The strange thing is, it feels as if she is singing only to me. I keep looking around, but no one else seems to notice. There is never any singing at the Sunday services at Mount Blessing. Singing, Emmanuel says, disrupts the flow of meditation, which is the whole point. We chant our "songs" instead, repeating strings of Latin phrases endlessly, until it is time for Emmanuel to preach. Here, everywhere I look, people are either smiling or crying with happiness. Some raise their hands to the ceiling along with the singing woman, while others clutch handkerchiefs to their faces, dabbing at the tracks their tears have made.

After the woman is finished singing, a man wearing a red robe (a *red* robe!) gets up from a chair alongside the altar and walks to the front of the church. He has dark curly hair cut close to his scalp and a strange-looking scar that makes the side of his face look puckered, as if it has collapsed beneath itself. He opens a small Bible and looks at something on the page. Then he shuts it again. I close my eyes. Emmanuel does the same thing just before he begins to preach. *Now we're getting somewhere*, I think. *Now we'll have a real Sunday service, complete with stern lectures from the Bible and commands to strive higher, reach farther, try harder to be perfect.* But then the man sits down. Right on the top step of the altar.

"I want to tell you a story," he says, smiling at us. The scar on his cheek disappears when he moves his mouth. People in front of me sit forward eagerly. Someone in the back says, "All right, Reverend!" My head snaps around. They're allowed to *talk* during Sunday service?

"There was once a boy named Zachary who had a terrible kidney disease," says the preacher. "It was so bad that if he did not get a transplant, he would die. His parents were frantic. Neither of them were a match, and when they asked their younger daughter, Josie, if she would get tested, Josie started to cry. She had a terrible fear of needles. But after a while she gathered her courage and shut her eyes and went for the test. She was a perfect match. If Zachary was to be saved, he would need to be operated on the very next day. Her parents were overjoyed but a bit apprehensive. They told Josie that if she wanted to, she could give her older brother one of her kidneys—but only if she wanted to. She would have to undergo a painful operation that would involve many needles. It was her decision. Josie listened quietly and asked her parents if she could think about it for a while. An hour came and went and when Josie approached her parents, they held their breath. She would do it, she said. Zachary could have her kidney. The parents cried with joy and hugged Josie tight. 'But,' Josie said, 'when I die tomorrow, will you promise not to forget me?' "

I look around as the sound of sobbing fills the church. A woman behind me is weeping openly, nodding and swaying in her seat. Across from her, the woman in the purple robe is sitting in a pew. Her eyes are closed and she is nodding as the preacher continues to speak. His voice gains strength suddenly, causing me to look up.

"If a child can love in this way," he says, pausing for a moment, "imagine what Jesus can do when we turn to him. All we have to do is ask. We don't have to be perfect or pure." He stands up. "Heck, we don't even have to feel *good* about it!" A series of murmured amens sweeps throughout the church. "All we have to do is ask. Just show up and ask." The man closes the Bible and presses it to the front of his chest. "Lord, here I am. Show me the way." He bows his head. "Show me the way."

A woman yells "Alleluia!" from the pew in front of us. She is wearing a pink dress and a matching pink hat, and she pumps her fist in the air. Honey giggles. Lillian pokes her in the shoulder.

"There is nothing greater than love," the preacher says, his voice gaining power. "It is stronger than any evil, any darkness." More shouts erupt from all over the church.

"Yes!"

"Show me the way, Jesus!"

"Love is the answer," the preacher continues. "If we love one another, then we need not fear anything else. Love"—he raises the Bible in the air—"is everything." His last word is spoken loudly, and as if that is the cue needed, the congregation rises as one and stamps and yells and claps. I glance nervously from side to side, only to see Honey, Nana Pete, Lillian, and Benny all on their feet. Benny is waving his good hand in the air and Lillian and Honey are howling and shouting along with everyone else. Nana Pete is standing there, grinning from ear to ear. I shake my head and press my lips together tightly. The woman in the pink hat stands up and points her finger at the preacher. "Ain't nothin' but the *truth*, Reverend!" she says, before sitting back down.

Finally the woman in purple comes back up to the altar, followed this time by the rest of the choir. They start off slowly, barely over a whisper, and then pick up speed, their voices rising to a crescendo over the shouting that is still coming from the rest of the church:

Walk together, children
Don't you get weary
Walk together, children
Don't you get weary
Oh talk together, children
Don't you get weary
There's a great camp meetin' in the promised land.

Benny takes my hand just as the song is ending and squeezes it tightly.

A myriad of emotions floods through me as the service comes to a close and people start to move for the door. I feel confused and sad and scared and a little freaked out by the whole thing. But I feel happy, too, and I don't know why.

As we are descending the steps, I notice the man in red at the very bottom, greeting and hugging people. The lady in the pink hat is standing next to him, doing the same thing.

"Come on, Nana Pete," I say. "Let's get out of here." But it's too late. As soon as we come into view, the lady in the pink hat swoops down on the four of us. She has a pair of tiny wire glasses balanced on the end of her nose and the largest breasts I have ever seen. When she presses herself against us, I worry for a moment that I might get smothered.

"*Visitors!*" She smiles hugely, exposing a single gold tooth along her upper gums. "Look, Reverend! We've got visitors today!" I stand rigidly under her embrace, watching as the reverend turns his attention in our direction.

"Welcome," he says, shaking our hands one by one. "I hope you enjoyed the service."

"It was wonderful," Nana Pete says. "Especially the story about the little girl." He nods, pleased with the compliment.

"I saw you shouting out," the woman in pink says to Honey. There is a twinkle in her eye. "You looked like you were having fun."

Honey grins and bows her head. "I was," she says softly.

"That's what shouting out is for, you know," the woman says.

"Oh?" Nana Pete asks.

"Yes," the woman says, nodding up and down. "The Lord knows we have things inside we can't keep quiet about, no matter how hard we try. That's why we come to church, to tell him about them. And if we need to shout them out, so be it. Sometimes, the longer the silence, the louder the shout." She grins, her gold tooth flashing. "Jesus understands."

HONEY

After Lillian drops her rental car off at a place near the church, the five of us get back inside the Queen Mary—Agnes, Benny, and me in the back, Nana Pete and Lillian in the front—and hit the road again. Lillian is driving. It's almost noon.

"We've got some ground to cover," Nana Pete says, opening her bottle of pills and throwing one in her mouth. "I don't know how fast you can drive, darlin', but it would be nice to get to Savannah before nightfall."

"It's only five hours," Lillian says. "I think we can do it."

Agnes slumps over on her side of the car and sighs deeply. Ever since she got up this morning, she's been acting all weird again. Maybe I'm crazy, but I thought we'd had a little bit of a breakthrough back there in Raleigh, talking about the barrette and running in the rain. But I guess not. Old habits must die harder than I realize. I gaze out the window as the North Carolina highway blurs by.

Nana Pete and Lillian talk softly up front. I wish they would turn around and talk to me. But hours pass and there is no indication of any shared conversation. I pull out my butterfly notebook and start sketching a White Skipper from memory. It ends up looking terrible, like a distorted balloon instead of a butterfly. I close the book, lean my head back against the seat, and pretend to sleep.

"He hasn't said a word since the operation," Nana Pete is

saying. Her voice is hushed and she is talking out of the side of her mouth. "Not one single word."

"He's in shock," Lillian says. "It happens to children sometimes. I think it's just because they have no words to describe certain things. It's too much."

"Do you think he'll snap out of it?"

Lillian nods. "I'm sure he will. We just have to give him some time." I glance over at Benny. He has his first two fingers of his good hand stuck in his mouth and he is sleeping soundly. For the first time, I realize just how young he is. I wonder how helpless he must have felt when Emmanuel lifted him off the table and carried him into his room. Like a lamb being taken to slaughter. I put my hand on his knee and keep it there until he stirs again.

After a while, Lillian pulls through a fast-food place called Captain D's and orders two buckets of fried fish, some weird little bally type things called hush puppies, and french fries with vinegar. I eat everything quickly, even licking the inside of the paper wrapper the fish comes in. It's delicious. Lillian, Benny, and Nana Pete eat their fish, too, but Agnes doesn't touch a thing. She's probably started another fasting period. Let her. I don't even care anymore.

"You wanna play Guess Who?" Lillian asks after everyone has finished eating. She's looking at me in the mirror.

"What's that?" I ask.

"It's a guessing game. I think of a famous person and you get to ask twenty questions until you think you've figured out who it is."

"I don't really know any famous people," I say.

"You could do saints," Agnes mumbles.

I roll my eyes. "Forget it."

"No, I think that's a great idea!" Nana Pete says, turning around. "Don't you, Lillian?"

Lillian slides a look over at her mother and nods. "I don't know how far I'll get, since I don't know much about them, but I'm sure I'll learn a great deal."

"You start, Mouse," Nana Pete says.

"No, I don't want to play," she says, shrinking back against the seat.

I turn, glaring at Agnes. "Spare me. You want to play so badly you can taste it. Now, just play. I'll even sit this one out."

So Agnes starts. Nana Pete and then Lillian ask questions until it's disclosed that Agnes's saint of choice is a girl who died when she was only twelve . . .

"Saint Agnes," I blurt out.

"Hey!" Agnes yells. "You're not even playing!"

"You're so predictable, Agnes," I say meanly. "Think of another one."

"Why did she die so young?" Nana Pete asks.

"Oh God," I say. "Here we go."

Of course Agnes tells her the whole story of her namesake, Saint Agnes, a story she has told me over and over again since she got *The Saints' Way*. I close my eyes and brace myself.

"Well, okay," she starts softly, but as she gets into it, her voice picks up. "Saint Agnes was a very beautiful girl. And a nobleman from Rome wanted to marry her—they married really young back then—but she said no, because she wanted to be a nun and devote her life to God."

"Like someone else we know," I murmur.

"Honey." Nana Pete glares at me. "Stop."

"Okay, okay," I answer. "Not another word."

"Go ahead, Agnes," Nana Pete says.

"So the man was really upset that Agnes wouldn't marry him and to get back at her, he accused her publicly of being a Christian, which was against the law in those days. She was arrested and brought before a judge and the judge tried to get her to deny it. He even went easy on her because she was so young. But she wouldn't budge. Then they threatened to torture her by peeling off her skin and burning her alive, but she still wouldn't deny Christ. Finally she was ordered to be executed. When she was brought up to the block, the executioner got really nervous, because she was so young and beautiful. He even begged her to reconsider, but she wouldn't." Agnes sighs and leans back in the seat. "And so she died a martyr for Christ."

"Good Lord!" Nana Pete says. "How terrifying! I wonder what that poor child was thinking as they led her up to the chopping block."

I stare out the window. Fields of wheat rush by in a haze of gold. I'd give anything right now to be standing in the middle of one of them, flying a kite.

"She was smiling, because she was so overjoyed to be dying for Christ," Agnes says.

I give Agnes as disgusted a look as I possibly can. "Agnes. Come *on*. The girl was twelve years old. She wasn't smiling. She was probably peeing in her pants! She was about to get her head cut off!"

Agnes narrows her eyebrows at me. "Well, that's what the book said, Honey. I didn't make it up."

"Whatever the case, there's certainly no doubt Saint Agnes

was incredibly brave," Nana Pete says. "I don't think I could be that brave if I was faced with execution."

"No one could," I retort. "And Saint Agnes probably wasn't, either."

"Don't you dare defame Saint Agnes!" Agnes shouts. "I mean it, Honey!"

"Girls!" Nana Pete grabs her handkerchief and starts blotting. The two of us sit for a while, seething in silence. I'm so sick of Agnes's holier-than-thou attitude about saints and martyrs that I could puke. I wish I could just rip that whole part of her out and toss it out the window. Instead, I watch the landscape pass by. There are no gold fields anymore; now everything is flat and green and still. I miss Winky.

"Here we are!" Lillian yells out suddenly in a singsong voice. She points to a green sign on the side of the highway. "Look—Savannah!" Twenty minutes later, she pulls into a wide gravel driveway. On the right is a weirdly angular yellow house edged with a white picket fence. She parks the car and looks over at Nana Pete. "Home sweet home." She smiles. "We made it, Ma."

The largest part of Lillian's house looks like a big box with a slanted roof. There is a door and two windows on the right side and a closed-in deck that protrudes out from a second-floor window. Next to the big box is a slightly smaller attachment with a single rectangular window in the middle. A large tree with draping, heavy boughs hangs over the side of the house like a dark green umbrella.

"That is one weird-looking house," I say, getting out of the car behind Lillian. She has her arm around Nana Pete and is helping her to the front door. Nana Pete is shuffling her feet and leaning her whole weight against Lillian.

"That's because it used to be an old carriage house," Lillian says over her shoulder. "Back in the day when people drove horse and buggy carriages, this is where they would store the carriages."

"Are there any carriages in there now?"

Lillian laughs and shakes her head. "I barely have enough room inside that place for myself and Mr. Pibbs. No carriages."

"You live with a man?" I ask.

"Nope. No guy. Come on in. You'll see."

Agnes, Benny, and I follow her through the front gate of the picket fence, stepping carefully along a set of cracked, flat stones that lead up to the front door. Big green bushes sit like boulders in front of the house. I pause, trailing my fingers over one of the strange fern-shaped spikes growing out of the top of the bush closest to the door. I've never seen anything like it before. Tiny buds cling to the tips of the spiky growth, hard and green on the outside with streaks of pink underneath.

"Those are my summer sweet," Lillian says. She is fiddling with the lock, watching me out of the corner of her eye. "They need a few more weeks to bloom, but when they do, the whole front yard will smell like apple pie."

I raise my eyebrows. "Apple pie? Really?"

Lillian turns the key in the front door. "Yep. And sometimes, at night, if you sit really still on the front porch here and watch, you'll see hummingbirds flying in and around the bushes. And butterflies, too." She gives the door a deft push with her hip. "Here we are, Ma. Come on in and have a seat."

Agnes takes Benny's hand and leads him inside, but I

pause as a cat darts out suddenly from behind the door and, weaving between my legs, makes a run for the front gate.

"That's Mr. Pibbs!" I hear Lillian yell from the inside. "Grab him, Honey, will you? He's not allowed out!" I grab the small animal around the scruff of the neck just as he is about to disappear around the picket fence.

"Gotcha, you little bugger!" He mews piteously, but I clutch him against my chest and walk back toward the house. The cat turns its head to look up at me and when he does, I almost drop him. He's a Siamese, with blue eyes and brown markings on his ears and face.

Exactly like George.

AGNES

The amount of space Lillian has inside her carriage house doesn't seem big enough to hold a horse, let alone a bunch of buggies. Or whatever it was they drove back then. Benny and I stand next to one of the bright red counters inside her tiny kitchen and wait while Lillian helps Nana Pete onto a large couch covered with a cabbage-rose print. I hold my arms out. My fingers can reach the countertop on the other side of the kitchen.

"I know. I know," Lillian says, walking in. She opens the refrigerator. "It's smaller than a gingerbread house in here, but it's home." She shrugs, holding a glass jar full of green liquid. "I'm getting Ma a drink. You guys want some? It's limeade. I just made it yesterday."

I don't say anything, but Benny nods eagerly.

Lillian blows inside a glass, shrugging as a pocketful of dust emerges from the bottom, and fills it with the limeade. "Don't worry," she says. "I'll take this one." Pulling out another glass from the cupboard, she rinses it out in the sink and fills it. Then, after plopping in several ice cubes, she hands it to me. "Come on in here. We can sit down."

We follow her into a slightly larger room with pale yellow walls. Lillian plops down on the couch next to Nana Pete. The arms are so threadbare that I can see pieces of wood beneath the stuffing. Nana Pete is perspiring more than usual and her mouth is drawn in a straight line. When we walk into the room, she looks up at us, but her lids are heavy, as if they are weighted on the inside.

"Listen, Ma." Lillian reaches over and smoothes Nana Pete's hair off her forehead. "I'm not gonna go into King's tonight so I can stay with you and—"

But Nana Pete cuts her off with a wave of her hand. "Don't be ridiculous, Lil. I'm tired from the trip, is all. You didn't go in yesterday to come meet us in Raleigh, and I don't want you to call in again. I remember the mess you came back to the last time I visited. Besides, it's no big deal. We're all just going to sleep anyway. It's not like I have to *do* anything." She glances over at me and winks. "Except maybe watch my snoring."

Lillian studies her mother for a moment and then sighs. "All right," she says softly. "If you're really sure . . ."

Nana Pete nods her head firmly. "I'm really sure," she repeats. "Now git. You have about twenty minutes to shower and get down there before they start panicking."

Lillian plants a kiss on her mother's forehead. "You really do remember from last time, eh?"

Nana Pete nods. "How could I forget? We barely got any time to visit."

Lillian hesitates again and then drains the last of her limeade. "Well, it won't be like that this time," she says. "I'll push through tonight and then I'll be off for three days in a row." She stands up. "We'll all have plenty of time together when I get back."

Whoopee, I think. *One big happy family.*

Honey comes in a few minutes later, carrying a little Siamese cat. Her face is pale for some reason, as if she has just seen a ghost. But Nana Pete sits up when she sees the animal, and claps her hands.

"Mr. Pibbs!" Honey releases her grip and the cat scrambles over next to Nana Pete. "Oh!" Nana Pete says, scratching him between the ears. "Hello, my little man! Mama hasn't seen you in so long!"

"Is he yours?" Honey asks softly.

Nana Pete shakes her head. "No, no. He's Lillian's. I bought him for her after she . . . came . . ." She bites her lower lip and looks up at us. Her eyes seem a little brighter than they did earlier. "He's been good company for her."

I watch as Benny sits down on the couch and starts stroking the cat's white fur. Mr. Pibbs tilts his head back and closes his eyes, clearly relishing the attention.

"Where'd Lillian go?" Honey asks suddenly.

Nana Pete rubs the animal's throat. "She has to go to work for a while. She'll be back in the morning."

"Work?" Honey repeats. "She's going to *work*? *Now?*"

Nana Pete puts her finger against her lips. "Shh . . . don't let her hear you. She'll feel bad. She wanted to call off, but I told her not to. She's been at King's for quite some time now. She works very hard. They depend on her. She has to go in."

Honey's face gets dark, like a storm cloud passing over the sun. Then she plops down heavily on a battered rocking chair in the corner and stares out the window.

"Are you all right?" I ask.

She nods but doesn't take her eyes off the window.

"It's late," Nana Pete says. "Come on, everyone, time for

bed." She kisses each of us and holds Benny close for a long time, stroking his hair. Then she walks up the stairs and closes the door.

Lillian has instructed Nana Pete to sleep in the only bedroom, which is on the second floor, so Benny, Honey, and I are sprawled out downstairs on the living room floor, on top of a stack of blankets. I'm a little spooked sleeping in this weird woman's house, even if she is my father's sister, and so I start my litany of evening prayers to help take the edge off. After a bit, Honey throws her blankets off and stands up.

"Hey," I whisper, leaning up on one elbow. "Where're you going?"

Honey whirls around. "To the kitchen, okay? I need something to drink." Her tone prevents me from asking anything more—or from following her after more than forty minutes pass and she doesn't reappear. I'm not sure what's bothering her. All of a sudden, for some reason, it seems like she's shutting down the way Benny has. Could she possibly be having second thoughts about everything?

I wonder what Mom and Dad are doing now. It's our third night away from them. Have they left Mount Blessing to come look for us? Has Dad tried to call Nana Pete? Will he be even angrier when he finds out that Lillian is in on this, too? And what will Emmanuel do when he finds out? Will we ever be allowed back inside Mount Blessing?

In the dark, I can hear Benny's hand rustle under the blankets as he reaches over for me. I slide my hand over his and hold it tightly.

. . .

Hours later, I am awakened suddenly by what sounds like a strangled sob. I sit up straight in the dark and listen, my body white-hot with fear.

"Oh God, please!" It's coming from upstairs. "Nana Pete! Get up! Please!" Throwing back the blankets, I race up the steps on the other side of the room. The scene inside Lillian's bedroom has the look and feel of a dream. A tiny, pear-shaped lamp next to the bed casts an eerie wedge of yellow over the room. In the bed, Nana Pete is lying flat on her back, her mouth open in a distorted *O* shape. Honey is straddling her, shaking her shoulders with both hands. "Get up!" she sobs again. "Please God, get up!"

"What are you doing?" I scream. "Get off of her! You'll kill her!"

Honey turns around, and in the partial light of the room, her face has acquired an ethereal, almost transparent look. Tears are streaming down her cheeks. "It's too late," she whispers. "She's gone."

PART III

HONEY

I get a weird feeling in the center of my chest when I see Mr. Pibbs, as if a curtain hanging over my life is about to be pulled wide open. It feels like Jell-O, nothing I can really stand on firmly or trust, and yet . . . it's there. It's real. Something is about to happen. I know it is.

My initial aggravation at Lillian leaving for her shift at King's disappears after Nana Pete tells me she's working so hard, that people are depending on her. She must have a really important job. The place is called King's—it sure sounds important. Maybe she is in charge of a lot of people, a boss of some kind. She left the house in a pressed white shirt and black slacks—pretty professional looking. I wonder if she is a nice boss or a mean boss. Would she order people around? Get mad if they come in late? Throw things at them? Curse? Or would she sit down and listen to what they had to say? Give them another chance?

I'm in a mood—all impatient and jittery and nervous and scared at the same time. I'm dying to get up and poke around a little, but Agnes won't stop with her insane praying. I figure leaving the room is a better option than leaning over and strangling her, so I head out to the kitchen and pour myself a glass of limeade. Then I climb up on one of the counters and sit there for another hour, staring out the window. I wait for Agnes to come out and start yelling at me for one thing or another, but she doesn't show. It's very dark outside. The drapey branches of Lillians's tree look like fingers behind the glass. I reach into my pocket and feel around for George. Just having him in my hand makes me feel better. Eventually I creep back into the living room. Agnes is asleep. *Finally.*

I start in the living room first. It doesn't take very long, since the room itself is about the size of a shoe box. The only piece of furniture aside from the couch and the rocking chair is a rickety old bureau pushed against the far wall. In the center of the bureau is a small glass bowl filled with seashells, sitting atop a delicate square of blue scarf. There are three small drawers underneath.

I pull the first one open with shaking hands. I don't even know what I'm looking for. Worse, the thing pushing me to find it might not even be valid. It might just be some kind of weird, screwed-up hunch. But what if it isn't? What if . . . ? I glance inside the drawer. My heart sinks. It's packed with old, dusty Christmas ornaments—gold and silver balls, ropes of beat-up garland, a half string of lights. The second drawer contains blue-penciled drawings on large, slippery sheets of white paper. I pull one out. It looks like the inside of someone's house. The rest of the drawings are similar looking. I put them back in, my heart starting to plummet.

But my breath freezes in my throat when I open the final drawer. It's full to the brim with pictures. Hundreds and hundreds of Polaroid pictures, loose and scattered, piled on top of one another. I remove the one from the top of the pile. It's of Agnes and me, when we were about four or five years old. We're sitting on the stone steps in front of the nursery, sticking our bare legs and feet at the camera, giggling hysterically, the way we used to do when things like stinky feet and toe jam were the funniest things in the world. I lean in closer, studying Agnes's face. Blue eyes crinkled at the corners, tiny button nose scrunched up, teeth as small and white as pearls. I haven't seen her face look like that in years.

I dig my hands through the rest of the pictures, letting them fall like leaves over my outstretched hands. Every single one has me in it. Some are just me alone, but most of them are with Agnes and Benny. They are all hot-weather shots, taken at the pool or in the frog pond. We are dressed in bathing suits and T-shirts and shorts, flip-flops and sometimes no shoes at all. There are pictures of us in the nursery, pictures of us on our bikes, pictures of us at the Field House, digging through the iris garden. My brain races. Nana Pete is the only one all of these years who has taken pictures of us. Of me. Every summer when she came to visit. So why are they here, in this drawer, inside Lillian's house? What does it mean that Agnes's aunt has an entire drawer full of . . . *me*? I scoop up a handful of the photos and race upstairs. If I can find just one more thing . . .

Tiptoeing quietly into Lillian's room, I place the pile of pictures on the bed and look around. It's a tiny room, almost completely filled by the bed. Nana Pete is on her back, as still as a shadow. Next to the bed is a dresser and then another door, which turns out to be a closet. I open the door, pushing the hangers aside slowly, and get down on my knees, feeling around in the dark. There are at least six pairs of sneakers, two pairs of brown work boots, and all the way in the back, a beat-up pair of black heels. I shove them aside impatiently and lean in farther. When my hand comes into contact with it, my whole body freezes. Slowly I pull out the violin case and rest it across my knees. It's smaller than I imagined it would be. The black leather surface is smooth and pebbled at the same time. I open the lid carefully, gazing at the slender instrument, my eyes filling with tears. Then I stand up. I need to know everything, right now. All of it, before Lillian comes home and . . .

But I stop cold as I turn toward Nana Pete. Something is wrong. There is no snoring coming from the bed, in fact, no sound at all. It is so quiet that it's like someone turned off a switch. Slowly, I put down the violin case and walk up to the bed. I know even before I crawl up on top of her. I scream and holler, beg her to wake up, but I know.

Agnes doesn't believe me when I tell her Nana Pete is gone.

"Get off!" she screams again. "You're hurting her!"

I slide my straddled legs off slowly, one by one, without taking my eyes off Nana Pete's face. Her eyes, frozen in their sockets, are slightly open, and there is a faint, blue pallor to her skin. I reach out to close her eyelids, but Agnes shrieks.

"Don't touch her! Don't you *touch* her! You don't even *belong* to her!"

My heart cleaves in two when she says that. It's the meanest thing she's ever said to me. Ever. I catch sight of Benny suddenly, who has awakened from the noise and is standing behind Agnes.

"Benny . . . ," I start, but he runs into the bathroom, slamming the door behind him.

Agnes comes around to Nana Pete's side, almost on tiptoe, as if she is afraid of waking her. She sits down next to her grandmother and reaches out for her hand, running the tip of her finger over a large green vein on the surface. "Hey, Nana

Pete." Her voice is just above a whisper. "Hey, I know you're tired, but just sit up for a minute and tell us you're all right. Come on, now. Sit up." She pats Nana Pete's hand over and over again as she talks.

I'm horrified. Can't she see the parted, unmoving eyes? The sickly shade of Nana Pete's dead skin? Does she not realize that the entire time she has been talking, her grandmother has not taken a single breath? She cannot possibly be this far gone. No one can be so out of touch with reality that they do not realize they are sitting beside—and talking to—a dead person.

"Stop it," I say, taking a step closer to the bed. "Agnes, stop it. She can't hear you. She's dead. Stop talking to her." But Agnes doesn't seem to notice that I'm even in the room anymore. She keeps talking in the exact same tone of voice, keeps rubbing the top of Nana Pete's hand over and over again. "Come on, Nana," she whispers. "Let's go now. Come on. Wake up."

And then she makes the sign of the cross over her, as if the gesture will somehow breathe new life into her. It's pure Emmanuel, and it freaks me out. It does. Before I can stop to think about what I'm doing, I reach out and shove Agnes as hard as I can off the bed.

"Stop it!" I scream. "Stop talking to her like she can hear you, you freaking lunatic! She's dead, Agnes! And nothing's gonna bring her back!"

Agnes cowers for a moment on the floor a few feet away from me. As I take a step toward her, I catch a glimpse of myself in Lillian's mirror on the wall. My face, flushed with rage, is framed by wild red hair, still unbrushed from the night before.

My shoulders are hunched, my fists clenched, and there is spit in the corners of my mouth. Maybe I'm the lunatic, I think to myself. Maybe we both are.

I hear Agnes crying beneath me and I move toward her, sinking to my knees.

"Oh, Ags," I start, reaching out to touch her trembling shoulder. But she raises her face and smacks my outstretched hand away from her. I don't mind being smacked. I probably deserve it, shoving her the way I did. But I'm not prepared for the look that creeps into her eyes as she starts talking to me.

"That's the last time you'll ever push me around, Honey Harper." Her voice is eerily calm, with a power behind it that I don't recognize. "I've spent the past fourteen years of my life putting up with you because I thought you were my best friend. But now I know the only reason is because I felt sorry for you." She spits on the floor, right between us. Some of it lands on my knee. "Emmanuel was right all along. You're nothing but trash, Honey. That's why you're always getting into trouble and being dragged into the Regulation Room and why my parents don't even want me associating with you." She glares at me with those new eyes of hers. I swear to God, they're practically pulsing with whatever weird energy is flowing through her. "And it's probably even why your own mother left you."

I haul off and punch her right in the face when she says that. It's the second worst thing she's ever said to me. There is a horrible sound as my fist connects with her jaw and then a scream as Agnes falls back, clutching her face. I lunge toward her again, ready to do God knows what, when Benny comes barreling out of the bathroom. He flings himself against the two of us, holding his bad hand in the air, grunting wildly like a baby pig. I back off then, not wanting to hurt him. But Agnes gets to her feet. Her eyes are still crazy. She's clutching the side of her mouth where I hit her with one hand and holding Benny behind her with the other.

"We're going," she says flatly. "This whole nightmare is over. I'm calling my parents and we're going home."

My teeth start working my lower lip until I taste blood. I decide to try again. Rationally, this time. "Agnes. Please. I'm sorry I called you a lunatic. I'm sorry I hit you." I take a deep breath, struggling to control my voice, which is on the verge of tears. "But please, we'll work something out. We'll call Lillian, okay? Please don't call your parents, Agnes. We've got to stick together. You know I can't go back there. Please."

But it's not working. Agnes starts shaking her head as soon as I start talking about sticking together.

"No, no, no, no, no, no, no." She pulls Benny out from behind her and grips him tightly around his shoulders. "*This* is my family," she says. "Benny and my parents and Emmanuel. They're who I'm sticking with, Honey. Not you. Not Lillian. You do whatever you want from now on. I don't care." It's the third shot Agnes has fired at me in less than ten minutes. I feel dizzy, as if I have been mortally wounded. I glance over toward the bed behind us.

"What about Nana Pete?"

"And Nana Pete, too, of course," Agnes replies. "She's always been family."

"She's my family, too," I whisper.

Agnes sneers at me. "She just let you think that because she felt sorry for you, too. You're not her real family. You're no one's real family. You're—"

"N-no," I stammer. "You're wrong. I just found—"

"Shut up," Agnes says. "I don't want to hear any more of your stupid rationalizations for the way things are. They never make any sense anyway."

I stare at her dumbfounded. Is this *Agnes* talking? I don't recognize her. "You don't have to worry about any of this anymore." I step forward with my last bit of energy and hold out my hands, palms up. "Agnes. Come on. Remember what Nana Pete said? When we were little and I wanted to leave you behind in the nursery because you were too afraid to go down to the frog pond with us?"

Agnes shakes her head and pretends to study the orange and brown geometric pattern on the rug. "No." Her voice is flat. "I don't."

"'Don't ever leave each other behind,'" I whisper. "'Not here. Not ever.' Remember?"

Agnes looks back up at me with her steely gaze. "Well, Nana Pete isn't around to tell us much of anything anymore, is she?"

And with that sentence, I know I've lost her. For real. It's as if she has gone through a door and locked it behind her. There's no key, no hope. Nothing.

Things move pretty quickly after that. I watch for a few minutes, in a stunned paralysis, as Agnes moves around the room like a wind-up doll. First she goes over to the bed and draws the sheet Nana Pete is lying under up over her face. Then she makes the sign of the cross over her and presses her fingers to her lips. Finally she kneels down and blesses herself. Benny does, too. They pray together in silence for a few minutes. Benny lays his head down on Nana Pete's sheeted thigh.

After a few minutes, Agnes reaches inside Nana Pete's leather bag and pulls out the cell phone. She dials a number, sits down on a corner of the bed, and holds the phone to her ear. I can tell she is making an effort not to look at me as the phone rings once, then twice. Finally someone picks up.

"Mrs. Winspear?" Agnes says. There is a pause. "It's Agnes. Yes, Agnes Little. Could I please talk to my father? Is he there?" She pulls on her earlobe as she waits. "Dad? Yes, Dad. It's me." Pink color fills her face as he begins shouting her name on the other end of the phone. She smiles and pulls Benny in next to her, holding him tightly. "Yes, we're here, Dad," she chokes out. "We're safe. Yes, Benny's fine. I know. I know. It was awful. I'm so sorry. Please, can you come get us, Dad? Please? We're at Lillian's. Yes. In Savannah. But we want to come home."

I turn away, staring out the window as she gives him the exact street address.

"Dad?" Agnes says in a small voice. "There's just one thing." She takes a deep breath. "Nana Pete . . . um . . . died." There is a long pause. I force myself not to turn around. "No, no, it wasn't anything like that," Agnes says. "It happened right here. We were sleeping. We all just went to sleep last night . . ." She starts to cry. "I don't know what happened. I really don't."

I drape my arms over the top of my head, shutting out the sound.

"Lillian?" she asks. "Um, I think she's at work. She had to go in last night. But she'll be back later, I guess. Maybe in the afternoon."

"Okay," she sniffles. "Yeah, okay, Dad. So you're gonna

take a plane? You'll be here by tonight, then?" She cries harder as he answers. "Okay, Dad. We'll be right here. We won't move." She wipes her eyes.

"And, Dad? Do you think we'll be in trouble? When we get back, I mean? With Emmanuel?" I hold my breath. Agnes is holding her breath, too, I realize, waiting for the answer. "Okay," she says finally. "Yeah, I know. Okay, Dad. We'll see you tonight." She closes the phone with a dull little click and stares ahead at nothing. I watch as Benny slides the tiny phone out of her hands, places it carefully inside Nana Pete's satchel on the bed, and then sits back down next to his sister.

I don't ask. I don't need to. I already know what awaits them when they return.

Something slides into place just then, like the last piece of a jigsaw puzzle, sealing something inside of me once and for all. This is the end of the line, I guess, for both of us.

"Okay, then," I say, lifting up my hand and backing out of the room. "I guess this is it." Agnes watches me with dull eyes. "I love you guys. I do." I nod my head over and over again, as if the action will propel me closer to the door. "Good-bye."

Benny buries his face in Agnes's shoulder.

And when she turns to stroke his head, I run like hell.

AGNES

The front door slams like a gunshot. In the silence, Benny and I stare at each other for what feels like an interminable amount of time. For the first time since everything happened, I'm glad my little brother has fallen mute. I know that sounds terrible, but I don't want to hear what he is thinking or what it means when his eyes race across my face, pleading silently with me. I hold his shaky gaze instead, willing him to see my own thoughts running like a train behind my eyes.

I know I've done the right thing. I know it. I know it. I know it. I know it. Let her go. Who cares if I never see her again?

My muscles strain under my skin, trembling with deprivation.

If I go after her, she'll think I'm making excuses. And if I give her even one opportunity to start talking again, she'll never stop. She'll start with all her crazy arguments and wheedling and I might not be able to stand up to her again.

Why did it take me so long to finally stand up to her in the first place? After all this time, the only thing it took to get her to back down was having a backbone. She's just a bully, when all is said and done. Punching me in the face like that. Like a crazy person. And always talking, talking, talking, talking. Blah, blah, blah. Why do you think this, Agnes? How can you think that? Don't you know there's no such thing as hell? Don't you know God is just some kind of slob, sitting on a bus? Yeah, right. Whatever, Honey.

. . .

She's gone. My father's coming to take me back and she's not going with me. She's gone. I might never see her again.

I bite my fists and then bring my legs up and cross them tightly under me, anything to quell the impulse to scream her name, anything to prevent my body from doing the opposite of what my mind is telling me.

Is this what it feels like not to give into temptation? Could Saint Thomas Aquinas have felt anything like this when he opened the door and saw the woman standing there? Is it possible that Saint Agnes struggled at all with denying her belief in Christ to avoid the sword on her neck?

No, it wasn't. Saint Thomas picked up the iron poker, hot from the fire, and Saint Agnes shook her head, even to her executioner, when he offered her one last chance to reject Christ.

After a while, Benny buries himself under a mountain of blankets on the other side of the bed, a good distance from Nana Pete and, no matter how much I plead with him, refuses to come out. He's humming a strange little tune I don't recognize and at first it kind of scares me. But then I leave him and walk over toward the window. He'll be okay. At least I know where he is. And that he's still alive. Every time I look over at Nana Pete, the only thing I can see is her nose protruding like a little tent from under the blue sheet. It scares me. She's dead. *Dead.*

My Nana.

My Nana Pete.

Why am I not crying?

I stare out at Lillian's wide, drooping tree, half expecting Dad to appear, although I know it will still be hours. I look at the clock on Lillian's dresser: 5:30 a.m. I want to get out of here. Now.

My hands are cold, and when I place my palm against my chest, I can barely feel my heart beating. How strange that Nana Pete is the dead one in the room, when right now, I cannot even tell if I am breathing.

Out of nowhere, Mr. Pibbs wanders into the room. He rubs himself along the insides of my legs and mews softly. He's probably hungry. Or maybe he misses Lillian. "Shoo," I whisper. "Beat it." He pushes the top of his head insistently against my calf. I stick my foot out and poke him away. He stares at me for a minute and then ambles out of the room again.

An hour passes like water leaking through a pinhole.

Drip.

Drop.

Drip.

Drop.

A soft crinkling sound from behind snaps me out of my stupor. Benny is sitting up on the edge of the bed, looking at something.

"Benny," I say softly. "What're you doing?" He holds a photograph out in my direction. His face is blank as a sheet. I take the photograph out of his hands and stare at it for a minute. It's of Dad and Lillian, taken years ago. Even with her flowing red hair and enormous belly, Lillian is unmistakable. Her left hand is resting lightly on the swell of her stomach and the other hand is around Dad's waist. She is smiling dutifully for the camera, but her eyes are turned down and her eyebrows are furrowed. Dad isn't smiling at all. His posture is erect and rigid, both arms firmly at his sides. I turn the picture over, looking for a date. There, in Dad's handwriting, are the words: "Isaac and Naomi, Mount Blessing."

Naomi? Who's Naomi? The only Naomi I've ever heard of is Honey's mother. This is Lillian. I'm sure of it. I turn the picture back over and study the face. Except for the long hair and the pregnant belly, the woman's features are definitely Lillian's. Why would the picture say . . .

Naomi?

"Where'd you get this?" I ask.

Benny points to the pile of pictures scattered around him.

I sit down slowly on the edge of the bed and pick up each one, studying them carefully. There is one of Honey and me sitting in our nursery crib, wearing diapers and nothing else. No more than two years old, we are huddled together over a book like two old women sharing a secret. I snatch another one, studying it closely. It's one Nana Pete took just last summer. We are standing in the bicycle ring in our summer shorts and T-shirts, smiling for the camera. I remember that day vividly. It was a month after I received *The Saints' Way*. Honey and I had argued just a few minutes earlier; she was angry with me because I would not race with her down the length of the field. My explanation for not wanting to run anymore wasn't good enough, she'd said; in fact, it was downright crazy. She had conceded bitterly, but in the picture her arm is flung around my neck, her cheek pressed against mine as if nothing had happened.

I grab the picture of Dad and Lillian back from under

the pile and hold it next to the picture of Honey and me. My eyes flick back and forth between the two so rapidly that my head starts to hurt. There's just no way. It's impossible. It has to be.

After a while, I throw the pictures down and run into the bathroom. Curling up into a little ball, I fit myself in the space between the tub and the toilet and stare at the white porcelain, trying to clear my head. I think back to the conversation Lillian and I had at the motel, when she asked me about Honey and Winky. Now, suddenly, I understand. Or do I? How can this be happening? What would it mean? The fear is overwhelming, like a heartbeat all its own, a new blood pulsing through every vein in my body.

I reach around and pull my little book from inside my waistband. Opening it to the story of Saint Agnes, I start to read. *She went to her execution cheerfully, knowing that she was to meet her Beloved Jesus soon.* I read the sentence again, trying to decipher the words behind my tears. Suddenly I close the book and hurl it as hard as I can across the room. It doesn't have far to go, and when it hits the opposite wall with a smack and then slides down against the floor, a sob breaks out of my chest.

My whole body begins to shake as I think about the punishment we will receive upon our return to the commune. Dad's answer—*One thing at a time, Agnes. Let's get you home safely and worry about the rest later*—had not been comforting.

In fact, every time I run it through my head, trying to search for hidden clues, I'm filled with dread. Why is it that he can never come right out and say what's really going on?

Why does he always present things under some sort of shroud, where in order to get to the truth I have to pull back layer after layer in hopes of finding it? Is he not who I think he is, either? Has everything been a lie?

"Help me," I whisper. "Someone. Please. Help me."

HONEY

The only thing running through my mind as I bolt out of the house is finding Lillian. If I can just find out where King's is and get her to come home, maybe we'll all still have a shot at this. Dawn is just breaking as I lunge through her front gate and run down the flagstone path. The air is pulsing with new, frail light. The sky is the color of an eggshell. I look around wildly, trying to determine which direction I should go.

And then all at once, out of the corner of my eye, I see it. A Zebra Longwing. She settles delicately inside the spiky fern for a few moments, collecting nectar with her nose stem. Her gossamer wings, elongated at the tips like fat teardrops, shudder every few seconds. The sun glints off the black-and-white stripes. I hold my breath. I'm afraid she will fly off if I breathe, and I don't want her to go anywhere. Not after waiting for so long.

But when she is done with the summer sweet bud, she does fly off and suddenly I am aware that I am standing there with no idea what to do or where to go next. Maybe I should go back inside. Try to plead again with Agnes. Tell her one more time that I'm sorry. Why do I always have to be so mean about everything? Calling her a freaking lunatic was going too far. No wonder she never wants to see me again. Why do I get so impatient with her? Especially since I love her more than any other person in my whole life?

I turn around and close my fingers over the doorknob. It's

small and cold in my hand. Lifeless. My fingers don't move. After a few seconds, I let go and sit down on the front step. I can't do it. I'm sorry that I've said things meanly and I'm sorry that I'm so impatient, but everything, every single word I've said about Emmanuel and Mount Blessing has been the truth. My truth. And I won't go back—I won't, I won't—and pretend that it isn't. Even for Agnes.

There is a scratching sound coming from inside the door. I open it carefully and stare into Mr. Pibbs's blue eyes. Scooping him up, I sit back down on the steps and turn him around so I can look at his face again. "Hey, buddy," I whisper. "I've got one just like you, only a little smaller. You know that?" The cat blinks his wide eyes and gazes back at me. "Has Lillian been a good mother to you?" I ask. Mr. Pibbs ducks his head and brings his left paw up to his face. With a tiny pink tongue, he begins licking his fur with small, short strokes. I press him tightly against my chest and bury my face into his silky white coat. He smells like wood and smoke and Nana Pete's perfume. I bury my nose in deeper, trying to smell Nana Pete again. Alarmed, the cat leaps out of my arms and runs for the fence. I don't stop him. I put my head down and sit there for a long time, not moving.

When I look up again, the first thing I see is Nana Pete's car. Her *car*. I run toward it at breakneck speed; maybe, maybe, maybe, yes! God, here are her keys. And that's how it happens. I don't know which direction to go in or even if Lillian's workplace is in Savannah. I don't even know what to do yet when it comes time to put more gas in the car. I know only one thing as I slip the silver key into the ignition and put the Queen Mary into drive.

It's time.

My time.

And I am outta here.

Lillian lives on a street called East Gwinnet. It's a pretty little street with exactly the kind of neat white houses I pictured when we left Mount Blessing. But it's so narrow that I almost hit the first car that comes driving down the other side. The guy behind the wheel leans on his horn and then sticks his middle finger out at me. I've never seen such a gesture before, but I'm almost positive it's not good. I ease up on the gas a little after that and then brake hard at the end of the street as two women cross in front of me.

"Excuse me!" I lean out the side window. The women are wearing white sneakers and shiny sweat suits that rustle when they walk. The slighter of the two has a pink foam curler in the middle of her forehead. "Have you ever heard of a place called King's?"

The women exchange a glance and then shrug. "No," the shorter one says. "Sorry."

"You're pretty small to be driving a great big car like that, aren't you?" the bigger one asks. I sit back down in the seat.

"It's my grandma's," I say, stepping on the gas and waving out the window. "She said I could drive it." I ease through three more streets, rolling the word over and over again along my tongue. "Grandma." It tastes good in my mouth, a new sweetness filling a bitter, empty space. Just as I am about to cross over West Charlton Street, I notice an elderly man putting a letter into a mailbox on the corner. I roll down the window again.

"Excuse me, sir? Have you ever heard of a place around here called King's?"

The old man's face, as worn and as wrinkled as a baseball glove, widens into a grin. "Eat breakfast there every mornin'."

"Breakfast?" I repeat. "You mean it's a restaurant?"

He leans against a brown cane and chuckles. "Yep. All-night diner. Good, too. Serves everything from eggs and bacon t' hominy and grits."

I sit back slowly. So she's a waitress. Why am I disappointed? I lean forward again. "Can you tell me how to get there?"

The man lifts his cane and points down the street. "It's right on the river. Get yourself down on Martin Luther King Boulevard and drive for a while, till you get to Broad. Then make a right. King's is right at the end."

I thank the elderly man and step on the gas.

I sit outside King's for a good ten minutes, trying to work up the nerve to go in. If I weren't sitting here staring right at it, I wouldn't believe you could make a restaurant out of a couple of old train cars. But King's is, in fact, three renovated train cars, each one shinier than the next, all hooked together on a neat, rectangular patch of green grass. A set of steps, flanked with two geranium-filled planters, leads up to the front door. Over the door, in curly, neon-pink letters is the word KING'S. I stare at the green-and-white checked curtains in each of the train windows. One frames a man spooning the inside of a soft-boiled egg into his mouth and gazing out at the river, which slopes quietly around the bend. Why am I hesitating? Nana Pete has just died! Agnes has just called her father, who is coming down as we speak to take her back to Mount Blessing!

Six faces at the front counter turn as I push open the front door. A little bell hanging from the top of it makes a tinkling sound. I shrink back, frightened by the stares. A woman in a pink shirt is behind the counter, rubbing it with a towel. She flicks her eyes at me and keeps rubbing. Her sleeves are rolled up to her elbows and her arms are as big as ham hocks. Despite the ceiling fans, the heat inside is overwhelming and the salty smell of bacon frying fills my nostrils. I take a few tentative steps forward. My sneakers make a peeling sound across the black-and-white floor.

"Hey, hon," the big-armed woman says. I jump a little at the sound of her voice. It's deep and oily. "You here for Lillian?"

I look at her curiously. She has a faint mustache over her top lip and her forehead is shiny with perspiration. "How'd you know?" I ask.

"Look just like her," she says. "You a niece or something?"

My heart does a somersault. The men at the counter turn around again to look at me. I drop my eyes and step on the rubber toe of my sneakers. "Um . . . uh . . . well, do you know if she's here?"

"Of course she's *here*," the woman says, rubbing the counter again. "She's always here. She owns the place."

I swallow hard, trying not to let my amazement show. "Yeah, I know. I just—"

Just then Lillian charges out of a back room, her eyes riveted on a small black calculator in her right hand.

"Hey, Lil," one of the men says as she rushes past him. "Someone here to see you."

"He'll have to wait," Lillian says, not taking her eyes off the calculator. She is punching one of the buttons furiously and her mouth is drawn into a tight scowl. I take a step backward.

"Willa!" Lillian says, beckoning to the heavyset lady with the rag. "Come here and do these numbers for me, will you? I can't get these two columns to match for the life of me, and I'm about ready to hit something."

Willa ambles over in Lillian's direction and then says something in her ear. Lillian's head snaps up. Our eyes meet and lock over the small room. Her lips part in a little O and her forehead crinkles.

"Honey?" she asks. "How did you get here?"

"You have to come home," I say. "Right now."

Lillian looks at a Coca-Cola clock on the wall above the counter. "I still have four more—"

"Nana Pete is dead," I blurt out.

Lillian's face contorts, as if I have just reached out and smacked her. "What?"

I take a step closer, suddenly aware of the hush that has descended over the room. I can feel two men's eyes on me as I move closer to Lillian and for some reason it feels as though I have to get through them to reach her. "Nana Pete," I say hoarsely. "She . . . died."

Without looking at it, Lillian lays the calculator down carefully on the counter. "What are you talking about?"

I open my mouth and then shut it again helplessly. I know she has heard me. "We . . . you have to come home, Lillian. You just . . . have to . . . come."

She is moving toward me, shaking her head back and forth, as if to stop a ringing in her ears. The only sound left in the room is the whir of the ceiling fans overhead. "Honey," she says, slowly moving toward me. "Is this some kind of a joke?"

I shake my head and take another step backward.

"What are you telling me? What's going on? How did you even find this place?" Her eyes are scary looking, like Agnes's just before she freaked out on me, and each question that comes out of her mouth grows more and more shrill.

Willa decides just then to intervene, and taking Lillian by the shoulders, leads her firmly out the front door. "C'mon, Lil," I hear her say. "Let's do this outside."

I follow, glad to be rid of the men's heavy glares, and catch the tail end of whatever it is Willa is saying to Lillian: ". . . Is she your niece or something?"

Lillian whirls around just as I stop dead in my tracks. Her eyes rove over my face, searching, it seems, for . . . what? I hold the tip of my tongue between my teeth and bite down hard. *She had laughed to see her hair on me. Saffron red with the same tiny curls just around the ears.*

"No," she says finally, not taking her eyes from mine. "She's not my niece."

"Then who—," Willa starts, but Lillian cuts her off.

"Get in the car, Honey." Her eyes are flashing and for a split second she looks exactly like Nana Pete did when she ordered me into the car in front of the Milk House. "Right now." I slide into the front seat, barely closing the door as Lillian puts the key in the ignition and guns the engine. "You got everything under control here, Willa?" she asks, leaning out the window. Willa nods, clutching her shirt collar at the base of her throat. She looks alarmed. "I'm going to be a while, I think," Lillian says tersely. "I'll call you." She squeals backward out of the lot and then throws the Queen Mary into drive. "Start talking," she orders, looking at me out of the corner of her eye. "And don't stop until you've told me everything."

AGNES

I'm still in my little curled-up position between the toilet and the tub when the door slams downstairs. I lift my head. It feels fuzzy, like it's been stuffed with cotton. Am I dreaming? Has all of this just been one long, horrible dream? There is a pounding of feet on the steps followed by a cry in the next room. "Ma! Oh, Ma!" It's Lillian. Her voice sounds broken, on the edge of cracking down the middle. "Ma! Ma!" It's the saddest voice I have ever heard and I stuff my fist into my mouth so that I won't cry. Then I hear another voice. I strain forward, my heart pounding loudly in my ears.

"Where's Agnes, Benny?" It's Honey. I lean my face against the door and push my knuckles farther into my mouth. She's back. A few seconds later, she is pounding against the door. "Agnes! Come on out. It's me!" But I don't move. Right now, the tiny bathroom feels like the only safe space left in the world.

For a long time, the only sound in the house is Lillian sobbing. It's a terrible sound, like a baby crying, and it makes my heart feel lopsided, as if part of it has been scooped out. After what feels like hours, the sounds of slow movement begin again. Honey comes over to the door once more and begs me to come out, but I tell her to leave me alone.

"Well, will you let Benny in, then?" she pleads. "He's scared, Agnes. For real."

I open the door a crack and let my little brother inside. He rushes toward me and collapses in a heap against my legs. I put my arms around him and hold him tightly, resting my cheek against the top of his head. "It's okay, Benny." I take slow breaths. Mom and Dad will be coming soon. I have to get ready. "It's all going to be okay. I promise." Through the thin walls, I can hear Lillian and Honey speaking in hushed tones. Suddenly Lillian's voice rises.

"Here? They're coming *here*? Now?"

I bite my lip and curl over my little brother until we are both tight as a little ball.

"Agnes? Benedict?" There is a blur of movement as Benny lurches out of my arms and runs out of the bathroom door. I can hear him run down the steps, hear Mom cry out, "Oh, Benedict! Benedict! Oh my God, how are you? How's your hand? Let me see your hand! Oh my God. Oh, let me look at you!"

"Where is Agnes?" Dad asks. There is a pause as Lillian says something to him, and then the pounding of feet on steps. Through the window, the sky is a dull gray color. I can't even imagine what time it is. I think hours have passed. We must have fallen asleep. I stand up on shaky legs, glancing at my reflection in the mirror as I do.

It's the strangest thing. For the life of me, I don't know who the girl staring back at me is. A friend, perhaps? Someone I used to know? I jump as fingers tap the door softly, not taking my eyes off the mirror. The eyes are bigger than any eyes I've seen before. And empty, as if I can see directly through the iris, the pupil, the cornea, all the way back into nothing at all. There is another tap at the door.

"Agnes?"

"I'm not ready." I watch my mouth move. Did I just say that?

"Agnes? It's Mom. Please, honey, come out. We're here. We want to take you home."

Home.

Let me take you somewhere safe, darlin'. A place where no one will ever hurt you like that again.

"Agnes?" It's Dad again. His voice isn't as gentle as Mom's. "Come on out now. It's just us. Come on."

Just us. He means no Emmanuel or Veronica. The eyes in the mirror get wider. Had they considered coming? What would I do if they were actually standing out there now, waiting for me to emerge? What would it feel like to hear Emmanuel's voice coming through the door? Or Veronica's?

"Agnes." Mom again. "I know it's been an incredibly stressful few days. I can't even imagine what you've all been through. But please come out and talk to us about it. Let us help you."

Let us help you until we get back to Mount Blessing. Then you'll be Emmanuel's problem.

"I'm not ready," the mouth says again. Dad sighs exasperatedly. Mom is talking to him in a low voice. They walk away from the door, probably going over to stand by Nana Pete in the bedroom next door.

"Mother," I hear Dad say in a low voice. There is the

squeak of bedsprings as he sits down. "Oh, Ma." His voice collapses into his throat.

My eyes jerk at the sound, as if awakening suddenly. It's the first time I've ever heard Dad's voice waver. I blink a few times. A shudder ripples involuntarily through me, and the tips of my fingers tingle. I watch the eyes in the mirror shrink down to their regular size. They're still empty, but I recognize them now as mine. I reach out for the bathroom doorknob and close my fingers around it. It's cold, like a ball of ice. I turn it slowly and open the door, following the sound of my father's fractured voice.

"Agnes," Mom whispers as I come into view. She is sitting on the opposite side of the bed, holding Benny on her lap. Dad looks at me, smearing the tears away from his face with the heels of his hands. I walk over between them as they hold their arms out and pull me in tightly. Above me, Benny sniffles into my hair.

"Let's go home," Dad says.

Home.

I close my eyes and nod, holding on to Benny's foot for dear life.

There is a female police officer standing in the hallway outside Lillian's bedroom when we emerge. She is talking to a short, fat man with a tweed cap on his head. He tips the hat in Dad's direction and sticks out his hand.

"I'm the Chatham County coroner," he says in a syrupy drawl. "If you're ready, I'll perform my examination." Dad nods somberly and adjusts the belt cord around his robe. "It won't take long," the man says, glancing over at Mom and

Benny, who are still in the room. "Why don't y'all just wait downstairs? I'll come down when I'm finished."

For some reason, Benny has a problem with this. When Mom takes his hand and leads him away from the bed, he pulls back and starts squealing. "Unnhh! Unnhh!"

Mom looks alarmed. "What is it, Benedict?"

He shakes his head and points his finger at Nana Pete. "Unnhh!" The coroner takes his hat off and places it on the sheet next to Nana Pete's feet.

"Please," he says. "I can't get started unless he is out of the room."

Without a word, Dad reaches over, scoops Benedict up, and carries him out of the room. Mom and I follow him down the steps. Lillian and Honey are sitting as still as statues on the yellow couch in the living room. Mr. Pibbs is curled up next to Lillian, sound asleep. Benny's *unhh* noises get fainter and fainter until, as the two of them disappear out the front door, I can barely hear them at all anymore. A faint terror, like a spider, crawls along the inside of my chest.

"He's having a hard time with this," the policewoman says, looking at me. I don't know if it's a statement or a question, and so I don't answer her. Mom puts her hand on top of my head.

"They both are," she says softly. "She was their grandmother. They loved her very much." Mom's hand feels like a rock. I step out from under it and walk away from her, out the front door.

I spot Dad and Benny a few minutes later sitting under the gigantic tree on the far side of the yard. It is very dark now; the air, heavy and warm, feels like a skin. Benny is cradling his injured hand in his lap, rocking it back and forth like a baby. As I get closer, I can hear him humming to himself. It's the odd little tune he started under the blankets in the room, something between a cry and a whine. Dad's legs are pulled up like a tent under his robe and his head is tipped back against the tree trunk. His eyes are closed.

"Stop it, Benedict," I hear him say. His voice is low and tired. I stop walking. Benny keeps humming, not even pausing at the sound of Dad's voice. The hum gets louder, more desperate sounding, as if he has lost something and the world as he knows it depends on it being found right now. Dad exhales sharply and without opening his eyes, grabs Benny's arms. "I said stop it!" he barks.

"Don't you touch him!" The words are out before I know they are mine or even that they are being said. I slap my hand over my mouth as Dad's eyes fly open. Benny stops humming, watching me fearfully. I rush toward my little brother, ignoring Dad's startled gaze, and sandwich myself between him and my father. Putting my arms around him, I guide his head to my chest and hold him there.

"It's okay, Benny. Shh. It's okay." I try not to flinch under Dad's stare three inches away from me. "It's okay, Benny. Just relax." I rock him until I can feel the rigid muscles in his shoulders begin to ease, the familiar drop of his chin against my chest. The humming begins again, but it's his regular hum now, not the frantic desperate sounds from before. Dad watches the two of us for a few minutes without saying a word. Then he brings his hands to his face and draws them down the length of it.

"I wasn't going to hurt him, Agnes." He pauses, waiting for

me to respond, but I don't dare look up. The sound of Benny's humming hovers between us like a tiny, wounded bird.

"Isaac?" Mom's voice comes floating out the front door. "Isaac, where are you? The coroner wants to speak with you!" Dad looks in the direction of Mom's voice and then turns to me. He puts his hand on my knee. I stare at the tiny black hairs sprouting from his knuckles, the curve of his thin gold wedding band on his fourth finger.

"Isaac!"

Dad takes his hand off my knee and stands up slowly. "I'm here, Ruth! I'll be right there." He looks down at the two of us. "You coming?" I shake my head.

"Okay." He crouches down in front of me so his face is level with mine. Something in his knee makes a popping sound. He studies me for a moment. "Okay." He stands back up, still looking down at me, and opens his mouth to say something else. But the words don't come. He shakes his head, turns on his heel, and walks quickly inside the house, back to Nana Pete and Mom and the coroner who will tell him how his mother died last night.

HONEY

I don't know why I'm surprised by Mr. Little's rude treatment of Lillian. I guess considering the circumstances, I thought he would be a little gentler with her, maybe a bit nicer. But he brushes past her the second he arrives and barely gives her a second glance for the next few hours it takes to call the police and the coroner and get everything in line to take Agnes and Benny back to Mount Blessing. Lillian tries a few times to get him talking, but the bastard won't budge. You'd never guess that at one time Lillian used to follow this guy around, worshipping the ground he walked on.

The coroner informs us that Nana Pete died of a massive heart attack.

"She was taking Lisinopril," he says, shaking the white plastic bottle in front of Mr. Little. "This is strong stuff. It's usually prescribed for people with high blood pressure or congestive heart failure. Did she have a prior attack?"

Dad gives him a blank stare and then barely, just barely, flicks his eyes over at Lillian.

"I don't know," Lillian says, getting up slowly from the couch. Her voice is thick with grief. "We'd only just started talking again. I didn't even know she was on medication."

The coroner hands Lillian the bottle of pills and then nods his head. "Well, I guess it doesn't really matter now." There are a few awkward moments of silence as everyone watches the coroner gather his things. He puts his hat back on, grabs his large black bag, and then tilts his head toward Mr. and Mrs. Little, who are standing side by side across the room. "Y'all just come from choir practice?" he asks.

Mr. Little clears his throat and straightens the front of his robe. "No," he says in an icy voice. "We did not."

The coroner looks stumped for a moment and then shrugs. He pulls a piece of paper out of his pocket and gives it to Mr. Little. "Well, I'm truly sorry for your loss," he says, tipping his hat. "That there is the name and phone number of the best funeral director in Chatham County. He'll take care of things for y'all from now on."

Mr. Little nods, but after the coroner leaves, he hands the slip of paper to Lillian. "You'll need this."

Lillian stares at the paper. "Yeah," she says after a minute. "I'll take care of it."

"If that's everything, then," Mr. Little says, "we have a flight to catch." He takes his coat off the back of Lillian's rocking chair, brushing invisible lint off the sleeve.

"You m-mean . . . ," Lillian stammers. "You're going back *now*? You're not going to stay? For the funeral or anything?" She searches his face. "It's *Ma*, Lenny."

"My name is Isaac," Mr. Little says brusquely. "And I have said my good-byes to Mother. I don't need any further sort of pagan burial ritual to put a close to things." He holds out his arms, one for Agnes and one for Benny. Agnes slides her hand into his, avoiding my eyes. "We're going." He stares at me for a minute. "I'm presuming you will refuse if I order you to come with me?"

I nod silently.

Mr. Little raises his eyebrows and then shakes his head. "Fine. You take care of yourself, then. You too, Naomi."

Agnes flinches when he says the name and pulls back a little on her father's hand. "Why . . . why did you just call her Naomi?" she asks. Instead of answering, Mr. Little turns around sharply and walks out of the house, dragging her and Benny with him. Mrs. Little follows, carrying the backpacks, her eyes fixed on the back of Agnes's head. Lillian and I stand in the doorway, watching as they climb into a compact gold car and shut the doors.

Look at me, Agnes, I plead silently. *Grab Benny and run out of the car. Don't go back there.* I know she can feel my eyes on her because as she sits next to the window, she brings a finger up and traces her eyebrow with it. She keeps her hand there, blocking us from view, until Mr. Little starts the car and with a loud, combustible sound, drives away down the street. The last thing I see is the glint of Agnes's golden hair through the glass, shimmering like a forgotten bit of sunlight on a cloudy day. My knees feel as though they will buckle from the strain of standing still.

I turn and look at Lillian. "You. Answer her question." My voice is shaking.

Lillian, who is still staring down the street at the gold car's taillights, startles when I speak. "What? What question?"

"Agnes's question. The one she just asked her father. Why did he call you Naomi?" Lillian's eyes squint into little slits. "I think I already know," I say. "But I want to hear it from you."

Lillian sits down slowly on the front step and runs her fingertips along the top of her forehead. "It . . . it was . . . the name Emmanuel gave me at Mount Blessing. You know, after I had . . . been there a little while and earned my spiritual status . . . or whatever it was they called it."

"That's my mother's name," I say, quelling the urge to sit down next to her. I pull George out of my pocket. "It's the only thing I know about her except for this." I hold George in my fingertips, waiting for Lillian to turn around.

She does, but slowly, as if she is afraid of what she will find. When she sees George, her whole face falls. She gives a little yelp and stands up, pushing her fingers against her mouth. "My God." Her voice is choked tight. When she blinks, tears fall in a liquid path down her cheeks. "Oh my God, Honey. You still have it."

"What does it mean?" I ask. "Why would you leave something like *this* behind?"

Lillian shakes her head. "It doesn't mean . . . It was just . . . something Ma gave me . . . when I was younger."

"Why? Because you liked cats?"

She shakes her head. "No. Because I used to be afraid of the dark."

I reach out and steady myself against the iron railing. "You were?"

She nods. "Terribly. I used to check my closet every night and have to sleep with the light on. Even when I was a teenager. Then Ma came home one day with the little cat and told me that if I kept him under my pillow, my fear of the dark would disappear."

"And did it?"

She smiles the tiniest bit. "A little. But I still check the closet at night before I go to bed."

I want to grab her so hard it aches. But I don't. I keep my fingers wrapped tightly around George and hope that she can't hear my heart thumping against my chest. "Well," I say, holding

George out in her direction. "You can have him back now. He never did anything like that for me."

Except for a vein that throbs in her forehead, Lillian doesn't move.

I shove him at her. Hard. "You know, what the hell is a ceramic animal gonna do for a kid whose mother has run off and left her behind at some commune?"

Lillian's nostrils flare. Her fingertips press white against her face.

"Take him!" I shout, pushing George against the back of her hand. "And answer me!"

She takes George from me with shaking hands. "Honey . . ." Her voice trails off.

"And tell me the truth!" I scream. "For once, I'd like someone to tell me the goddamned truth!"

She pushes me inside, through the door, and leads me over to the couch.

"There is no need to scream," she says. "And no need to use that kind of language, either."

"Then *tell* me!" I grab my braids with my hands. I feel like I could pull both of them out by roots and I wouldn't feel a thing. "Just tell me why you left! Tell me why you went away and forgot to take me with you." I can tell by the expression on her face that each of my words is like a knife in her heart, but I don't care.

"I didn't forget," she whispers. "I've never forgotten, Honey."

"Oh yeah? You coulda fooled me." I fold my arms over my chest and sit back hard. "I don't know you from a stranger on the street."

"But you will," she says quickly. "I mean, you can. Now." She looks at the top of the steps across the room. "You know, the last thing Ma did with her life was bring you back to me."

I tighten my arms against my chest. "You're gonna have to start from the beginning, *Lillian*. I don't have the faintest idea—"

"She was never allowed to reveal herself to you. It was Leonard's biggest rule. If she wanted to visit you and Agnes and Benny at the commune—and she did, desperately—she had to promise him that she would never tell you the truth."

"But *why?*"

Lillian looks down at the floor and bites the inside of her cheek. "I think it was Leonard's way of just erasing me—from his life and yours. You know, when I first came to Mount Blessing, I was a big hit." She laughs, a weird, strangling kind of sound. "After Emmanuel found out that I could play classical violin, I sort of became this . . . this little star of his. He waived all the rules and made me part of his inner circle right away—something that usually took years. Leonard said it was because he respected my talent. He knew how hard it was to learn how to play like that." She takes a deep breath. "And Leonard was just . . . over the moon about it. He was so proud that Emmanuel had taken me in and changed my name and included me in everything. You know, it was like a reflection of him or something." She draws a finger along the bridge of her nose. "But there was one person who wasn't very happy about it."

"Veronica," I say instantly.

Lillian nods. "Yes, Veronica. I don't know if it was a jealousy thing or what. But she didn't like the fact that

Emmanuel thought I was talented. Or that he was showing me attention. I didn't realize it at first, because she just never talked when I was around. But then one day when I was playing for the two of them, I caught a glimpse of her over my violin bow. She had this awful scowl on her face and her eyes were just blazing. I got this feeling in the pit of my stomach, like she was biding her time when it came to me, just waiting to pounce."

"And did she?" I ask.

"Well, you know, the whole reason I came to Mount Blessing in the first place was because I had just found out I was pregnant. I was in my senior year of high school and while Ma and I got along okay, I didn't want her to find out. She had big plans for me, you know? Wanted me to go to college, get my degree in architecture . . . Anyway, Leonard was calling me regularly by then, telling me that I should drive out to Connecticut to visit him and meet everyone at Mount Blessing. I always stalled and made excuses why I couldn't go because, frankly, the whole idea of a commune sort of weirded me out. But all that changed when I found out I was pregnant. I figured it was my way out of having to tell Ma, or by the time I did, it would be too late for her to do anything about it. So I came to Mount Blessing. I was only two months pregnant, so it took a while before I began to show. After a while, of course, my belly started to pop out. I tried my best to hide it, especially since Emmanuel was calling me in at least four or five times a week by then to play for him. I wore those horrible blue robes for days at a time and tried to take as few showers as possible, in case anyone saw me. But pretty soon it just became impossible to hide. When Leonard found out the truth, he went ballistic. And then, a month before I gave birth, Veronica found out."

I am holding my bottom lip so tightly between my teeth that it feels numb.

"It was just what she needed. She went straight to Emmanuel and told him."

"And?" I ask, releasing my lip.

"It was as if I or my violin had never entered his life," Lillian says softly. "He referred to me from then on as the harlot."

My mouth tastes hot inside. "Harlot?" I repeat.

"Yes," Lillian says. "And a few days after I had you, Leonard came into my room and said that I had to leave. Apparently Veronica had told Emmanuel that she wouldn't tolerate my presence any longer, that I was an insult to the rest of the female Believers who were trying to live pure lives."

I want to cry, scream, bite, kick, spit. I don't know if I have ever hated anyone more than I hate Veronica right now.

"But that still doesn't explain why you didn't take me with you," I press.

"I should have," Lillian says. "I know that now. But Leonard convinced me to let you stay. Veronica had told him that harlots didn't deserve to be mothers."

I snort. "Ha! She should talk!"

Lillian nods sadly. "I didn't want to do it. I told him no at first, that I couldn't bear to leave you. But he promised me that he would look after you, that you would grow up in a comfortable, loving environment, and that your cousin Agnes, who had been born only a few weeks earlier, would become your soul mate."

"But he didn't!" I scream, leaping up from the couch. "He

never looked after me! Agnes and I never knew we were related or that—" My voice breaks, thinking of it. "Or that Nana Pete was mine, too."

"I was a fool to believe him," Lillian says, searching my face. "I thought I was doing the right thing, but you were my responsibility, Honey, and I failed you."

"You're damn right you did," I say bitterly. "Why didn't you at least come to visit? Like Nana Pete did? Even if you weren't allowed to say who you were?"

Lillian shakes her head. "I wasn't allowed anywhere on the grounds. Emmanuel forbade it. And after I left Mount Blessing, I had a terrible time of it. I never touched the violin again. Ma and I lost contact and I began to drift around, in and out of work, struggling to get by. I was just massively depressed. I didn't want to . . ." Her voice drops to a whisper. "You know, go on anymore. I just didn't see a way out."

I have no time for her sob stories. "Well, you're obviously still here."

"Yes," Lillian whispers. "And the thing that kept me going was all those pictures Ma took of you every summer and mailed to me at whatever address I was living at at the time. Then last year we started talking again, trying to rebuild things between us. Ma bought that restaurant for me so I could start over, and then, just a few days ago, everything happened with you telling Ma about that horrible room . . ."

"The Regulation Room," I say. "Did you ever see it when you lived there?"

Lillian shakes her head. "No," she whispers. "He liked me at first, remember? And then . . . well, I guess there was no need for it later. I was as good as dead to him."

"I hope I'm dead to him," I say, and I mean it with my whole heart.

The room is silent except for the sound of Mr. Pibbs padding over the floor. I sit up suddenly as a cold dread, like a hand, wraps itself around my throat.

"We have to go back," I say, standing up. "Right now. Agnes and Benny will never make it at Mount Blessing without us."

"Now?" Lillian asks.

"Yes," I say firmly. "Right now. We can't waste another minute."

AGNES

Thirty thousand feet below me, the world looks like a patch-work quilt. I press my forehead against the smooth bit of window next to me and stare at the different squares of green, the rectangular fields of gold, teardrop-shaped swimming pools, and narrow rivulets of water, which, even from this distance, I know are moving. A strange sensation builds inside of me as I peer at the miniature topography below. I don't know what it is at first, maybe fear, maybe trepidation, maybe just anxiety. I reach around, pulling my shirt up a little to remove my book before I realize it's not there. Panic fills me like water. Where is it? Suddenly I remember throwing it across the bathroom floor in Lillian's house. How could I have forgotten to go back and get it before we left?

The plane dips to the right suddenly, turning in a wide arc, and my stomach falls with it. I close my eyes and bite my tongue, trying to push the photograph of Dad and Lillian out of my mind's eye. Why did he call her Naomi just before we left? It will be a two-hour flight back to Newark Airport in New Jersey. Dad says that someone from Mount Blessing will be waiting there to pick us up for the two-hour ride back. I wonder if my heart will survive the distance.

I glance down the row we are seated in. Dad is on the edge, his feet sprawled in the aisle. His chin is propped against his hand and he is staring pointedly at the seat in front of him, lost in thought. Mom is next, her head on Dad's shoulder, small hands loose and open in her lap.

I look over at Benny, who is sitting cross-legged in his seat, although Mom has already told him twice that he can't sit that way. He has taken his seat belt off and is fiddling with his shoelace. He's also rocking back and forth. But at least he's not humming.

I nudge him a little with my elbow.

"Hey," I whisper, jerking my head toward the window. "You wanna see something?"

He closes his eyes and shakes his head.

"You don't? It's kind of amazing. Come on, get up here on my lap and you can look."

Benny doesn't move.

"You might not be able to see it again, if you don't."

His finger stops twirling his shoelace as he glances over at the window. I can see the fear in his eyes, behind his glasses. I put my arm around his shoulder. "Come on, Benny. Right here. Right on my lap. Come and look."

He crawls over slowly, peering out the tiny window with a rigid expression on his face.

I point with my finger. "See over there? That tiny little blue circle? That's someone's pool." I grin as Benny's eyes widen. "I know! It's so tiny, right? Can you believe it? It looks like a pin!" He nods. "And look over there. See that dark little winding thing? The one that goes up and down, all over? I think that's a train track. Like a real train would run on." Benny nods, his face getting pink. "Look over there, at those little red dots. I'm pretty sure those are barns. Just like the horse barn at Mount Blessing."

But Benny's face darkens at the mention of Mount Blessing. He crawls back off my lap and rearranges his legs so they are crossed over each other again.

I watch as he starts to rock back and forth, fiddling once more with his shoelace. Leaning my head against the window, I fight back tears. God, I miss her. Oh my God, it's been only three hours and I miss her. A tear rolls down the side of my face and I lift my hand to wipe it.

But Benny reaches out as I do and pulls my hand into his. Without looking at me, he lifts up the armrest between us, scooches himself down against my thigh, and curls around it like a little squirrel.

At the airport, I spot the midnight blue Honda Accord with the sunroof on top and the orange rust stains along the edge of the front wheels, and something settles a little in my stomach. I've never been inside Claudia's car before, but I've seen it a hundred times parked alongside the Field House. Its familiarity is comforting. Dad gets in the front with Claudia, while Mom arranges herself between Benny and me in the back. The car smells like peanuts and lemon peel. There is a tiny rubber hummingbird hanging down from the rearview mirror. It swings gently from side to side as the car begins to move.

Dad talks the entire time about getting back to work at the mattress place, what he had to tell his boss about the time off he took, and the possible sales he missed during his absence. He's worried about not making his monthly quota. Claudia listens next to him, her jaw clenched so tightly I wonder if she will crack her teeth. I reach down and unzip the front pocket of my book bag, looking for the pink barrette. I just want to hold it. But my fingers come into contact with something else, something flat. I pull out the Polaroids as carefully as I can, staring at the pictures of Honey's lacerated back with horror. Where did these come from? And how did they find their way into my bag? Did she do this? Is this how she wants me to remember her? Mom turns her head, glancing in my direction, and I hide the pictures as quickly as I can under my leg, away from her prying eyes.

Claudia cuts Dad off midsentence suddenly, looking at me in the rearview mirror. "How's Benny's hand, Agnes?"

Mom shifts uncomfortably in her seat and looks over at me. Dad frowns at Claudia and then gives me a look.

"Oh, it's great," he answers for me. "I checked it out just a little while ago." He gives a short, harsh laugh. "I can't tell anymore which is Emmanuel's work and what they did in the hospital, but it looks pretty good, I'll tell you that."

I fold my hands in my lap. "Actually, they had to undo everything Emmanuel did," I hear myself saying slowly. "I talked to the surgeon. He said Emmanuel butchered Benny's hand. And that there was no miracle. None at all."

The silence in the car is so loud that I am aware of the whoosh of tires coming from a car twenty feet behind us. Then Dad smiles, one of his bright, quick smiles that makes me cringe inside. Fear flickers in his eyes.

"Of course he said that. He's not a Believer, Agnes! Non-Believers can't see miracles, even when they're staring at them in the face. You know that."

I look down. Close my eyes. Wait for the voices battling inside my head to stop:

But I asked him! I asked Dr. Pannetta. Twice! Right to his face! And he's gone to medical school. He knows. He must know! He fixed Benny up right.

Did he? Or was he already healed? There are many temptations out in the real world, which, if I embrace them, will cause my faith to weaken and then disintegrate. Was Dr. Pannetta a temptation, trying to turn me away from all I believe in?

What do you believe in?

I don't know.

Yes, you do.

No. I don't.

"Agnes?" It's Dad. I raise my face to look at him. His face is shiny, practically glowing with my anticipated response.

"Why did you call your sister Naomi?" I ask.

Dad's fake smile fades against the dark interior of the car. Next to me, Mom freezes.

"Naomi?" Claudia says. "Now, that's a name I haven't heard in a while. You're talking about Lillian, right?"

Frightened, I try to hold Dad's gaze. But his eyes are cutting through me. "I don't know," I croak out. "I think so."

"Yeah," Claudia says, unaware that Dad's breathing has become rapid and shallow. "I remember her." She glances over at Dad. "How's she doing, anyway? She still play the violin?"

Dad turns toward Claudia. "You mind your own business, Claudia," he says in a terrible voice. He points a finger at me. "And *you* are not to utter another word until I permit it." There is a pause. "Do you understand me, Agnes?" Something in me folds in on itself, like a pair of wings closing. I nod, silent and obedient. It's what Saint Agnes would do.

Dad sits forward anxiously as flashing red and blue lights slice through the darkness at the top of the hill in front of the Great House.

"It's the police," he whispers. "Why in God's name are they here?"

"What do you think it is, Isaac?" Mom asks. "Do you think it has anything to do with us?"

Dad looks at her sharply. "Of course not. How could . . . ," his voice trails off. "Unless Naomi . . ." His face pales. "Oh my God." By now Claudia has parked the car behind the Great House, along with all the other cars. Dad pushes open the door and disappears around the front of the house.

"Well," Mom says, putting her arms around me. "We're home." She gives me a tight smile. "Let's go."

My knees feel like Jell-O standing in front of the Great Door again. Benny makes a whimpering sound and buries his face in the side of Mom's leg.

"He's scared," I say, stepping forward. "It reminds him of . . ." But Mom only picks him up silently and walks through the door.

Although all two hundred and sixty Believers are present in the large room, it feels like a tomb inside. Dressed in their blue robes, some of them are kneeling in front of the crucifix on the wall, silently mouthing desperate prayers. Christine is among them, but she is just staring at a point on the wall next to the crucifix. She is not praying. Her face is pasty, her lips trembling. Dad is already in one of the far corners, whispering with Amanda Woodward's father. Everyone else is sitting at one of the long tables, staring ahead, not saying a word. Mr. Murphy lifts his head as we walk back into the room, but gives no expression of recognition. Iris is sitting next to him, swinging her feet under the bench. Mom pulls a clean blue robe over Benny's head and then hands me one. I slide into it carefully and tie the cord.

"What's going on, Samuel?" she whispers.

Mr. Murphy looks scared and tired. "Some kind of police investigation," he says.

Mom's face darkens. "Why? Who made allegations?"

Mr. Murphy shrugs. "No one knows. The police drove up here out of nowhere, just about an hour ago."

Mom takes a deep breath and then closes her eyes. "We must pray." Taking my hand, she begins to chant in Latin. Mr. Murphy joins her. I stay silent, staring first at Benny and then at Iris, who are looking at each other across the table.

"Are you okay?" Iris mouths.

Benny nods.

"Does your hand hurt?"

He shakes his head from side to side.

"I'm glad you're back."

Benny smiles sadly at her.

I look at my brother, really look at him, for maybe the first time. What is he trying to say? What does he need to tell me? Why won't he talk?

Dad comes over then and sits down with his back to me.

He stares grimly at my mother. "No one seems to know any-thing just yet," he says in a low voice. "We'll just have to wait and see."

Just then something bounces off my arm. I look up. Winky is sitting two tables over, waiting for me to look at him. He points toward the Great Door. "I have to tell you something," he mouths.

I sit back a little in alarm. Aside from when I came to get Honey from his garden, Winky has never said more than "hello" and "good-bye" to me. He scares me a little, if you want to know the truth. I don't like looking straight at his face.

"Please." His lips form the word carefully.

I look over at Mom and Dad. They are still deep in con-versation.

Winky is waiting for me outside the restroom when I get there.

"Honey's not with us," I whisper. "She stayed behind in . . ."

He shakes his head and pushes a piece of paper in my hands. As I open it and see Honey's handwriting, my hands start to shake.

> Dear Winky:
> Please don't be mad at me. Nana Pete and Agnes and Benny and me are all running away. Bad things have been happening to us. Emmanuel has a secret room called the Regulation Room that he takes us to and beats us with belts in. I have marks on my back to prove it. Nana Pete found out about the room and she

is taking us away from this horrible place. I think
we are going to Texas, but we haven't really worked
everything out yet, so I will let you know when we get
there.

There is one thing I need you to do for me. I
think there may be a slight possibility that Agnes will
come back. Even if I don't come with her. I don't have
any proof; it's just a gut feeling. And if she comes
back, Emmanuel will make her and Benny pay in a way
that I can't even let myself think about. I'm afraid he
will hurt them terribly. So please, if you find out that
Agnes is returning, please call the police and tell
them what I have told you. Tell them about the room.
Tell them that all of the kids here are being hurt.
Please, Winky. If I can't save Agnes, please help me
do it for her.

All my love,
Honey

P.S. I'm sorry I was too chicken to say good-bye to you
myself. But I know I will see you again and when I do,
I will be able to do it the right way.

"It was you who called the police when you found out we
were coming back?" I ask when my voice finally returns.

Winky nods.

"And you . . . you told them about the Regulation
Room? And everything Honey said?"

Winky nods again, more vigorously. "They already talked

to me," he whispers hoarsely. "But I didn't show them the note yet. I figured you'd want to see it first. I told them you would know more. When they find out you're back, they're gonna talk to you, too." He nods toward the back of the Great House. "They're in there now, poking round that Regulation Room." He takes a step toward me. "Please, Agnes. I didn't know anything about that room. I swear on God Almighty. I never seen it. Not once. And Honey never told me nothing all these years."

It's as if a hand shoves me forward, right into Winky's heavy arms. And even though it's the closest I've ever been to him and I'm scared to touch him, I hold him tight around the waist. He smells like sun-warmed starch and wet dirt, just like Honey used to after working in the garden all day.

Two policemen, one tall and thin, the other round and chubby, walk out of Emmanuel's room just as I return from talking to Winky. Emmanuel and Veronica are behind them, following closely at their heels. Emmanuel's bearded chin is jutting out over the collar of his robe and Veronica keeps clasping and unclasping her hands, which, for some reason, are red and bleeding. Both of them look as if they are on their way to a funeral. The policemen, too, seem grave. The chubby one is studying the front page of a tiny notebook in his hand, while the tall one is scanning the crowd.

"We need to talk to the children," the tall one says finally, facing us in the middle of the room and hooking his thumbs behind one of his belt loops. "Just the children. No one else."

There is a rush of whispers among the adults, as the children look up at their parents fearfully. Benny slides closer to Mom. Dad is glowering at the tall policeman. No one moves.

"*Now*, please," the policeman says. "Children only."

Still no movement.

Emmanuel takes a step forward. "It's all right," he says. His arms are lifted high above us, as if he is going to start preaching, but his voice sounds weird, like it is rupturing around the edges. "Let all the children come forward. Have faith and do not be afraid."

Little by little, kids of all ages step away from their parents, some by themselves, others holding their brothers' or sisters' hands. At the front of the pack is Iris Murphy, standing alone, her little arms folded across her chest.

I glance over at Benny, who is still sitting close to Mom. Then I see Dad, who is staring at me in a way I've never seen him stare at anything before. It's even worse than the stare in the car, like actual heat is radiating out from behind his eyes, pulsing in waves throughout the air between us.

I lean down nervously toward Benny. "I think we have to go, Benny. Come on. It'll be okay. I'll stay right next to you the whole time." Mom glances worriedly at me as she helps Benny off the bench. I take his hand in mine and lead him toward the group of children, pretending not to feel Dad's white-hot gaze in the middle of my back.

"Remember, children!" Emmanuel's voice echoes in my ears. "Remember we are Believers."

The two policemen lead the sixty or so children, including Benny and me, into a side room near the front of the Great House. I don't recognize the room, since I have never been in it before. It is sparsely furnished, with a wooden desk on one side, a single bed on another, and a white, knotted throw rug in the middle. A large cross hangs above the bed.

"Sit anywhere," the chubby policeman says, surveying the lot of us. "Get comfortable. We're just going to talk."

Iris Murphy and a few other little girls scramble on top of the bed. Amanda Woodward settles herself down in the desk chair. Peter stands against the wall, his arms crossed against his chest. The rest of us sit cross-legged on the floor. No one speaks.

"Okay, then," the tall policeman says. He is standing in front of the room, his legs askance. For some reason, he looks familiar. A small silver bar pinned to the breast pocket of his navy shirt reads CAPTAIN MARANTINO. Could this be the same police officer who came a few years ago? "We just want to ask you guys some questions, okay?" Silence. He clears his throat. "How many of you have ever heard of something called the Regulation Room?"

Benny buries his face in the side of my arm at the mention of the room, but no one else moves. Not a hand raised, not a word spoken. I look over at Iris. She is picking a scab on the front of her knee. Peter has turned his head in the opposite direction.

"No one here has ever been inside something called the Regulation Room?" the policeman presses. "Not even once?" Silence. He shoots a sidelong glance at the other policeman, who raises his eyebrows, rocks back on his heels, and then clears his throat.

"Okay, why don't we start from the beginning? How many of you like living here?"

A small forest of hands rises up from the group of us.

Captain Marantino nods approvingly. "Anybody *not* like living here?"

Iris's hand shoots up.

Captain Marantino pounces. "And what's your name?" he asks.

But Iris bows her head, absorbed once again with the scab on her knee.

"Sweetheart?" he asks again. "Can you tell me your name?"

Iris shakes her head.

"Why not?" the chubby policeman barges in. "Are you scared of something?" Silence. I know exactly what Iris is scared of. "You know, we can help you if someone here is hurting you," the policeman pushes. "We can make it stop. We can make sure it never happens again."

All I have to do is stand up. Take out the Polaroids in my back pocket. My neck feels tight. What should I *do*? I look at the crucifix on the wall—will it tell me anything? Will I get a sign, a hint of some sort? The blue uniform in front of the room is starting to blur. My nose begins to wiggle as I think about the preacher in the church in Greenville.

All we have to do is ask. Lord, here I am. Show me the way.

Was it any safer out there? With the red and orange foods and the awful songs on the radio and the vanity-promoting hair products? All temptations to sin, to blacken the soul, permanently erase any chances of ever becoming a saint. But what about the word on Honey's bruised back, the belt marks on mine? What does it mean that Honey is my first cousin— and I have never known it until only a few moments ago?

And why, if the world is so evil, as Emmanuel is constantly telling us, did it provide me in the past few days with the first sure footings of safety, something I have never felt—not once—in all my years at Mount Blessing? How else to explain the strange happiness I felt after leaving that church service, or the terrible security I felt locked in Lillian's bathroom? How could a world so evil have such a beautiful statue of the Blessed Virgin in the mountain? Or let people cry and shout out in church?

A tug on my shirt tears me away from my swirling thoughts. Benny is staring up at me. "Tell them, Agnes," he says.

I look at him dumbly, shocked at the sound of his voice after all this time. "Benny," I whisper.

He pushes himself closer against my arm. "Please." His voice, soft and urgent, throbs in my ears. "Please tell them."

The Lord knows, the woman in that church had said, *we have things inside we can't keep quiet about . . . Sometimes, the longer the silence, the louder the shout.*

The story of Saint Agnes races through my head for maybe the hundredth time. She was just about my age when she stood up in front of the emperor of Rome and told him that she would not believe in his pagan gods. I have always, I realize suddenly, imagined myself doing the same thing, for God, and for Emmanuel, who in some inextricable way, have become the same thing. It has never occurred to me until this very moment that perhaps they are separate, that maybe the God I want to stand up for is not the one Emmanuel represents. Maybe Emmanuel is the pagan god. Would the real God send children to hell if we messed up on that road he keeps asking us to travel? Would the real God have a Regulation Room?

Have you ever tried to trust yourself to do the right thing? Instead of always waiting for some sign or trying to figure out what Emmanuel thinks is right for you?

My sign is right in front of me. All I have to do is open my eyes.

Slowly, on trembling legs, I stand up.

HONEY

After making sure that Nana Pete is safe at the Jackson & Sons Funeral Home, Lillian and I get into the Queen Mary and drive all night and most of the next day to get back to Mount Blessing. It takes me a while to convince her to let me get behind the wheel, but her exhaustion from working all night at King's finally takes over and she gives in—especially when I remind her Nana Pete let me drive on the way down. She sleeps soundly in the front seat, her head slumped down against her chest.

For a while I'm pissed that she's sleeping. I mean, I haven't seen the woman in fourteen years and now that we're alone in the car together with a fourteen-hour trip ahead of us, she conks out? But when I calm down, I realize that I'm actually kind of glad she's asleep. I mean, I don't even know where to start to *feel* when it comes to the fact that I am actually sitting next to her. Shock and happiness and rage and fury are all balled up into this gigantic . . . thing inside my chest. Mostly it just feels unreal. I keep looking over, as if maybe she is simply a mirage and when I get close enough, she will vanish into thin air. But she doesn't. For hours, little whistling sounds blow in and out of her nose, and her hands lie limp as sleeping kittens in her lap. Every time a car passes, its headlights flood her profile with a brief, sweeping light, making her hair look like an electric halo around her face.

I wonder if I will ever feel any love for her—now, or later, after some time passes. But I guess I shouldn't worry about that. The real question is if I am ever going to trust her after everything that has happened. Mr. and Mrs. Little did a horrible thing, keeping the truth about my mother from me all these years—but then, so did Lillian. Her explanation for it made sense, and a part of me feels bad for her, having to go through all that rejection from her own brother and then Emmanuel. But I was her baby. I *am* her baby. And I should have come first. Before either of them. How do we get past the fact that I didn't? That she listened to two men who told her she wasn't good enough instead of her own heart? And then, just as I'm starting to feel really lousy about the whole deal, I remember one of the last things Nana Pete said to Agnes and me:

We've got to stay on the same team if we want to make it, okay?

Maybe all I've got to do, at least for now, is just try to stay on the same team. Slowly, I reach out and slide my hand inside Lillian's. It is warm and soft.

As we pass Raleigh, I try to quell the anxiousness rising inside. Have things already been put into motion at Mount Blessing? Could Winky have possibly come through for me? Or have Agnes and Benny been snatched from Mr. and Mrs. Little upon their return and sent to Emmanuel's room? I get a shooting pain in the front of my head when I think of the latter. Emmanuel will destroy Agnes completely if he gets his claws into her one last time. And there's no telling what will become of Benny. I glance in the rearview mirror at the empty highway behind me and step down hard on the gas.

Lillian wakes up just outside of Baltimore as the sun is

coming up. She rubs her eyes and stretches and then looks over at me. I turn the radio, which I have been listening to for the past six hours, down low.

"God, how long have I been asleep?" she asks.

"Five hours. Give or take."

"*Five* hours?" she repeats. "Are you okay? Why didn't you wake me?"

I shrug. "I'm fine. I'm a pretty good driver."

Lillian rubs her eyes again. "I guess you are. Geez, Louise! I can't believe you drove all that way without stopping!" She peers out the window. "And you know where you are?"

"I've just been following signs for 95 North," I say.

Lillian shakes her head. "Amazing."

"You hungry?" I ask.

Lillian rolls her eyes and pats her belly.

"Yeah. But I'm always hungry. *Always*. Ma used to say I had a tapeworm in my belly." I smile when she says that. "Pull over at that Burger King," Lillian says, pointing to a sign. "We'll get something to eat and I'll drive the rest of the way."

We order the works at the Burger King drive-through: French Toast Sticks, two Croissan'wiches with eggs and ham, Cheesy Tots, hash browns, a large coffee for Lillian, and two orange juices for me. Lillian eats with one hand, steering the car with the other, and takes big bites without pausing for breath. She slurps her coffee, even though it is scalding hot, and sighs after the first sip.

"I miss Ma already," she says in a quavering voice. I stare out the window at a green sign that says WASHINGTON, D.C. 25 MILES. In a little while, we will be back at Mount Blessing, hopefully to get Agnes and Benny out of there for good. But going back there without Nana Pete suddenly feels ominous, like going into battle without any armor.

"I still can't believe she's gone," I say.

"How was she on the trip?" Lillian asks, taking another gulp of coffee.

"What do you mean?"

"The only road trip I ever took with her was just that short drive from Raleigh down to Atlanta. You got her for two whole days on the road. What was it like? Did she drive fast? Did she stop a lot? Did she tell you stories?"

I tell Lillian everything, starting at the very beginning with Nana Pete throwing us all into the Queen Mary and tearing out of Mount Blessing as if our shoes were on fire. Then the McDonald's and Wal-Mart stops, the motel, me driving, her exhaustion, the discussions about God, Agnes's waist string, and the pink barrette. To my surprise, I wind up talking for over an hour. My voice is raspy when I finish, but for some reason, I feel exhilarated. It is the first time since everything began that I realize I feel different. Older, maybe. Quieter.

"She was something," Lillian says softly. "Wasn't she?"

"Yeah," I answer. "She really was."

Five hours later, Lillian pulls on to Sanctity Road. She sits forward, practically on top of the steering wheel, and drives slowly. Tiny beads of sweat have broken out on her forehead. "God," she says, surveying the empty landscape. "This is when I wish I still smoked."

"You used to smoke?" I ask, glancing out the window as the Field House looms into view. There is no one in sight.

"Oh yeah," Lillian answers. "Lots. Ma made me quit last year, after we started spending time together again."

I press myself flat against the side window, straining to see the Milk House, which is next in line. There is no sign of anyone inside. I hold my breath as the car passes the house, waiting for the butterfly garden to appear. It's empty. Where is everyone?

"Cops," Lillian says as we make the turn toward the Great House. "Lots of them."

I count five police cars—blue and white with FAIRFIELD POLICE DEPARTMENT in gold on the sides—parked in front. We are about ten yards from the Great Door when a policewoman steps out from one of the cars. She strides toward us, waving us aside. Lillian rolls down her window.

The woman peers in at both of us. A large mole sits on her cheek like a bug. "You two live here?" she asks.

"No," Lillian answers. "We don't."

The policewoman frowns. "Well, you're not allowed here, then. This is private property."

I lean forward. "Why are the police here?"

"We're conducting an investigation," the woman says vaguely. "But I'm not at liberty to—"

"You *are*?" I yell. Getting out of the car, I slam the door and run around to where she is standing. "Did someone call you guys to come investigate what's been going on with Emmanuel?"

The woman's mouth contorts into a grimace. "Like I said, I'm not at liberty to discuss the details. And I'm afraid you're going to have to . . ."

Lillian gets out of the car. She is a good foot shorter than the policewoman, but she looks her straight in the eye. "We have family here, ma'am. Children. And we need to know what's happening to them."

Behind the policewoman, I catch a glimpse of the Great Door opening. My knees go weak when Winky emerges from behind it. He grins when he sees me and holds out his hand. I run to him, clutching his fingers ferociously and let him pull me into him. He smells like the garden. I am breathing hard, trying not to cry and laugh at the same time. "Winky," I whisper.

He pulls a rough hand down over my braids. "They're all in there," he says hoarsely. "Still getting interviewed or something. Been going on for hours. They're done with me, I think."

"Agnes and Benny, too?" I ask.

Winky nods. "She looks different."

I take a step backward. "Who does?"

"Agnes."

"Different how?"

He shrugs. "Bruised a little. Not so perfect anymore." I hug him again tightly. "Who you with?" he asks softly, nodding toward Lillian. I lead him over to the car, where Lillian is biting her nails and stepping down hard on her other shoe.

"This is Lillian Little," I say. "My mother."

Winky nods slowly. He sticks his hand out and shakes Lillian's gnawed fingers.

"I remember you. Sorta." Lillian swallows hard. Her bottom lip is quavering. "Thank you for being so good to Honey," she finally whispers. "It means the world to me."

Winky smiles.

"Hey, Winky," I say. "Guess what?"

"I can't guess," he says. "After all them questions, my head hurts."

I laugh. "I saw my first Zebra Longwing! Down in Savannah, where Lillian lives. It was beautiful!"

"Yeah?" Winky asks. "Male or female?"

"Female. With great big stripes up and down her wings, just like in the book."

"I'm glad," Winky says, pushing a piece of hair out of my face. "God, I'm glad for you, Honey."

The Great Door groans once more.

"Agnes," Lillian whispers. I step out from behind Winky. Benny is with Agnes, clutching her hand. They both look frightened and exhausted. I take a small step in their direction.

"Ags," I whisper. She raises her face. Her eyes are tired, but blue and fair as a summer day.

"I told the truth," she says. "I had to."

I catch her just before she falls, collapsing against me like a little rag doll. "It's what Saint Agnes would've done," I whisper into her hair. "You know that?"

Her shoulders sag heavily. When she begins to sob, I can feel her ribs move up and down her sides. Benny and I close ourselves around her like a tent and hold her up off the ground.

"I love you, Agnes," Benny says.

His voice, small and clear, rings out above us like a bell.

Agnes

Staring at Benny at the opposite end of the park, with his arms stretched out on either side and the sun glinting off his white hair, it seems impossible that only three months have gone by since we left Mount Blessing. Some nights when I lie in bed and wait for sleep, it feels like three years.

Honey looks at me and shoves her sleeves up past her elbows. "You ready?" I lift my leg, bringing my heel up against my butt. "In a minute."

"Come on!" Benny yells, waving his hands. "My arms are starting to fall asleep!" I smile a little when he says that. It's been a while now since he finally got the bandage around his injured hand taken off and all the stitches removed, but his hand is still stiff. But, the doctor down here in Savannah praised whoever had operated on him, saying that Benny would regain full use of his fingers in no time.

Honey kicks the ground with the toe of her new sneaker and hops from side to side like a boxer getting ready to fight. "These new sneakers might give me some leverage against you," she says, watching me out of the corner of her eye. "Maybe for the first time."

I pull on the toe of my own new sneakers, which Lillian bought us a few weeks ago. They're blue and white, with little swoops on the side. Something called Nike's. Lillian's got a lot of money now, since Nana Pete left her everything in her will. I never knew Nana Pete was so wealthy, but then, I guess there were a lot of things about her I didn't know.

The three of us live with Lillian right now, after a judge in Connecticut said that we couldn't have any contact with Mom and Dad until the trial starts, which is sometime next year. Emmanuel and Veronica are the ones who are really on trial, but Mom and Dad are considered "accessories," which basically means that they didn't do enough to help us when we were being hurt all the time, and so they have to go, too.

I hate thinking about it, but of course I do. All the time. We'd all still be together if I hadn't stood up that day and showed the policeman the pictures of Honey and then lifted my own shirt to show him the marks on my back. Once I did that, all the other kids began to come forward. Pretty soon the police had people from Children's Services Center called in and by the end of that day, sixty-four separate charges of child abuse had been filed against Emmanuel, complete with photographs, documentation, and sworn, signed statements. After the investigation, Mount Blessing was shut down completely.

"Okay," Honey says, placing her fingers on the edge of the grass and kicking her legs out behind her. "This is it, Agnes."

I stare out at my little brother, who is hopping up and down in the sun, still waiting for us to come toward him. Since we moved to Lillian's house, he sleeps next me every night. I don't mind. If you want to know the truth, it actually makes me feel better, too. He keeps a picture of Nana Pete under the pillow and after he falls asleep, I pull it out and tell her good night. And thank you.

Honey was a little freaked out for a while after we moved down here, with no news of Winky or where he ended up. She pestered the pee-willy out of Lillian to find out what had happened to him, and then just a few weeks ago, we found out that Winky and his older brother had reunited and bought a farm in upstate New York. Apparently there's lots of room for a butterfly garden.

Now I bend over and raise my hips to the sky.

Waiting for the trial has been hard, but not nearly as hard as being separated from Mom and Dad. Emmanuel's cruel ways may have been exposed, but my parents are still my parents. And no matter how many mistakes they made, that's not going to change. No matter what. Still, I don't know what I would say if I saw them just now. For as much as I miss them, I also feel betrayed. All those lies about Lillian and Honey and Nana Pete. It just doesn't make any sense, especially since we were all supposed to be trying to live like saints and lying is such a terrible sin. Keeping the fact that Honey and Benny and I are all family hidden from us was just so . . . wrong.

And so maybe the distance between us right now is a good thing. Until I can sort things out, try to make peace with everything that has come between us. Lillian's been trying to help me do just that by having me talk about everything to a therapist. Benny too. Her name is Dr. Tipper and I've been to see her only twice so far, but I think she's going to be okay. She's got a huge fish tank in her office, full of blue and orange fish and she lets me feed them before we start talking. Lillian told me that the courts have also ordered Mom and Dad to see a therapist. She keeps using the word "brain-washed" when she talks about them, which sounds like someone went inside their heads and scrubbed their brains clean. But I guess that's exactly what Emmanuel did to them, making them believe he was so powerful that they couldn't object to anything he said—even if it was wrong. They lost the ability to think for themselves. I hope the therapist they are seeing helps them figure out how to get it back.

"On your mark!" Benny screams. I lift my face to the sun, stare down the length of track we are about to explode upon.

I've even put away *The Saint's Way* for now. I haven't looked at it once since we left. It's not that I've turned my back on saints as a whole; it's just that I personally don't think I fit into their group. I don't want to be Saint Agnes anymore. I just want to be Agnes. Whoever she might be.

"Get set!"

Next to me, Honey tenses. Her red braids hang in front of her shoulders like ropes. She glances quickly at me. "The barrette looks great on you."

I grin and stare straight ahead, trying not to think about the pink flower petals clipped to the top of my ponytail. "Don't try to distract me, goof."

"Go!"

From here, the distance seems long. But as my arms pump up and down and my legs carry me over the soft grass, the space between us gets shorter and shorter until all at once, despite everything, I am there.

ACKNOWLEDGMENTS

I could not have written this book without the support of many people. I am forever grateful to my agent, Jessica Regel, whose faith in me, not to mention her unbelievable persistence, has, in my eyes, set her far above the rest. Thank you to my editors, Melanie Cecka and Elizabeth Schonhorst, whose keen eye for detail and sense of humor helped me create a richer, more sensitive story, and to all the staff at Bloomsbury, whose enthusiasm for my work continues to both awe and humble me. It was my parents who gave me a love of writing, as well as supportive, enthusiastic feedback throughout all my years struggling to get it right, and for that I am forever indebted. Thank you to my dear friend Joe Biondo, who believed in me from the very beginning; Donna and Lou Rader; Judy Plummer; Gina Marsicano; Lynn Chalmers; and Don McMillan, all of whom read early drafts of my work and pushed me to continue. Thank you so much. To my brother, Dr. Samuel Plummer, who helped me with the medical terminology, and P. J. Adonizio, for his specific advice on funeral arrangements. Thank you to my children, who have made my life richer than I could have ever dreamed possible. My husband, Paul, is the one who, with his patience and love, has helped me realize one of my biggest dreams; thank you, love, from the bottom of my heart.

A CONVERSATION
WITH CECILIA GALANTE

The Patron Saint of Butterflies is a work of fiction, but according to your bio it is inspired by personal experience. Can you explain?

My biography states that I was raised in a religious commune, which is indeed true. My parents met, married, and settled down in a religious commune in upstate New York in the late sixties. In 1971, they had me (and seven other children) and for the next fifteen years, we lived within this existence. It was not until 1985, five years after the leader of the commune died, that the last vestiges of the place finally disintegrated.

Soon after, my parents moved our family to Wilkes-Barre, Pennsylvania, where I still live now. Personal experiences aside, however, I think it is safe to say that all writers of fiction draw on some facet of their history. Where else do you start, really? Writing about what you know—or knew—comes the most naturally, or at least it did for me. Being able to draw on things I remember as a kid being raised in a religious commune helped shape this book enormously. But it wasn't the only thing. And it wasn't even the most important thing. The most important thing was getting the characters—who, while figments of my imagination, are still very much their own persons—to matter to the reader. The thing that matters most to me as a writer is to create characters that people will care about long after the last page has been read.

**What made you want to write about this experience in
novel form in the first place, and then specifically for
teens?**

The novel form appealed to me because I think this story
works best as a fast-paced narrative. There needed to be a solid
beginning, middle, and ending. I also wanted to write it as a
novel because I thought it was important to get inside the girls'
heads, to let the reader know what they were thinking—especially during some of the times most fraught with danger
and/or fear. I originally began the book just from Agnes's per-
spective. But about 150 pages into it, I realized (with a sinking
feeling!) that Honey was demanding to be heard as well. She
was practically yelling off the pages! And so I went back to
the beginning and started over.

As far as writing for teens is concerned, I didn't start the
book thinking about a teen audience. I just wrote from these
girls' perspectives, and they just happened to be teens. I'm
thrilled that it has found a YA home and can't wait to hear
what teenagers across the country think about it.

**The terms "religious cult" and "religious commune" are
rife with negative connotations. From your experience,
do you agree? Why? Were there any aspects of that life
that were positive?**

I think when people hear the term "religious cult," they immediately connect it to frightening, apocalyptic events they have
heard on the news, such as David Koresh and Waco, or the
Heaven's Gate members who committed mass suicide waiting
for Halley's Comet. Such drastic, violent movements were not
included in the commune I grew up in, but I will say this: I

think it is safe to say that any time a given number of people turn over their lives to one person, not much good will come out of it.

The single most positive thing that came out of my experience is my family, who have proved, over and over again, that love is stronger than evil. My family is my rock, from my parents to my seven younger siblings. None of what we went through was easy. But getting to where we are now was worth every bit of it.

Given your history, when writing your novel were you careful of whom and what you were depicting so that it would not appear as if you were replicating any facet of your own life, or was that never a concern?

The bottom line is this: I didn't want to write a story about my life. I just wanted to write a good story. I remember a certain time, maybe in my early twenties, when I realized suddenly that my history was rife with possibility. Storytelling possibility, I mean. I spent a good deal of my life feeling ashamed of being so different. (I have yet to meet a person who shares a past similar to mine, although I know they are out there.) My childhood circumstances were unique and it took me a great deal of time to embrace that, instead of trying to hide it from the world. But when I accepted it, when I realized that my history was what, in fact, made me who I am today, it was much easier to start appreciating it for what it was: a really interesting, at times even fascinating, account, instead of something I had to keep a secret. And so I began to write about these interesting, fascinating things. Eventually, they took on a life of their own and as I delved more deeply into it, the characters began to tell me what it was they wanted to do and say, how they wanted to think and feel.

I think when all is said and done, while facets of my own life may have been drawn upon, this story belongs to Agnes and Honey.

Do you consider yourself a religious or a spiritual person? If yes, do you think it is because of or despite your childhood experience?

I had a hard time with religion for a long time after we left the commune. I felt betrayed by God in general and wanted no part of Him—or anything else for that matter. Forget the church. I didn't set foot in one for years. But I was also aware of a deep sadness inside of myself that nothing—not medicine or running or even my beautiful children—could fill. I started reading books with religious themes in them—books like *Looking for Mary* by Beverly Donofrio and Anne Lamott's *Traveling Mercies*—and I began to realize that religion could be a very quiet, personal thing—the opposite of what I had been taught. I wouldn't classify myself as a religious person now, but I will say that the deep sadness that nothing could fill is getting full again.

When assimilating to life off the compound, what was the most difficult adjustment? The easiest?

I think the hardest thing was going to school. I went from a three-room classroom with four other kids in my grade to a public school with hundreds and hundreds of kids. I didn't know anyone. I didn't know what a lunch line or even homework was! And the kids were exceptionally cruel. Word got out about the commune and I was shunned. People don't like outsiders, especially ones they don't understand. It was one of the most difficult times of my life.

The easiest adjustment was the fact that my family remained intact. There were a number of families from the commune who fell apart after it split up. But my parents made a commitment to us to stay together and try to rebuild all the years we had lost. And they did. I don't think I would have had a chance without them.

You now teach high school English and work with kids on a daily basis who are the same age you were when you were adjusting to major cultural and lifestyle changes. What differences and what similarities do you see between your teenage years and your students?
I think the major difference I see between myself at that age and the kids I teach is the maturity levels. Kids know so much now—so soon! The world that they are exposed to on a daily basis is rife with violence and sex and drugs—stuff I wasn't aware of and probably wouldn't have been aware of, even if I hadn't grown up where I did.

As far as similarities go, I think that despite the technological advances and the rising maturity levels, when all is said and done, kids are just human. They are still very vulnerable and desperately in need of love and protection—just as I was. Every once in a while, I will see a kid being teased or bugged at school—and it is no different from the teasing and ribbing I experienced after we moved. As a teacher, I always step in, because I know too well what that kid is feeling. I won't tolerate bullying or rudeness in my classroom. Life is too short to be mean.

Have there been any stories that you'd like to share of people's reactions when they first learned that you did not have a "typical" childhood?

I have one that sticks in my mind, if only for its exclusivity. After we left the commune, I had a very difficult time adjusting. After a while, I fell into a deep depression and went to see a therapist. He was a sweet, gentle man with a manner about him that put me immediately at ease. He took my information down rapidly, jotting down details here and there—but then stopped cold as I mentioned the commune. He crossed his legs and sat back in his chair. "Can you tell me a little bit more about this commune?" I talked for an hour without stopping, all the while dreading his response. He was not the first therapist I had gone to see about growing up in a commune. And I was sure he was not going to be the last one who would stare at me blankly, maybe shake his head in amazement, or even tell me, as one female therapist did, that my situation was "too complex to take on."

When I finished, he closed the file, uncrossed his legs, and leaned forward, resting his elbows on his knees. I held my breath.

"I'll tell you what," he said. "I've never had anyone with this kind of case history. But if you let me figure out how to help you, I'll do my best."

Some people may think that that's an odd reaction, maybe even a weakness, for a therapist to admit that he was unsure how to treat me. But what he said put me immediately at ease. It was the first time a professional had admitted they weren't sure what to do with my situation, but that they would try to figure out how anyway. And I believed him. When I look back now, that day was really the beginning of my healing process.

Agnes and Honey are your two main characters in *The Patron Saint of Butterflies*. Do you see yourself in either girl? If so, in what way?

Agnes and Honey are very much their own persons. I tried to make each girl as different from each other as possible, from their mannerisms to their beliefs to the way they reacted to the outside world. That being said, and to echo an earlier answer, I think there are probably parts of me in both girls. I try very hard to write as accurately as possible. By that, I mean that I try to get down on paper how people talk and act in real life, right down to the smallest details. Still, the person's head I can most easily tap into while doing this is mine. So there are most likely sides of myself in Agnes and in Honey that even I don't realize!

What do you hope people will take away from their reading of *The Patron Saint of Butterflies*?

I think what I said earlier: I hope that my characters are engaging and thoughtful and interesting enough for my readers to care about them. And when all is said and done, it would be great if someone put the book down and said, "What a great story!"

What's your favorite kind of pie?

Peach. But if there are no fruit pies available, I will lick the plate clean of a peanut butter pie.

A Reading Group Guide for
The Patron Saint of Butterflies

1. The book begins with a quote from Czeslaw Milosz, a Polish poet and academic: "In a room where people unanimously maintain a conspiracy of silence, one word of truth sounds like a pistol shot." Did this quote add to your understanding of the story? How do you think it relates to events in the book?

2. What do you think of the Big Four (strive for perfection; clothe the body, adorn the soul; waste nothing; tempt not lest you be tempted) of the Believers? Do you think they are achievable? Desirable? How are they violated in the story?

3. Agnes explains that Honey is Mount Blessing's only orphan. Does this knowledge make life easier or harder for Honey?

4. Honey says at one point, "The whole point of being human is to make mistakes" (page 13). Do you agree? If yes, how so? If not, do you think perfection is attainable?

5. Agnes loves to run, especially in the rain, but she does not allow herself to for most of the story. What does running mean to her, and why does she feel that she should deny herself this pleasure? Have you ever denied yourself something pleasurable, and if so, why?

6. Admitting that the abuse at Mount Blessing was wrong took all of Agnes's conviction. What was Agnes giving up when she told the police about the Regulation Room? What would you have done in a similar situation?

7. What was your reaction when you learned that Agnes's parents let Emmanuel abuse their children and that they had allowed him to do the same to them? Do you think they should be punished for their actions? If yes, how so? If not, why?

8. What do you imagine Agnes's dad's story would be? What about Agnes's mom?

9. What qualities do you think Emmanuel has that attracts so many people to him? What personality traits do you think make some people more susceptible to Emmanuel than others?

10. Agnes and Honey struggle to figure out what makes a person good and how it relates to their community's ideals. Honey frequently berates Agnes for her stoic belief in what the community says and what sometimes seems like a lack of natural sympathy for her loved ones. Have you observed in your own experiences a difference between goodness and morality? What are the differences, if there are any?

11. How does Nana Pete's death affect the different characters? What do their reactions show us about Agnes, Lillian, and Agnes's dad?

12. Do you think that both Emmanuel and Veronica deserve to go to jail? Is Veronica another victim of Emmanuel's magnetism, or has she too become culpable over the years?

13. If you were to produce a movie of this book, whom would you cast in the roles of Honey and Agnes?

Jane Spurrier

CECILIA GALANTE was born into and raised for the first fifteen years of her life in a religious commune in upstate New York. She received her BA in English from King's College, Pennsylvania, and her MFA in creative writing from Goddard College, Vermont. Cecilia lives with her husband and three children in Kingston, Pennsylvania, where she teaches high school English. *The Patron Saint of Butterflies* is Cecilia's first young adult novel.

Don't miss these extraordinary novels starring girls like you.
They live in your world . . .
but they're dealing with issues you won't believe.